Dear Romance Reader,

Welcome to a world of breathtaking passion and never-ending romance.

Welcome to *Precious Gem Romances.*

It is our pleasure to present *Precious Gem Romances,* a wonderful new line of romance books by some of America's best-loved authors. Let these thrilling historical and contemporary romances sweep you away to far-off times and places in stories that will dazzle your senses and melt your heart.

Sparkling with joy, laughter, and love, each *Precious Gem Romance* glows with all the passion and excitement you expect from the very best in romance. Offered at a great affordable price, these books are an irresistible value—and an essential addition to your romance collection. Tender love stories you will want to read again and again, *Precious Gem Romances* are books you will treasure forever.

Look for fabulous new *Precious Gem Romances* each month—available only at Wal★Mart.

Lynn Brown, Publisher

HALF THE BATTLE

Lynn Christopher

Zebra Books
Kensington Publishing Corp.
http://www.zebrabooks.com

ZEBRA BOOKS are published by

Kensington Publishing Corp.
850 Third Avenue
New York, NY 10022

Copyright © 1999 by Lynn M. Bulock

All rights reserved. No part of this book may be reproduced in any form or by any means without the prior written consent of the Publisher, excepting brief quotes used in reviews.

If you purchased this book without a cover you should be aware that this book is stolen property. It was reported as "unsold and destroyed" to the Publisher and neither the Author nor the Publisher has received any payment for this "stripped book."

Zebra and the Z logo Reg. U.S. Pat. & TM Off.

First Printing: February, 1999
10 9 8 7 6 5 4 3 2 1

Printed in the United States of America

One

July, 1864

The last of the Kentucky sour mash was in Sander MacCormack's tumbler. He held the cool length of it up to his aching temple, then stood by the railing of the porch, looking into the Missouri twilight, doing what he did every evening. He looked for ghosts.

They came at this time of half-light, to flit through the trees as the sunset dimmed and the mourning doves called. Maybe some folks would be afraid of ghosts. Sander gave a brief chuckle, feeling the burn of the liquor. These ghosts stirred no fear in him. He knew them like old friends.

Billy Perkins was out there. Some nights he stood full in the moonlight and looked at Sander accusingly, as if he blamed his commanding officer for dragging him away from home into that skirmish at Mingo Swamp that blew off the top of his nineteen-year-old head. The first three men to die under his command were out there, looking as puzzled as they had at Wilson's Creek when they were all fighting for Price. There were others, shades in gray clothing that nearly matched their shadowy faces. In uniform or homespun, they stared out of the grove with Billy Perkins.

All of them seemed to ask why they were there instead

of in a hundred more pleasant places. Sander couldn't answer. He wasn't even sure why he was here himself anymore. There didn't seem to be any reason to recruit men for the Confederate army for a grand invasion of Missouri. The state seemed determined to remain Union. Still, General Price had ordered him to recruit troops and form a company and supply that company. In slow times, when there was nobody to recruit and nothing to supply anybody with, the ghosts came. So Sander stood of an evening on the porch and drank until they went away.

After tonight he'd have to go without or drink that rotgut Yancey had found. Again, as he did every night, Sander praised the foresight of Judge Fox, who had owned this house, in putting by a store of good whiskey.

A bunch of ragtag Confederates were the only ones who used the dining room these days, and the judge was planted in the family plot. He'd been there since last winter according to his tombstone, so Sander didn't think he would mind much what happened to his whiskey. At least Judge Fox didn't seem to be part of the shadow company that traveled through the grove.

But then, neither did Sander's mother, and God knows she was good enough at haunting him even though he hadn't laid eyes on her for twenty-seven years.

Sander smiled grimly as he sipped a little liquor out of the tumbler. Perhaps the judge wouldn't be quite so complacent if he knew who was drinking his whiskey. The papers left in the judge's desk seemed to indicate that he was steadfastly Union. He was probably twirling in that hole out back at the thought of a rebel company using his house as their headquarters. Let him twirl, Sander thought as he sipped the whiskey, welcoming

HALF THE BATTLE

the liquor-burn in his throat that took his mind off his headache. He needed the whiskey, and no one from the judge's family was here to object.

Sander speculated about the whereabouts of that family during his evenings on the porch. The wife was dead, planted beside Judge Fox's grave years before. Neighborhood gossip and the contents of the house told him there should have been a son and a daughter.

The son was easy. He'd heard the name of Tyson Fox himself on the field. Followed the old man's Union sympathies right into command of the local reserves. Had his hands full where he was now, ol' Tyson did. But the daughter was another matter. Even though some of her possessions were still in the house, neighborhood gossip refused to divulge her whereabouts. There was just the portrait over the mantel.

When he'd seen it that first day in the parlor it had given Sander a shock. Rooted to the spot he'd traced the deep gold hair with his gaze, taken in the familiar planes of the face, the flashing eyes. Although he'd never seen this young woman, this Lila Fox, he knew this face. It looked like his Evie—or like his Evie would have looked if she'd been brought up in a fine house with servants. Those delicate hands would never have survived the chores in a dogtrot cabin.

Evie. She was out in the clearing every night. The portrait teased Sander about the whereabouts of the mistress of the house. Evie haunted him. He could catch glimpses of her dress, the worn green calico turned to gray in the fading light as she tripped barefoot between the oaks.

Sander wondered what Evie saw, looking up at him from out there in the gloom. He was thinner than he'd been last winter, and nobody ever got on him to trim the ragged beard and scraggly hair that covered the frayed collar of his uniform. He suspected he looked as bad as Yancey, a thought that should have made him wince. It didn't, not dulled with as much liquor as he was. There was no one here to care about his appearance, and he cared least of all himself.

Evie flitted, never staying to face him. No pale face looked up at him, demanding to know why Sander had murdered her too. He had killed her, even if his hadn't been the hand that lit the fire. Without Sander and his interference, Evie Harvey would still be alive.

Sander's head still throbbed, even as the whiskey path burned down to his stomach. There was noise in the front parlor, Yancey and some of the men joshing with Fay. Their raucous laughter came through the open windows. Fay had won another chunk of somebody's pay with a crooked hand of poker. He would have to turn her out soon. The woman couldn't cook, did no work except on her back, and was a general nuisance. But it would mean a row with Yancey when she went, and Sander had trouble enough without that.

When he turned back to look at the clearing, Evie was there. This time it wasn't a scrap of cloth disappearing behind a tree. She stood still next to the tallest oak. Her hair was lit by moonlight that brought out pale highlights in tresses falling past her shoulders. Her eyes were huge in her pale face. When Sander looked at her, all he saw was terror reflected in them.

The contact was riveting. So many things ran through his mind, the myriad things he had wanted to tell her. "I miss you," he wanted to say. He wanted to tell her of the perfectly formed, all too tiny boy he'd buried beside her. "I didn't name him anything. I couldn't." He wanted to hold her, to talk to her one more time.

But most of all he wanted to ask her to forgive him. Now, looking at her across the darkening clearing, time froze while Sander's mouth went dry and his hand trembled.

The tumbler slipped through his fingers and shattered. Like a deer, she started and was gone. "Hold there," he called, taking the three steps off the porch in a bound.

When his feet hit the solid-packed earth below the last step the force jarred him to his liquor-fogged senses. He was chasing a shade.

Evie was dead. He'd buried her himself. There was no warm, willing girl running from that clearing. There were only his memories, wicked and willful. And now there wasn't even any bourbon left to quell them.

"Anything out there?" Yancey stood at the window.

"Nothing but a damn fool, and I'm coming in the house," Sander said, swallowing past the bitterness.

The porch steps creaked as he went up them. Sander looked down at the shards of the tumbler resting in a puddle of pale brown liquid. He kicked the mess off the porch into the azalea bushes below.

The door closed behind him with a sense of finality. Ignoring the laughing group in the parlor, he went into the room on the other side of the hall. Sitting heavily in a chair, he took down a book and found where he'd left off reading last night. How far would he get tonight before the Latin phrases and heavy thought would overwhelm him? Outside, lightning bugs flickered in the grove instead of ghosts.

Lila Fox burst into the cave, making Chloe jump where she sat in front of the fire. "Lila, girl, don't do that. If I drop this needle and have to hunt for it, we're both in a world of trouble. This is the last one I've got left."

"I'm sorry, Chloe, I truly am." The words came out with ragged edges. "At least this time you didn't take the ax to me."

Her friend scowled, making her face resemble an African mask in the flickering firelight. "Only did that the first time you came back last week. I didn't expect you. You could have been a whole tribe of bushwhackers for all the noise you made."

"Bushwhackers don't make that much noise," Lila said quickly.

"Sorry," Chloe said, looking down at the sewing in her lap. "I didn't want to make you think about . . ."

"That's all right, Chloe. I'll think about those bushwhackers for a long time yet, no matter what anybody says." She'd thought about them since the moment weeks before when she'd gotten off the mule outside her aunt and uncle's cabin.

Instead of the warm welcome Aunt Ruth would have given her, she was greeted by charred earth and a very new graveyard. Lila was sure she was going to lose her mind right there.

She'd progressed from standing in front of the four graves to sitting beside Evie's, talking to her cousin just the way she would have if she'd met her at the cabin door. The mule wandered off because in her daze she hadn't tied it to anything. And, of course, no matter how long Lila sat on the cold ground letting the damp soak into her skirt, Evie hadn't answered back. She couldn't tell Lila how she came to die, or why there was a tiny grave next to hers that spoke volumes.

Chloe scowled again. "At least now you're where they can't get to you so easily. Why you didn't come home that very day you got there, I'll never know. Where was your sense?"

"The same place yours was when you talked Marcus into letting you stay in this cave instead of going to Illinois like you promised you would," Lila retorted.

One corner of Chloe's mouth twisted. "I like this cave. It's safe and quiet, and near home. From what you've told me that cabin was neither safe nor quiet."

"When the bushwhackers weren't around it was very quiet," Lila said.

She'd stayed there a few weeks, then come home. Traveling at night, planning to live in the cave on her father's property until she could see if Ty had been right about the Confederates taking over the house the moment it was empty. Walking into a screeching, ax-wielding Chloe instead of an empty cave had terrified her into blurting out more about the weeks of horror than she had planned.

Chloe was still treating her like someone who needed care and humoring. She put aside her sewing and laid a hand on the surface of the chest she used for a seat, trying to get enough leverage to hoist her swollen body.

"No, you stay sitting. It's hard enough to haul you up and down now," Lila said.

"I'll get up if I want to," Chloe declared. "What do you think I did before you came along last week?"

"Waddled, I expect. You sure there's only one baby in there, Chloe?"

"Only feel one set of elbows, or knees, or whatever it is kicking me in the ribs," she said with a grimace. "If he's as big as my Marcus must have been newborn, one will be plenty. But stop trying to pull me away from what's going on. They saw you up there, didn't they?"

Chloe's perceptive dark eyes demanded a response.

Lila sighed and lowered herself to the cool floor of the cave. "I think so. One of them was standing on the porch. He yelled something but he didn't follow me."

"You're lucky he didn't shoot you. Don't you think they post sentries?"

Lila pushed aside a stone with one bare foot. "I know they don't. There wasn't a living soul outside, except one fellow down in the stables and one heading for the privy, and he wasn't too steady on his feet. I think they found Papa's store of liquor."

"I expect they did, probably the first day they moved in there," Chloe said dryly. She pulled the thread through the cloth one last time and knotted it. Nipping off the end close to the fabric, she threw the mass at Lila. "Here, try this on. If you've got to go get caught over there, you might as well do it dressed in something that fits."

Lila spread out the fabric in her hands. A dress without holes in it. A dress that didn't have a ragged bottom instead of a hem, one with armholes that held together all the way. Her eyes filled with tears. "I can't take this, Chloe."

"You can and you will. That thing you've got on has another hole in it. Are you hurt?"

Lila shook her head. It was only one more tear to join the dozen or so others in the faded calico. "I caught it on something, but that's all right. Besides, this will never fit me. You're so much smaller than I am . . ."

Chloe gave a hoot of laughter. "You're wrong. I'm not small anymore, and you're no bigger than I started out."

"That can't be," Lila argued. "Even when I wore that infernal corset we bought in St. Louis, that had steel ribbing instead of my regular whalebone stays, I couldn't ever get my waist as small as yours was in just your chemise."

Chloe tilted her head back, half a smile tugging at one corner of her thin lips. "Uh-huh. And you say you've been eating what for the last month and a half, Miss Fox?"

Weeds, mostly, but she wasn't ready to admit that to Chloe. "It wasn't that bad. When I had the cow, there was milk every day. For the first two weeks there was even one jar of Aunt Ruth's jam they'd missed." The awful memories caught up with Lila, and tears stung the backs of her eyelids. "It was blackberry . . ." she managed to get out before she gathered the dress up and buried her face in it.

"Oh, Lila, honey, I didn't mean to make you cry. You take that old dress and stop arguing. I can't wear it anyway. Look at it, girl, and be practical. It buttons down the back."

"So," Lila said, trying to stop sobbing. "You could put gussets in it, and it would still fit. You're not that big, Chloe, you're carrying low, anyway."

"I am so that big. I feel like a house on legs. Besides, that's not what I meant," she said, brushing a stray hank of pale hair from Lila's wet face. "It buttons down the back. In about eight weeks, I'm going to have no use for anything I can't open a dozen times a day. From the front."

Slowly what she was saying sank into Lila's brain. "Oh, the baby. Feeding him." She shook herself. "Him. Now you've got me doing it too, Chloe. What makes you so sure that's a him?"

"I don't know. I've called him 'him' since before I finished losing my breakfast every morning," she said softly, sitting beside Lila. "Marcus laughed at me too before he took off with that brother of yours. He said there's no way of knowing. Said it might be a girl and as ugly as his Aunt Hattie."

Lila managed a little croak of laughter. "Did you hit him with something?"

"The bed pillow. It was handy at the time." Chloe's mouth twisted again. The half-smile and the firelight combined to give her a wizened appearance that stirred Lila's maternal instincts.

"You've sat here all evening sewing on this, haven't you? And tomorrow your back is going to hurt. I'm going to go find you a cool drink of water before you go to bed. I'll even get enough so that we can both have a spit bath."

"Be careful. There may be rebels down by that spring. Or snakes. And I'd sooner trust the snakes."

Lila nodded. She stood and picked up the bucket next to the wall. "So would I. I'll watch out for both and be back real quick."

Walking to the spring in the dark made Lila wary. It reminded her of hiding from the bushwhackers. Even though the soldiers around her house were likely to be much friendlier than the cutthroats who'd murdered her cousin, they were still rebels. She wasn't taking any chances on any of them finding her.

There were no rebels here; especially none like the dark, haunted man on the porch. Remembering the way he'd looked at her made Lila shiver. This man was made of darkness, she thought. Not just the heavy hair and beard, the deep hollows that shrouded his eyes. There was darkness around him as he'd stood on the porch, looking out at nothing, in the twilight. Until he'd seen her.

Lila could still see that look if she closed her eyes.

Something about the intense quality of his gaze had frozen her then and now made sweat trickle down her sides at just thinking about him.

Lila shook herself and headed to the spring, trying to avoid any sharp rocks in the dark. Thinking of her Confederate watcher, she needed that spit bath worse than ever.

The next evening at about dusk Chloe was more snappish than usual. "You're going again, aren't you? I've watched you pace and fidget for an hour. Shall we pack you a bag, Lila?"

Lila blew out a most unladylike snort. "Of course not. I'll just look around a little."

"And what if they look around a little and find you?" Chloe's posture, with her hands on her hips, might have looked more intimidating if her belly hadn't bulged out so far.

"Just what we talked about before," Lila said, trying to force the words out. "I'll tell them I'm the Foxes' cousin Evie, come for a visit. None of them are likely to know anything about her."

Lila splashed water on her face. "Will you come with me?"

It was Chloe's turn to snort. "Me? I don't want to see anybody. Especially a troop of rebel soldiers, Lila. I'm staying right here. You'll get word to me."

"I'll be back after dark, most likely. If not, you know I'll be all right. I'll leave a message in the blackberry bushes."

Chloe stood to look at her as Lila fastened her shoe. "I'll be waiting. Take care." She hugged her tight, and the babe showed what he thought by delivering a kick Lila could feel. She laughed at her friend's grimace.

"You be careful too." She swallowed the tears that threatened to well up, as they did all too often these days. Damn those bushwhackers. The least thing put her in tears.

Taking one last look around, she slipped out of the cave. She spent the walk to the house trying to convince herself that she was Evie, or could pretend to be. Except that even if Evie hadn't been dead, Lila wasn't sure she would have known how to be Evie anymore. There was too much mystery to Evie's last year.

Evie would have been pregnant at Papa's funeral last winter. Thinking back, Lila knew that Evie had looked like she'd wanted to tell her things, but they'd never had time alone to talk.

Surely one of those things would have been about the baby's father, whoever he was. He wasn't one of the bushwhackers. Lila had seen them at a distance, and she knew instinctively that Evie would not have let any of those men touch her that way.

But without Evie, or her journal, she'd never know for sure what had happened. There had been only scraps of the ruined journal in the burned-out cabin. Lila had read one over and over: ". . . even tho' I was scandalized at the time, Zerelda was right. It is better than Christmas. I can hardly wait to tell Lila."

Except she never did. Lila didn't see a soul on the way to the house. Not that she expected to, for she crossed no roads and spent all her time on Fox property. It was mostly property that was pretty bare since the hay had been brought in. Lila got grim satisfaction at the thought of those Confederates sweating in their wool uniforms, struggling to get hay cut and into the barns. In any case, someone had had the good sense not to let it all rot in the fields.

Walking there alone, Lila promised Evie again that she'd find whoever killed her. She'd made the promise out loud, at Evie's grave. Nobody had heard her then but a crazy woman.

Prue had watched her the whole time she'd lived in the dogtrot. She hadn't been right in the head even before the war started, and nobody bothered her now. Her comments chilled Lila to the bone. "They killed them, you know. That MacCormack and the one he rides with. And now they've come back. We should hide."

"I know," Lila said, swallowing a scream.

Getting ready to leave the cabin, Lila wished she'd paid more attention to the mule that first day instead of letting it wander off while she sat in shock. She went out in the pale sunshine to tell Evie good-bye. "I'll find them," she told the rude carving over her cousin's bones. It was still hard for her to equate that patch of scarred earth with her laughing, vibrant cousin. "Whoever did this, I'll find them."

"It was that MacCormack. I saw him standing over her, plain as day. Wasn't day, though. Night. Black night," Prue went on.

Lila patted her hand. It felt like a handful of twigs in a kid glove. "I'll look for him, Prue, all right?"

The old woman's eyes cleared to the pale green of creek water as she looked up at Lila. "Won't need to. He'll find you." Her pronouncement haunted Lila all the way home. It haunted her now as she got closer to the house.

It was dusk when she reached the grove. The man on the porch was there again, leaning against the rail, silhouetted in the near dark. Lila pulled back behind a tree while she watched him.

He stood, staring out into the night. Lila wondered what color his eyes were. She stood still and willed his gaze away from her, not sure what she would do if that intensity lit on her again. He looked into another part of the grove, one arm above his head, forehead resting on the porch pillar as he stared. What did he come out to think about?

Whatever his thoughts were, they certainly put a damper on her plans to try to get inside the picket fence and shinny up the tree that stood outside her bedroom window. She'd never get past him, not when she could feel those intense eyes raking the yard.

There was a noise inside the house, and the man turned his head. He said something, then walked into the house. Lila saw her chance. She slipped from behind the tree, through the grove and past the gate. She eased the gate closed so it wouldn't squeal. She was halfway to the tree before he appeared in the doorway. Her heart stopped.

Being this close to the man in the doorway, she could smell a hint of the white lightning in his tumbler, feel the physical power of him. She planned to stay where she was, rehearsing the careful story that she and Chloe had concocted. Instead she whirled and turned, dropping the little bundle she was carrying. She fled through the gate before he reacted. He shouted, then behind her Lila could hear the solid thump as he vaulted off the porch in pursuit.

Running hard, she plunged into the grove. Here in the half-light she had the advantage of knowing where every tree was. She and Tyson and Chloe had chased each other through here for years.

Playing tag had never made Lila's heart race like this. This chase pulled the breath out of her body in ragged, tearing gasps. Her pursuer didn't seem to be breathing as hard as she was, and now she could hear his every breath. He was in good condition, she thought crazily as she scrambled ahead of him, for a man who seemed to spend a lot of time drinking on her front porch.

She cleared the far edge of the grove now, still running. It was then that Lila panicked. Ahead of her stretched nothing to conceal her, only the stubble of hay fields. She was out of hiding places, and her pursuer was still behind her.

She nearly sobbed for breath. A hole made her stumble and she clutched at the air to try to stay upright. She kept going, listening to the man behind her. His breathing was as heavy as hers now, his boots making a steady drum on the ground behind her.

"Stop." She could almost feel the push of air it had taken for him to shout, he was that close to her back. Beyond thought, she kept running. The uneven stubble pulled at her skirt, and she ran blindly. When she could feel the heat of the man behind her, smell the acrid scent of him, she knew the chase was over.

He had strong hands that closed in on her shoulders, making her breath escape in a high sob. The weight of his solid body bore them both to the ground. Lila struggled to keep her face out of the sharp stubble as she fell. Her knees and elbows struck the ground, and the rough ends of the hay scratched her skin, drawing blood.

The fall knocked the air out of her. For a minute all she could do was fight the heaviness of the man on top of her. As she struggled to make her legs work in the tangle of skirts, she could feel the muscular length of him along her back, trying to turn her around.

Lila pushed, wanting to get up again and run. Even

though his breathing was as tortured as hers, he would not be moved except to wrap long arms around her and turn her body. Rolling, she tried to push him away. But his lean, well-muscled body still bore down on her as she looked up into his face. There were little lines at the corners of his eyes, and his chest heaved mightily. His eyes were dark brown, and they regarded her with an expression Lila could not fathom.

He was still holding her hands to the ground when he spoke. "You're not Evie." The shock was so great, Lila felt as if the ground slid out from under her.

Two

For a moment they both lay twined on the ground, and Lila could feel his heart pounding. She tried to draw a good breath, but it was impossible with him still on top of her. Her struggle seemed to shake him out of his shock. He rolled off her onto the ground and knelt, still holding her wrists.

When she could catch her breath, Lila pushed as hard as she could and sat up. "I most certainly am not Evie," she said, stopping only to suck in another welcome breath. "I'm her cousin Lila Claire Fox, and I'll thank you to let go of me."

"And if I do?"

"I intend to retrieve my belongings and go into my house, sir. The house you and your . . . friends seem to be inhabiting." It was hard to sound haughty with this infuriating man's tight hold on her wrist and hay stickers poking through her drawers.

He let go of her. "Ma'am, my 'friends' as you so quaintly put it, have secured your house as Confederate States Army headquarters for Madison County."

Lila clenched her fists, ignoring the pain inflicted from dozens of scratches. "Oh, it is my house, sir. And I intend to have it back."

The stranger made a sound that might have been a

laugh. "It would take a great deal more than one young woman, no matter how angry, to convince us to cease inhabiting that house. If you would care to accompany me back, I shall instruct my men to let you enter unmolested."

"How generous." Lila resisted the desire to rub her wrist. "And if I choose not to accompany you?"

A slight drawl was more evident now that he was getting his breath back. "I could drag you, but I see no point in it. If you don't come, you will lose whatever belongings you dropped so hastily in the yard, and I shall be much more deliberate about posting sentries in the future."

Lila thought. It would almost be worth parting with her only clean chemise to be rid of this man. She might have found him almost handsome, with his glittering dark eyes, if he had been a Union man.

He wasn't. He was a Confederate officer, and if she left he would continue to inhabit her home. She would lose not only her spare chemise, but also the keys to the strongbox still in the house somewhere. Lila made her decision and rose from the ground. "I will accompany you, sir."

He stood up as she did, and somehow they bumped, both grappling for balance. Lila's hands still stung from the scratches, and the one that brushed against the front of the stranger's shirt throbbed. But it was the damp warmth of his body through the thin cloth that made her drew back as if scalded. The man looked concerned. He put out a hand to steady her. "You're able to stand, Miss Fox? No injuries from our fall?"

"I can stand. Unassisted, sir." Ignoring her tumbled hair and the sweat trickling down her back, Lila tried to sound cold. Still the overpowering, warm male aura of her captor surrounded her. "I fear you have me at a disadvantage. You know who I am, and who I am not, but I have not a clue to your identity except the uniform you wear."

"And only half of that. Hard to even tell my rank without the tunic, I expect," he said, looking down at his open white shirt. "Captain Sander MacCormack, the Army of Missouri, Confederate States of America."

Whatever he had expected from her, the attack he got wasn't it. Lila flung herself at the man before she thought, her fingers like talons. When her vision cleared, they were on the ground again, this time with her on her back and her captor above her, panting and dazed.

"MacCormack. No wonder you know I wasn't Evie. You're the one who killed her."

He let her go as if he'd been shot. In a moment he was standing, while she tried to pull herself into a sitting position. "Get your things from the yard and go, Miss Fox. Go anywhere you like, I won't bother you or send my men after you. But go."

"I can't. You're in my house."

"If it were up to me, I'd give you the damned house back," he said, looking out over the field stubble. Lila slowly stood, her reeling senses trying to make some logical order of everything she'd found out in such a brief time.

"I was wrong. You didn't, did you?" What she'd seen on the man's face had not been the remorse of a killer. It was a pain much more intimate. "You didn't kill my cousin, but you know who did. Who was it?"

He said nothing, would not look in her direction. "I'm going back to get my things, Captain. And then I'm going in that house."

His eyes, when he turned to face her, were filled with disbelief. "Why? If you go in there, I cannot promise you safety."

"I know that. But in there somewhere is the answer to my question. And I'm not going to be happy until I know."

His answering sigh was one of long suffering. "Young lady, you're not going to be happy, even if you do know." And then he walked ahead of her into the growing dark.

They crossed the grove in silence. When they reached the gate, Sander opened it for her and Lila went through, retrieving her bag. "You'll come in, I trust, Miss Fox?" The irony in his voice was thick.

Still, he held the door for her as Lila sailed into the front hall. And then she stopped. The force of knowing that rebel troops were living in her home hit her like a blow.

She stood in the hall, trying to collect herself. There were cobwebs above the chandelier and the mirror was horribly streaked, but nothing here seemed to be broken. It wasn't the condition of the rooms that unsettled her so.

It was the sound and smell and feel of her home. It reeked of cigar smoke and unwashed male bodies—and other invasions. As she stood, there was a roar from the family parlor, and a huge bear of a man threw down a handful of playing cards and stood up. "Damn, Fay, even without sleeves, I swear you've been putting aces someplace." The large, disheveled figure nearly ran into them as he strode from the room. He stopped abruptly in front of Lila. She could smell the raw spirits on him, and the obvious fact that his last bath had been too long ago in this summer heat. "Look here, boys. The captain has done caught himself the picture lady."

The demeanor of this big ruffian made Lila want to slap him. Before she raised her hand she heard old Prue's voice in her head. "MacCormack and the one he rides with." The captain couldn't have killed Evie, but the man standing in her parlor could kill the way most people would swat a fly, of that she was certain, looking at his little, piggy eyes.

Her backbone stiffened even as she felt a cold chill go over her. "You can address me as Miss Fox. And I'll thank you not to swear in my house." He gave a hoot that told her what he thought of her little speech, but he stepped back to see what would happen next. Lila wasn't sure she knew herself.

The picture lady. Sander hadn't been thinking of her quite that way, not in a plain cotton dress and tumbled hair. She carried herself like a lady, even with hay stubble sticking to her skirt. Sander wondered how he could have mistaken her for Evie, or Evie's shade, even at a distance. She didn't have Evie's lush, swaying hips or her air of continual amusement. This was no image of the girl he'd thought of as a wood nymph.

Instead of Evie's girlish nature there was a careful control here, and he found himself wondering what he would face when it was broken. Did that full mouth with its red lips tremble, or did it compress into a narrow line? He wondered how a loss of composure would change the color of her eyes, not green like Evie's but gray as summer thunderclouds. Unlike Evie, who had held a trace of a child's softness almost to the end of her life, the figure before him possessed more maturity.

Trouble had made this one a woman even if she was still young.

The hair was the same, abundant and honey colored. Evie's had perhaps a touch more gold, but that was probably because she never covered it no matter how much time she spent outside. Lila looked as if she'd acted the lady, with gloves and a sunshade, until recently. Sander wondered what she'd been through since she'd left this place. Whatever it was, she hadn't taken to her hardscrabble role with much grace. She'd fought like a wildcat when she'd thought he was a killer.

He was a killer, but not the way she'd thought. He still felt responsible for Evie's death, and sooner or later this young woman would know that just from watching him. He looked at her, wondering how much she'd seen already in his eyes.

Whatever she'd seen, it was gone now. Looking at her, Sander was aware of her shock, and he reminded himself of how this place must seem to her. That parlor table had probably never been used for anything more challenging than whist or chess when she'd occupied these rooms. And no woman had ever sat at it, Sander was sure, barefooted and with a light wrapper over her petticoat and corset cover, as Fay Culpepper was doing now.

Sander took in Lila's posture when she faced Fay. Her back was stiff, her head held at a tense angle. Even with tousled hair tumbling down her back, she managed to seem haughty in front of the blowsy older woman.

Fay broke the silence first, leaving one arm languidly draped over the soldier next to her. "That right, Yancey? This gal really live here before?" Fay rose, straightening her skirts a little. There wasn't much else

HALF THE BATTLE

to her attire that could be straightened, a fact that Lila seemed to be taking in with contempt.

"I did. And I do, as of now. Do you live here, then, a lone woman among a troop of soldiers?"

"Right smack among them most of the time," Fay said, challenging her.

Sander was somehow reminded of two cats, fur bristling along their backbones, getting ready to spit and hiss. He wondered how to avoid a human catfight. "Fay, why don't you go upstairs?"

"To my room," she said with somewhat of a sneer. "I must say, Miss Fox, you have excellent taste in linens." Fay swept out of the parlor with all the dignity she could muster. Lila watched her go, then turned to face him.

Sander marveled at her eyes. There was none of the gentle softness that the portrait painter had captured. Instead they were dark and flashing. "Am I to believe, Captain, that not only are there twenty men living under this roof, desecrating the property, but that . . . that *woman* lives here as well?"

"Shares my bunk," Yancey piped up, coming through the doorway with a fresh jug. "Whose you plan on sharing? Space is sort of at a premium right now."

Sander grabbed Lila's wrist before she could hurl herself at Yancey. Under the warmth of her skin was the strength of steel in those small bones. Sander had no doubt that she'd try to bring Yancey down if he didn't step in. "Sergeant Phillips, Miss Fox has my word that she will be unmolested here. This includes remarks that might be more suitable for the stable. Is that clear?"

"Sure enough, Captain. But I haven't heard you this formal since Wilson's Creek." Yancey made a mock bow, made even cruder by his shambling height and the fact that he came up scratching his scraggly red beard. "Please forgive me, Miss Fox. But begging the captain's pardon, where you going to put her, Sander? We've got ten men in tents out back now."

"Captain"—the voice came from the corner—"Miss Fox can have my room if she wants it. Ma's been after me to come home nights anyway."

Sander looked over to the skinny lad sitting on the leather chaise. Hoskins. Blainey Hoskins. His one-and-only prize Madison County recruit. "That would be highly unusual, Private Hoskins, but given the circumstances, I'm going to allow it, the nights you don't have guard duty. Be back by sunup."

Hoskins leaped up and saluted. "Yes, sir."

Lila's answering smile was wry. "And where has Blainey Hoskins been sleeping, Captain? The loft?"

"The, uh, suite behind the kitchen, I believe," Sander said, avoiding those flashing eyes.

"I'll take it. It offers the advantage of not being under the same roof as any members of the Confederate States Army," Lila said coolly, crossing the threshold into the hall.

"You going to let her stay, Sander? Won't it be a lot of trouble?"

The evening's activities were making Sander's head throb at the temples. He tried to remember where he'd set his tumbler before all this happened, and couldn't. He hoped he hadn't dropped another one. There were only three left. "I fail to see, short of violence, how we can keep the rightful owner of the place from remaining, Yancey."

Yancey scratched some more. "I guess you're right." He stood, looking at Lila for a moment, and his face brightened. "Hey, maybe she can cook. Can you cook, gal?"

HALF THE BATTLE

"I can. But how do you know I wouldn't put arsenic in the stew?" The tilt to the woman's head as she looked up at Yancey made Sander marvel. Even on his best days he didn't provoke the testy bastard unless he had to, and this young woman who barely reached Yancey's chest was doing it with impunity. The two enlisted men that were still in the room read the signs the same way their commanding officer did and slunk out.

Surprisingly, Yancey smiled instead of growling. "You wouldn't poison us. There's twenty of us and one of you."

"Not for long. I suspect whether I poison you or not is of little consequence. In a few weeks, when the Union forces know of your existence, my brother and his troops will be pulled back from Tennessee, and you, sir, will be heading for whatever hills you came from."

Yancey roared with laughter. "Tennessee? Gal, who told you that? Hell, that whole bunch is probably scalped balder than billiards by now," he said with a laugh.

Sander watched the flush of triumph on Lila's face fade. She looked bewildered. "Scalped? What does he mean?"

Yancey straightened up. "The troops that left here ended up in Indian Territory, chasing old Stand Watie. From what I hear the Cherokee haven't left many of them with their own hair."

Of all the things Sander had expected, the shriek that came out of Lila before her legs buckled wasn't one of them. He stood dumbly in the darkening room as she sat on the floor, the unearthly noise coming from her throat echoing off the walls.

It was too much. Knowing on top of everything else that Ty was out in Indian Territory, he and Marcus both probably dead, was too much. All the fear and sorrow that Lila had been holding in since the day she had gotten to Evie's and found the dogtrot in ruins poured out.

Only a part of her was conscious of the shadowed walls of the room around her, the gritty feel of the wood floor under her as she sat on it. The rest of her retreated into a howling mess. Her throat ached, and she couldn't even lift a hand to stop the tears that ran down her cheeks. Tears for Evie, for Uncle Ernest and Aunt Ruth, as well as Ty and Marcus. All those feelings she'd held back, out of terror that bushwhackers might hear her let go, were pouring out now.

It was this horrid bunch of rebels that was making her cry. Especially the sergeant with his ugly demeanor and even uglier stories. It strengthened her conviction that he was Evie's murderer. He was probably the one who had used Mama's little painted dish with the violets on it for an ashtray and then left it on the table. Crying felt good, a release of the awful wrenching in her chest. And she couldn't stop, she found, even when she tried.

Forcing herself to see the room around her, the cards dropped on the littered floor, the faded draperies, didn't help. Instead new waves of anger at these men overrunning the place just fueled her hysteria. The sobs rolled over her, engulfing everything else.

The large, coarse man who had been taunting her was gone. She hadn't even noticed him leaving, but the room was empty. No, not quite empty. Captain MacCormack was sitting on the leather chaise behind her. Through the haze of tears that still kept coming, Lila saw him sitting there, still and rather pale above the dark beard. He looked as if he would rather be anywhere else.

"I don't have one either. A handkerchief, I mean." Lila snuffled and wiped the back of her hand across her wet face, which seemed to discomfort him even more. "We're soldiers, Miss Fox. Few of us know anything about the niceties of ladies, and I never expected one tonight."

He reached out as if to touch her, but drew back his hand before it got to her shoulder. "Do you need anything?"

"Nothing you would get me," she choked out, trying to get the tears to subside. They turned to shuddering sobs that broke off sharply and then started again, as would an overtired child. Lila leaned her head against the chaise, gulping a deep breath between sobs.

Instead of cool leather her head and shoulder found warmth and rough wool and prominent bones. A kneecap, she thought with that odd detachment that comes after crying so hard. She hadn't meant to lean against him. But she was too tired to move and he wasn't objecting, so she stayed, absorbing the solid warmth of him through her dress. His trousers were worn, his boots dusty.

Being this close to him made the still air in the room feel even more still. Her last trembling sigh sounded loud. She pushed her wet hair off her face. "It's true, isn't it? What your sergeant said about Ty."

"In part. He's definitely in Indian Territory or someplace in Kansas, depending on where Watie and the Cherokee nation have been leading the Union. But the casualties there haven't been much worse than anywhere else." His voice sounded tired but calming, and Lila kept listening, her head leaning back against the seat of the chaise, her shoulder still against his trouser leg.

There was a hand in her hair, large and tentative, but incredibly gentle. He was stroking the waves at the crown of her head. As someone would gentle a restive horse, Lila thought. She wondered if he thought she was going to bolt.

"Your brother probably isn't dead, or scalped, but he's not likely to be back here anytime soon, either, Miss Fox."

She drew away from him, and the hand left her hair as he continued to speak. "So where does that leave you? Is there other family in the area?"

"None. This is my home, Captain MacCormack, and I intend to stay here." Lila brushed a sleeve across her face, more in control again now. "If nothing else, to make sure that rebel fools with cigars don't burn the place to the ground." For emphasis she pushed herself off the floor and stubbed out a smoldering remnant. She looked around and saw her bundle in the hallway.

"Now, if you'll excuse me, I'll be retiring." Lila tried to sound as if taking her leave of a Confederate commanding officer in her own parlor was something she did every night.

He was already on his feet, following her. "I'll accompany you. There are men in tents billeted near the kitchen, and I want to make sure they understand the situation."

Lila nodded. Walking mechanically, she got through the back door, across the porch and down the steps before she stopped on the flagstones in front of the open door of the kitchen. There was no light except that which filtered through the streaked windowpanes, and Lila shuddered to think what a troop of soldiers had done to her kitchen.

The noise of what someone, or rather something, was

doing there now was unmistakable. "Captain, there is a pig in that kitchen."

Incredibly, there was laughter in his voice when he answered. "A very small pig, I believe, ma'am. I'll chase him out." He ducked in front of her into the darkened room. In a moment the pig trotted out, followed by the captain.

"It's empty now, ma'am." He stood at the doorway, a smile playing around his lips.

"I should hope so!" Lila went through and slammed the door, sending the bolt home. She went straight through the kitchen, preferring to discover by daylight what havoc twenty men and a pig could wreak.

Chloe and Marcus's attached room seemed unharmed. Blainey Hoskins had cleared out and was gone. Other than a cloaking of cobwebs and mud on the floor, it looked as Lila remembered it. There was a rough bedstead in the corner, with a bare shuck mattress. The dresser was no more scarred than before, though the mirror was cracked crazily. Lila went to prop the window open to let in any stray breezes.

There was a knock on the door beside her, on the outside wall of her room. Lila shot the bolt, then answered. "Yes?"

"Captain MacCormack, miss. I've posted sentries, and no one should be bothering you. If they do, I wish to know of it immediately."

"You needn't worry, Captain. I suspect you would hear the results if anyone bothers me. You'll remember, this is my kitchen, and I'm familiar with the use of the knives and cleavers there."

There was a sound from the other side of the door that might have been a chuckle. "I've no doubt you are, Miss Fox. Sleep well."

When he was gone, and she'd heard the door to the house close, Lila tiptoed into the kitchen. It didn't take her long to find her favorite knife; the one Marcus always wanted to use for pig butchering. The heft of the handle was reassuring as she slid it under the corner of the bed that would be closest to her hand in the dark. It was probably rusty, but that wouldn't deter its effectiveness against Confederates. She could hear the noises of men settling in for the night as she took off her shoes and stretched out on the mattress, fully clothed.

She wondered which room upstairs Captain MacCormack had chosen for his own and how he slept there. Images of him in any of the big walnut bedsteads made her shiver in the sudden cool breeze that came through the window. She pushed the image away, reached down to check on the handle of the knife one more time and slept, one arm drooping over the side of the bed.

Three

Lila lay on her back, looking up at the windowpane. The morning sun that filtered into the room only emphasized the filth. Cobwebs in every corner, floor unswept since Chloe had done it last and dust so thick she could have written her name on the furniture. She pushed her hair away from her face, trying to find the energy to get up. That windowpane was going to be clean before she lay down again at night. Lila pulled on her shoes, tied her hair back and completed the rest of her toilette as quickly as possible. She closed the door on the cobwebs and the dirt in the corners. That would have to wait.

Like it or not, twenty men would rise, scratching and yawning, in a few minutes. It was either let them in her kitchen, perhaps bringing a pig for company, or fix them breakfast.

The supplies were plentiful, if not varied. A large sack of cornmeal, flour in abundance that appeared to be weevil free and coffee. Lila got a bucket of water from the well, thankful that no one had fouled it. She started water boiling for coffee as soon as there was a fire in the stove. Just as she was rummaging under the table for a basket, Blainey Hoskins flew through the door.

"Your mother feed you before she rushed you on over here?" she asked.

He nodded, a skinny Adam's apple bobbing in his neck. "Even sent a biscuit and bacon for once I got my breath back."

She shoved the basket at him. "Good. Then go into the chicken house and get me eggs. There *are* still layers in there aren't there? Surely they haven't all hit the dinner table yet."

Blainey shook his head, wrinkling his freckled nose. "Oh, no, ma'am, Miss Fox. Captain MacCormack is particular about that. We haven't eaten anything on the hoof, except what we bought from farmers."

"Good. Then go get the eggs, and if there's still bacon in the smokehouse, get me that, too." Blainey pulled at the front of his cap and took off.

The Hoskins boy had come with the eggs, and Lila was already frying bacon, a double batch of biscuits in the oven, by the time Sergeant Phillips came dragging through the doorway, still scratching his disreputable undershirt.

"Well, I swan . . ." he drawled, looking at Lila. "You're cooking breakfast?"

"Yes, but only because I didn't want you in my kitchen," she said, brandishing a fork that kept him at a distance. It wasn't quite enough distance for Lila, even this early in the morning when the air was still cool. "Do you bathe, Sergeant?"

"When I feel the urge."

"Well, until you feel the urge, stay downwind of me and out of this kitchen." Even the pig would have been preferable. It was easy to imagine the sergeant as a killer. Anybody that filthy must have numerous vices.

He grumbled and spat, but he left. A few minutes

later Blainey was back, sticking his head in the doorway. "Smells mighty good in here, Miss Fox."

"Just call me Lila. Then I won't have to mess around calling you Private Hoskins, all right?" She wiped her forearm across her face, moving hair and sweat away from her eyes.

"Suits me if the captain don't find out. Around him it'll be Miss Fox." The respect in his face showed clearly, and Lila wondered what there was in Sander MacCormack that made these men follow him this way.

Whatever it was, it led to organization and far less looting than she'd expected. The place was filthy but basically intact. She loaded the bacon and biscuits on one of Mama's biggest platters and handed it to Blainey.

"How do you have meals, usually? The dining room wouldn't seat twenty."

"The enlisted men have just been hunkering down on the porch, once we get our food. And it hasn't looked this good. Sergeant Phillips ain't found anybody who could cook worth a damn."

"What about Fay?"

Blainey snorted. "Her? She couldn't boil water. They didn't even bother asking. She eats plenty. She sits inside, with the officers and such."

He seemed to read her look of panic. "Oh, she doesn't ever come down for breakfast. Half the time she don't even make an appearance before noon. Want me to take this in there?"

"If you would, Blainey. There's more biscuits when those are gone."

When he had left, Lila realized she'd forgotten to tell him to come back for the coffeepot. Using toweling to swing the hot, heavy pot off the stove, she started up the stairs to the dining room.

Captain MacCormack was sitting at the head of the table, one hand protectively at his right temple. He seemed to wince when the coffeepot hit the table with a thump. "It's hot. And you look like you need some," Lila said, going to the corner cupboard to get a cup.

She put it in front of him and poured a cup. "And good morning to you too, Miss Fox," he said, still moving his head gingerly. "I trust you slept well."

"For sleeping in a pigsty. You keep this bunch orderly, but their cleanliness leaves something to be desired, Captain MacCormack."

"We are soldiers—" he began.

"And filth will breed disease among soldiers just as quickly as among anyone else," Lila said, running a finger along the greasy surface of the table. "This is going to change, sir."

"It will. I should have gotten to it sooner."

"We'll get to it *now*, Captain. I do not intend to see my home collapse around my ears from neglect. Do these men have more than one uniform issued?"

"In most cases, they're lucky to have an entire one. Private Hoskins's was made by his mother when he joined," Sander said, taking a sip of his coffee. "They have some change of clothing about them, for the most part."

"Good. I haven't seen anything that needed burning yet, but then I haven't met all the enlisted men."

MacCormack's chuckle was mostly hidden by his coffee cup. Then he straightened up and looked up at Lila. His hair curled in dark brown profusion much longer than it should have. His beard was clean but scruffy. She had intended to say something tart, something about his own need for a wash and trim to be an

HALF THE BATTLE

inspiration to his men. Then the full force of those eyes hit her.

His eyes were magnificent, a deeper brown than any she had ever seen. When he smiled, which she suspected was not often from the lines beginning to etch a path between his dark eyebrows, there was a sparkle to his eyes. It wasn't golden, exactly. Lila tried to put a name to that sparkle. Bronze or copper. In that sparkle she began to get an idea of why his men followed Sander MacCormack.

He, too, seemed mesmerized for a moment. The sparkle in his eyes stayed even when his smile faded. He moistened his lips as if to speak, then there was a noise in the doorway and his eyes narrowed. "It looks as if you're about to meet the enlisted men, Miss Fox. Best stand out of the way of their breakfast if you don't wish to be trampled."

Lila knew enough about hungry men to do just as he said. Sander made some introductions. Lila wondered if she would be around long enough to sort out the mob. For the most part the names rolled over her, and their owners just seemed to be an identical horde of brown-haired, ragged young men.

When the soldiers had trooped through the dining room filling plates, and she'd put out the last of the biscuits, Lila turned to their commanding officer. "That lineup settled it for me, Captain MacCormack. If you would be so kind, when you're issuing orders, tell the men to stack all clothing they can possibly spare in a pile under that oak at the corner of the kitchen, and spare me two to keep the fire going and help wring. I plan to spend most of my day doing laundry." It was bad enough having a mob lounging on the parlor furniture. It didn't have to be a filthy mob.

"And I plan to spend mine rounding up some supplies," MacCormack said, rising. "But I will tell them before I leave. And, Miss Fox? I appreciate this, truly. I know what this must be doing to you. I'm sorry to be a part of it."

He looked at her again, with that intensity, and Lila had to swallow hard to get her tongue to move again. "You have no idea, Captain, what this is doing to me, and if I have my way you'll never find out," Lila shot out, her empathy with the man's lame apology gone. Her pain at seeing her home overrun with Confederate soldiers was going to stay her own, no part of it becoming this stranger's, no matter how expressive his brown eyes. She turned and walked out. Right now she had a fire to build.

Lila judged it must have been about five in the evening when she quit doing laundry. Her hands were raw, she'd gone through all the lye soap she could find, as well as two sets of helpers, and that wasn't counting the two young men she'd set to kitchen work in the middle of the afternoon so that she could have stew with dumplings ready by the time everyone was prepared to eat.

She was beginning to tell some of the men apart. One of the Davis boys—George, Lila thought it was—came back from tipping the tubs over in the herb garden. "You got anything else for us to do, Miss Fox?"

"Yes, I believe I do. Unless Sergeant Phillips has something to be done, I want you and anybody else who's free to go get a handful of that soft soap out of the barrel, take it down to the creek and bathe. Understand?"

"Yes, ma'am." George spread the word, and within minutes there wasn't a gray uniform to be seen anywhere except draped over the wash lines or the bushes. As she stirred the stew and added a touch more salt, Lila noticed that even Phillips dug a handful of soap out and slunk down the road with the rest. She resisted crowing.

Now all she had to do was wait for MacCormack and his supply detail to return. Lila felt odd, putting supper on the table without the commanding officer. She stepped back into her room for the first time since she'd left it that morning, aware that there were still cobwebs in the corners and dust on the floor, but she had no energy to change that.

However, there were two dripping rags in the kitchen, hung over a chair. Both were clean and wet, and there was enough vinegar to dampen one of them and begin on the filthy window. At least that would be done before she went to bed.

On the last pane, as she looked out, she saw the little band up the road returning. The two privates were driving a scrawny brindle cow. Corporal Reed seemed to be limping slightly, and Sander brought up the rear. Lila, wiping the last of the window, noticed that the front brim of his hat had an odd, lacy effect.

She went out to meet them. The warm air in the yard seemed even warmer as she got closer. "Captain MacCormack. I've been holding supper until you returned in case you had some orders."

"No orders, and precious little to add to the supper," he said, sounding tired. He took off his hat to beat the dust off it, and Lila had to stifle a laugh. "Would that be buckshot damage, sir?"

Sander handed the reins of his horse to the private who came back to take them and lead the animal away. "It would. I made the acquaintance of yet another of the fine citizens of this county—of German origin, they all happen to be Uncle Abraham's finest supporters. I suppose *verdammte Rebell* needs little translation into English. Even if it did, the buckshot spoke for itself."

"Eloquently," Lila said. "I expect your men can be glad you profess to be a gentleman, sir."

He looked puzzled for a minute; then, staring at his damaged hat, he understood. "I expect. If this had been on my head instead of in my hand, I'd be minus a nose. That woman is a good shot." The glint in Sander's eyes challenged her to share his laughter.

He looked around the yard. "When I left here, Miss Fox, I had twelve men around the place set to various jobs, and two more detailed to help you. I know you are determined, but you couldn't have done away with or driven off the lot of them."

"They're all down at the creek, taking a much-needed bath, Captain MacCormack."

"And I think after supper I will follow their example," he said. "For now I'll just avail myself of the pitcher in my room. If, in fact, it's still my room?"

His question made anger flare in Lila. "I've been busy enough out here today, Captain, not to have made it inside the house once, much less to have rummaged through your room. I sent your orderly in for any clothing that seemed to need washing. You can claim yours if you recognize it. Now I need to finish up supper."

Lila turned and walked across the yard into the stuffy little kitchen. The dumplings were steaming on top of the stew that was heavy on carrots and cabbage out of the garden to stretch out the chickens she'd culled out after Blainey had pointed them out as two who'd stopped laying. Still, the herb garden had yielded good things, and it would be a decent meal for all of them.

Rebel or not, she couldn't see them starve, not on her property. Especially not Sander MacCormack after the day he'd had. Thinking again of his hat gave her a vicious satisfaction as she got dinner on.

He was perceptive. It wasn't for lack of desire that she hadn't rooted around in his quarters. She'd just gotten so busy she'd never had the time. At least now they'd all smell better.

The kettle was heavy, and it was a considerable effort to get it into the dining room. The reward for that effort was to see Fay breeze down the stairs in Lila's best summer frock. Her hair was done nicely, she smelled of lavender and her arms, instead of looking plain old fat as they had last night, looked plump in the white muslin.

"Oh, good. I was getting pretty peckish," Fay said, going to the corner cupboard and getting a bowl.

"You could at least wait for Captain MacCormack and the men," Lila said, not bothering to hide her aggravation.

"I expect that would be the mannerly thing to do, wouldn't it? And I'm going to have to stand more on manners, I can see, if I don't want you yowling at me every step of the way." Fay's eyes narrowed. "I've got too good a thing here to let you ruin it."

"It is good for you, isn't it? Plenty of food, no work, and a roof over your head. Didn't it ever occur to you to do something to earn it?"

Lila regretted her remark the moment she finished speaking. A sly grin spread across Fay's face. "Oh, I earn it all right. Just not the way you'd ever think of doing."

Lila brushed past her and took a bowl out of the cabinet. She ladled herself some stew and headed for the door. "It's too warm in here. Tell Captain MacCormack I've gone to my quarters."

"I'll do that and see if he gives any notice," Fay said.

Lila went to sit in the creaking rocker in the corner of her room. The bowl of stew didn't really tempt her, but she knew she'd worked all day and needed the food. So she ate, noting that next time she'd add more rosemary. If there was a next time. With any luck she'd get inside the house, find Ty's money and be gone to St. Louis soon. She wondered how often MacCormack left the place all day.

She dipped into her bowl again, imagining him confronting Katie Wilhelm and getting a load of buckshot for thanks. It must have been a blow to his earnest dignity to have to leave that fast. Still, he'd told the tale with some humor. There was something engaging about him. Why couldn't he just be oafish and abrasive like Phillips? That way she could rifle his things without feeling bad.

As it was, she felt compelled to answer his dignity with her own. That was about all she had left at this point, a little pride and dignity. And it wasn't going to get her to St. Louis. She scraped the bowl clean and set it in the kitchen. The last of the men were disappearing into the house. Lila grabbed up the little basket she'd set aside earlier and moved. She ambled in the direction of the privy and hoped no one noticed that she just kept going.

This time she managed to make enough noise that Chloe wasn't surprised when she entered the cave. "You settled right in, didn't you? Got them doing laundry. And you were the one telling me you couldn't get organized again," Chloe said, her dark eyes dancing.

Lila set her basket down. "Chloe, the whole place is

HALF THE BATTLE 45

filthy. If we're going to keep things going until Ty and Marcus get home, I have to do something."

"You're doing plenty," Chloe said. "I was worried about you for a while, but once I saw two of those boys hanging wet clothes, I figured you had the situation in hand."

"Well enough in hand to bring you a bowl of chicken stew with dumplings. How are you feeling?"

"Fine," Chloe said. "When I'm not being kicked in the ribs, I'm almost cheerful. You find Ty's hoard yet, or the rebels already get to it?"

"I don't think they've found it. The operation seems to be short on cash. That or they're mighty poor traders." She told Chloe about the skinny cow in the barn. And about her suspicions regarding Phillips. Chloe stayed silent, listening and eating.

Chloe finished her stew and handed back the bowl. "You'd better get back there before they start wondering where you are."

"Nobody will come looking for me," Lila said.

"Nobody?" Chloe questioned.

Lila wondered why the image of Sander MacCormack flashed instantly to mind. "Well, perhaps the commanding officer. He might think I've taken off for good, and I don't want to give him that satisfaction yet."

"Then get on back there."

Lila went over and gave her friend a quick hug. "I won't be able to do this every day, but I'll come when I can. And remember, if something happens and you need me, tie a red rag to that stump out there. I'll get here as quick as I can."

"Don't worry. I'll try."

Lila stopped at the doorway with her basket. "I almost

forgot. Do you still have any of that lotion from Mama's recipe that we put up last winter?"

"The glycerin and rose water? I took both bottles that were left. They're in the trunk over there. Go ahead and take one. I figured once you saw a mirror again you'd come looking for a bottle. It's automatic, the way your Mama raised both of us. We move along just fine until we start thinking about things. Then I don't know about you, but I hear her voice saying 'Child, just look at those hands.' "

Lila laughed while she was rummaging in the trunk. "I do too. And after I finished that much laundry today, I couldn't think of anything else."

"There's more to it than that," Chloe pressed. "That woman is still there, isn't she?"

Lila sat up straight on the rock floor where she'd settled. "Does that mean you leave this cave once in a while?"

"When I know it's safe," Chloe said between bites. "I can sneak over to the Rogerses'—across the ford and through the woods. Sallie is still there, and we talk some."

"And naturally you talk about the rebels."

Chloe nodded. "Of course. Neither Sallie nor I would talk to them, so we might as well talk about them. And Fay makes the most interesting subject. Talk is, she says she's a widow woman." The emphasis she put on the last phrase told Lila what Chloe thought. "Don't let her get under your skin."

"That's easy to say. She's not wearing your best dress."

"From what I hear, she won't wear yours long enough to get it wrinkled," Chloe said with a hoot. Lila grimaced at her as she left, hurrying across the field in a zigzag in case anyone noticed her coming.

The men were still all too busy with their supper or their relaxation afterward to pay her any attention. Lila went into her room and stowed the lotion in the dresser. Then she went into the yard and found the few pieces of her own clothing that she'd laundered. It was easy because she'd hung them herself, not wanting George Davis to turn red up to the ears from having to touch her things.

When the sun had almost gone down and the men seemed to be settling in at hands of cards or other pursuits, Lila found a piece of toweling and her own handful of soap, and headed for the creek. She looked around twice to make sure she was truly alone before she found the place where the water deepened at the bend, making a pool where she could stand and wash her hair.

She slipped out of her shoes and unbuttoned the dress, letting it slip to the ground, followed by the rest of her clothing. At the last moment she couldn't strip naked, imagining some errant rebel heading down for a little fishing. So she kept on her chemise as she went into the cool water, telling herself she would just go back to her room in her drawers and dress.

The water was warm at the surface, but deeper down it was cold and welcoming, and Lila plunged under it to feel the coolness on all of her skin. Coming up for air, she lathered her hair, working the soap through it. Even the plain soft soap she would normally use for dishes felt luxurious.

She plunged under the water again, working the soap out of her hair, coming up for a breath, then going down again. When she stood again, feeling the mud and pebbles of the creek bottom under her, Lila wanted to hug herself, not from cold but just from a burst of gladness. She was alive and the moon was rising clear above her and the stars were coming out.

She soaped her arms and rinsed, the cool water making hard buttons of her nipples under her chemise. Frogs were beginning to plop in the shallows nearby, and there was another noise, of something larger. Lila hoped it wasn't a fat blacksnake sliding off the bank in search of the frogs.

As she shivered, something did pass by her leg, something warm and sleek, and she shrieked. The surface of the water broke about six feet away, and a man rose, head and shoulders, out of the water. It was MacCormack, his dark curls flattened by the water streaming around him.

Lila nearly shrieked again. "You about scared me to death," she said, knowing she sounded on the verge of a scream. "Couldn't you let me bathe in peace?"

"I didn't realize there was anyone here until it was much too late to leave politely, Miss Fox." MacCormack's voice was low.

"Oh, for heaven's sake, call me Lila. Formality just doesn't go with sharing a creek. Which I have no intention of doing any longer," she said, arms still folded protectively across her chest.

"I see. Which one of us do you recommend to scramble buck-naked up the bank, Lila?" There was a humor in his voice that made her name sound different than when anyone else said it.

"Naked? You mean to tell me you are standing there. . . ."

"You mean you aren't? People generally bathe without their clothes on."

"I was afraid someone might come down to the creek

to fish, but I certainly didn't think anyone would be bathing. Especially not you."

"It's my second in command who seems to be averse to water, not me. And I noticed that you even convinced him to take a swim this evening. The widow Culpepper has another reason to thank you." Even in the near dark Lila could catch the sparkle in Sander's eyes by way of the moonlight. She could sense that he was using teasing to hold her at bay as successfully as she was using her position, close to the bank, to keep away from him.

"Turn around, MacCormack. I can trust you, can't I?"

"You may, madam. Just as much as I can trust you."

Lila decided that put a new light upon the situation, but the moment his back was turned, she scrambled up the bank. Grabbing the rough toweling, she rubbed her hair, her arms and shoulders. It was useless to dry herself any further with her dripping chemise still on.

She had two choices. She could put her dress on over the wet undergarment and hope they both dried by morning. Or she could trust that the tall rebel in the water would keep his back turned while she changed. Lila looked over her shoulder. It was a fine back, pale in the moonlight which defined all the muscles of his broad shoulders, and his torso narrowed to the water line. It was still turned.

Lila stripped off the dripping shift and quickly rubbed herself dry. Her skin reacted to the rough toweling and to the man behind her by raising the biggest goose bumps she had ever seen, or felt, and she shivered as she pulled her dress on and struggled to fasten the buttons in back.

Still struggling she looked back again. Sander had turned sideways and was watching her. His white grin flashed in the moonlight. "Caught you peeking," he said before he dove under the water and was gone, surfacing far out of reach on the other bank. Lila stalked home, leaving a dripping trail behind her.

Four

Sander listened to the rustle of the leaves and twigs as Lila got farther from the creek. Hadn't she been a treat in the moonlight? Pale skin glistening with water droplets, hair streaming over one shoulder, she had looked like those classical Greek statues the head of the military school back in Boonville had in his garden. And just about as accessible, Sander reminded himself.

He swam to the other bank, where his clothes were piled, and thought about the disturbing Lila. More than likely he was the only one she disturbed. From her reaction to the widow Culpepper, Sander could tell what Lila's conduct would be around his men. That was just as well. He had his hands full right now with Fay, trumped-up and playing cards with the men every night.

He had been looking forward to Lila's company at supper and had been disappointed when Fay was there instead, looking like an overripe peach stuffed into that summer dress. He could imagine what it would have looked like on Lila. On her, the thin muslin would have floated and clung in just the right places instead of being the unflattering second skin it had become on Fay. The image of Lila in the dress had cut down considerably on the amount of supper he consumed and had pulled him here to cool off in the creek.

What he'd seen was not relieving. Lila's body had stirred things in him he didn't know were there anymore. Those desires had gotten him into the worst trouble of his life less than a year ago. Not a day passed that he didn't regret his actions with Evie, and that had all started with a chance encounter in the moonlight. He had no use for desires. He had a command to lead. Still dripping, he pulled on his clothes.

His shirt was missing a button again. Sander wondered idly if Lila would find one and sew it on if asked. He laughed. The woman didn't trust him farther than she could throw him, and he felt the same way about her. Judging from this little episode tonight, both of them were right in their feelings. He still savored the look of surprise she'd worn when she'd turned around and looked straight at him. No, he couldn't quite trust her. But Sander would still ask her to sew on a button for him, and more than likely, she would do it. It was a funny world that war created.

There was a lamp burning in Lila's window when Sander got back to the house. He thought about going straight up the stairs instead, then found himself drawn to the rough door. He knocked and called softly. "Miss Fox? Lila?"

"Just a minute." She was dressed when she opened the door; barefoot in the cotton dress that was the only one he'd seen her wear since she got here. Her damp hair was twisted into a roll on either side of her head, then coiled tight in the back. In the lamplight Sander could see short golden wisps springing up, begging to be smoothed down. He stood for a moment, just looking at her hair, and his hand moved slightly toward it before he mastered himself.

"I was wondering if you could tell me if there might be some buttons about," he began, showing her the gap in the middle of his chest. "I seem to be short one or two."

"Probably lost them trying to move so quickly this afternoon, dodging that buckshot. You weren't hurt, were you?"

"Not a scratch." She honestly seemed to care about the answer. "But I am minus a button."

"That we can fix. Come in and sit down. I'll go see if my sewing box is still where I left it." She walked out and Sander went to the only chair in the room, a low rocker in front of the fireplace.

She'd been working in here. There weren't any cobwebs in the corners, and the windows threw back the gleam of the lamp. It gave Sander a little pang to see the homey way Lila had settled into this small space. Here he was, overrunning her house with a company of infantry. She should be the one in that big bedroom upstairs, and instead she had a shuck mattress and a cracked mirror behind the kitchen.

Still, he was only doing his job. He had found a large, unoccupied house when he had eighteen men to keep housed and fed. That Lila had come back to try and claim the place was her problem. She shouldn't have left it in the first place.

Lila opened the door softly and walked down the hall. There was another card game going on in the parlor. It seemed to be all that Sergeant Phillips and some of the other men ever did. And it was definitely the Culpepper woman's favorite form of recreation. Or favorite save one, Chloe would say. The thought made Lila smile crookedly to herself.

The floor under her feet was gritty. Didn't any of this bunch care that they were destroying her home? She made a mental note to start working in here before the hardwood was damaged. She went into the parlor, looking for her workbasket. It was pushed into a corner by the chaise, and she bent to get it.

"We dealing you in?" Yancey called.

"I believe not, thank you." No sense in rising to his bait, Lila reasoned. After all, he was going to be here for a while. No, she'd worry about Yancey when she had enough evidence to see him hang. An argument each time they spoke would be tiresome. "Just retrieving my workbasket."

"Ah, domesticity," Fay murmured, to the laughter of the men. "If you feel that much like sewing, there're a couple of things in the corner in my room that could use a few stitches."

"I'll go look," Lila said, taking the basket and going swiftly up the stairs. Fay was in the middle of a hand of cards, and there would be no better time to get a first look without being bothered.

The whitewashed perfection that Lila had left behind was gone. Clothes in various states of cleanliness and repair were flung everywhere. Lila made a note to burn the sheets if Fay and Yancey ever vacated the place.

She went through the closest pile of clothing quickly. Fay would never miss a few underthings, and even if she did, the woman wasn't stupid enough to ask for them back. With a few scrubbings and a good sun bleaching Lila would nearly double her wardrobe.

There were still more rooms to look at, and she hadn't much time. Walking into her parents' bedroom

HALF THE BATTLE 55

made her fists ball around the material she was carrying. Even after Ty was the man of the house, he'd never moved in here, and now there seemed to be three rebel soldiers inhabiting it. Her anger would have to wait, because she couldn't do anything about it now. Lila slipped across the hall.

Ty's room was not much different than he'd left it, save for a thick layer of dust and a few sparse belongings. The pile of laundry, clean and sharply folded, that she'd earmarked as Sander's, was on the bed. Lila's fingers itched to start looking in the desk drawers, but there just wasn't time now.

She went to the old nursery. Even the trundle bed in there seemed to be used to accommodate a Confederate. She wrinkled her nose and walked on. In the cupboard in the corner was the crock she'd been looking for, stuffed full with buttons. She grabbed it and started down the stairs.

Lila went swiftly out the back door before Fay could notice her armload of white goods. The room behind the kitchen looked like a haven compared to the stuffy house full of noisy people. Through the window, she could see Sander sitting in the chair, his head was lolling back on the rocker, one leg stretched out in front of him. It was a long leg, lean and muscled, in worn trousers.

Lila had noticed last night how scuffed his boots were, and now the other memory, of the firmness of the muscles under the cloth and leather, came flooding back as well. His shirt gapped where the button was missing. His skin was darker than it had looked in the moonlight at the creek, and the curling hair on his chest that peeked through the gap was even darker.

She shook her head. This was ridiculous. She'd seen

naked male bodies before. The last three months, taking care of Papa, she'd seen more of a male body than she'd ever wanted. But she'd never invited a male to sit in her bedroom and take off any of his clothing before as she was about to do now.

Would his chest be as magnificent as his back had been in the moonlight? Could she sew on a button with him watching without jabbing a needle through her finger? Of course she could. There was no sense in having vapors like a schoolgirl over some ragged rebel.

She pushed open the door and he jerked awake, grabbing the arms of the rocker. When he saw her at the doorway, he relaxed a little, settling back into the chair. Lila wasn't sure what unnerved her more, his smile or watching him ease back into comfort, stretching one leg in front of him. "Must have dozed off. Sorry."

"Don't apologize to me, Captain. I was gone quite a while." She left the door open a little to get the night breeze. This room, with him in it, needed to be cooler than it was.

"Well," she said, going over and sitting on the bed. A pointed look in the captain's direction wasn't having much effect. He just looked back at her, blankly, as if he'd forgotten the purpose of his being here. "Your shirt, Captain. Take it off. I can hardly sew on the button with you still wearing the shirt."

It was hard to tell if the flush on his high cheekbones was a trick of the light or the beginning of a blush. "I can give it to you and come back if you want."

Lila discovered that wasn't what she wanted at all. "Just slip the shirt off and hand it to me. While I'm sewing the button on, why don't you borrow my scissors and trim up your whiskers?"

"Part of the plan to bring order out of chaos?" he

asked. But Sander slipped off his shirt and handed it to her. Lila hadn't counted on his nearness while she cut herself a length of thread. He held out a hand to take the scissors, and she gave them over gladly just to have him farther away.

His chest was broad and sprinkled with a forest of coarse dark hair. The thought of the combination of textures that would provide made Lila's fingers tremble as she sewed. She worked out a neat little rhythm. First, she pushed the needle into the cloth at the right spot. It took a while to draw the thread through the material, and each time, as she pulled the thread, she watched the man intent on his work in the mirror. Then it was a quick stick of the needle, and back to the sight of Sander.

There was a vast difference between her father's wasted, white old flesh or the ropy muscles Uncle Ernest had displayed when Aunt Ruth had made him wash outside before trooping into her clean house of an evening and what Lila was seeing now.

This was a man in the prime of his life, lithe and hard with the exercise that went with the physical training of a soldier. As he leaned over the dresser close to the wavy mirror, Sander's muscles were taut, his flesh firm and golden. Lila wondered if she should offer to trim the overlong hair at the back of his neck when she was done. Just the thought of what that skin would feel like made her reject the idea.

He whistled tonelessly between his teeth, seemingly unaware of Lila as he concentrated on his task. She shifted in discomfort, suddenly aware of the heavy fabric of her skirt around her legs, the lack of breeze in the room. The shuck mattress rattled with her every movement.

Lila's next pass through the shirt plunged the needle deep into her finger. Her high yelp made Sander drop the scissors and wheel around. "Did you stick yourself?"

"Humph." It was the only noise she could make with a finger still in her mouth. "Of all the inane questions. Of course I stuck myself. Do I look like someone who would squeal otherwise?"

He was beside her. "You're bleeding. Are you sure you're all right?"

"I'll be fine. But take the shirt off my lap. I don't want to stain it."

Sander picked up the shirt and dropped it onto the rocker without ever moving from his spot next to her. He took her finger in his hand. The warmth of the contact made her flinch.

"Does it still hurt?" His eyes were so deep and so close to her that Lila's tongue cleaved to the roof of her mouth.

"It's getting better," she finally managed.

"Good. I wouldn't want you hurt on my account." But he didn't let go of her hand. In fact, Sander leaned in toward her. He had found a sprig of mint somewhere between the creek and her room. As his face drew nearer she caught the spicy cool smell of peppermint.

Then he came even closer, and the illusion of coolness vanished. His mouth was hot, tasting of mint, but with a fiery note as his lips searched hers. He still held her left hand between them, but as the kiss deepened Lila let her right hand trace the path it had been aching to follow since she'd started watching him in the mirror.

Sander's skin felt even more like warm velvet than she'd imagined, and his muscles rippled slightly under her touch. Past his shoulders, up the column of his neck, damp tendrils of hair met her fingers where her hand came to rest, caressing the back of his neck. It was the strangest sensation, the back of her hand cool as little drops of water teased down her fingers from his hair, the palm almost feverishly warm with the touch of his skin.

Then as he leaned into the kiss, brushing his lips over hers with more force, his hand in her lap closed over her fingers by reflex right on the spot she'd stuck. Lila couldn't stifle the whimper she made in the depth of their kiss. Sander pulled away from her quickly, his dark eyes dazed.

He swallowed hard, then found his voice. "Forgive me. I didn't mean to . . . I'll take my shirt and go."

"You'll wait just a minute. My needle is still attached to that shirt," Lila said, jumping up and getting the scissors he had dropped. Neatly finding the tail of thread, knotting it quickly and snipping it, she handed the shirt back. "Now you can go, Captain."

He backed out of the room, eyes wide. The back door of the house slammed behind him before Lila thought it would have been possible to cross the flagstones and leap the steps to the porch. Somehow she knew he was heading straight for the sanctuary of one of those jugs she'd seen in the dining room. She wondered what sanctuary this warm little room would offer her.

Her room was the closest she got to a sanctuary for days. Everywhere else she seemed to run into Sander. Always the back of him, quickly leaving a room when she entered it. At times when he couldn't leave, he was suddenly in deep conversation with someone. It certainly surprised Blainey Hoskins one morning at breakfast to suddenly have the full attention of his commanding officer. And one evening at dinner Fay Culpepper was so amazed to have Sander ask a question about her earlier life in Tennessee she nearly choked.

Lila found it harder and harder to bite back a grin. At first she had been mortified that simply sewing on a button had resulted in an embrace with a near stranger. Especially since the near stranger was a Confederate officer. But then, when she realized that he was even more upset over it all than she was, Lila's tension eased.

Judging from the actions of those around him, Sander didn't usually fluster easily. The men brought every small problem to him, bypassing Yancey whenever possible. A dozen times a day, Lila would pause from stirring a pot, sweeping a floor or hanging clean curtains to watch someone seek him out.

Few of them walked away discouraged. Lila's store of knowledge about Sander grew daily, fueled by each encounter with his men. Chloe, when told all this, was not properly sympathetic. "He's not Moses in the Promised Land, Lila, just a rebel soldier. And not even high ranking. You could at least find yourself a major," she said, scraping the bowl clean from the dinner Lila had managed to spirit away.

"But he is honest and fair," Lila said. "Too fair, I think. If I were him I'd make some changes around there."

"Like throwing Fay out a window," Chloe muttered.

"I'm not sure she's even worth hauling to the window."

"She won't stay around forever," Chloe said. "First sign of any trouble, she'll be gone."

"That's the only thing I'm afraid of," Lila said, stirring Chloe's small fire idly with a stick. "Trouble's bound to catch up with us soon."

HALF THE BATTLE

"What makes you say that?" Chloe leaned forward awkwardly, with the growing bulk of her middle pressing out in front.

"They've started drilling every day. Sander knows something. They all do."

"Well, keep listening. And keep looking for the money. Are you sure they haven't found it?"

"Positive," Lila said. "Ty left me over thirty dollars. That would get us to St. Louis and keep us there a while."

Chloe scowled. "What do you mean, us? I'm staying right where I am until this baby is born and for a while after."

"Then I can't be making any trips to St. Louis," Lila said firmly. "I'm going to be here too."

"Fine pair we'll make," Chloe said, trying to hide a quaver in her voice. "You ever seen a baby being born?"

Lila shook her head. "I've heard about plenty. Mama and Aunt Ruth used to talk when they thought we weren't listening. Evie and I would hang out of bed in the loft trying to hear. What about you?"

Chloe shook her head. "Not exactly. Even when your mama would take me with her, it was always just to help out for a while. But it's all natural, isn't it? Women been doing this since time started."

Lila, looking at the huge bulge of Chloe's middle and those narrow hips below it, tried to sound as cheerful. "When the time comes, we'll do just fine."

Hurrying back to the house in the dark, Lila prayed fervently that it would really be that way. That even without a proper midwife or doctor, or anybody except the two of them, Chloe's baby would be born safe and healthy. And Chloe would stay that way too. Lila didn't know what she would do without her. Since her mother had died when she was fourteen, Chloe had been her constant companion.

With Mama gone, and now Aunt Ruth and Evie, there was only Chloe left. If she died too, Lila would feel like the only woman left in the world.

"We'll do just fine," Lila told herself again as she got to her room. "We'll do just fine."

"Some of us better than others." The sly hiss near her shoulder made Lila start when she realized she'd been talking to herself aloud and someone else had answered. It was Fay, melting out of the shadows on the path. "Where is it you go, anyway, so many nights? You hiding some Union deserter who slunk back here? I'll bet Yancey would love to know about that." The woman's eyes looked small and glittered in the faint light from the back of the house.

"I don't know what you're talking about," Lila said, trying to slip the small bundle with Chloe's bowl into the bushes near the door, where Fay wouldn't notice.

"Sure you don't." She pushed a surprisingly bony finger into Lila's chest. "You've got somebody out there in the woods. It can only be one somebody or we'd have heard about it by now. But a person's out there."

"You can't prove anything." Lila willed herself not to tremble.

"I can't prove anything, but I can make plenty of trouble with the folks that can," Fay said. "That is, unless you want to make a deal."

"Deal? What are you talking about?" Lila could almost hear the clicks and whirs in the machinery of the other woman's mind as she smiled.

"Where's your jewelry? You don't need it out here in the yard. When all is said and done, you won't need it anyway. Even if all of this crew up and leaves tomorrow, you've still got this house. You won't starve."

Lila stared at her dumbly. "My jewelry?"

"I've gone through everything, and I still can't find it."

"That's because it's not there." The numbness was spreading, making her light-headed.

"What did you do, bury it? I could probably get all the way back to Tennessee on just that one necklace you wore in that pretty picture. Where is it?"

Lila tried as hard as she could not to start giggling hysterically. "It's buried out back. Just walk down to that big hackberry tree down the hill and dig about six feet down. Of course, it won't look the same . . ."

"Not if it's been buried for a while," Fay said thoughtfully. "But we could rub it with salt and potato water."

"No, it won't look the same at all," Lila said, trying not to twitter. "It has brass handles now and it's black."

Fay stared at her as if she were speaking a foreign tongue. "What on earth are you saying?"

"Papa's coffin. That's where my necklace went, and the earbobs and the two rings I had left. We sold them all for the funeral."

The older woman seemed to explode in a fury. "You mean I've been looking for a month for things that aren't even here?"

Lila leaned against the side of the stone building, the tight laughter building up inside her leaving her weak. It escaped in something between a laugh and a wail. "You can look until Christmas if you want, Fay. It's all gone."

Her hilarity was too much for Fay. With a shriek the woman flung herself at Lila, shaking her shoulders. "You're lying. You have to be. Where is it?"

Lila was just as loud when she answered. "It's gone. Sold for granite and marble and brass and ebony. And they're all rotting in a hole in the ground."

They tussled now, drawing a crowd of bewildered soldiers. Yancey thundered down the stairs, swearing. "Somebody get a bucket of water from the well. That ought to cool them off. Or maybe we should take bets first. Anybody know if Fay is as good at scrapping as she is at poker?"

Lila was trying to keep her opponent's claws away from her face. Fay had lost whatever pins she'd had in her hair. Yanking the tress of it streaming over her shoulder made her pull back, but not long enough for Lila to get away.

"What is going on here?" Sander's voice thundered through the noise of the assembled men and Fay's screeching. The yard around them was suddenly silent as he pushed his way down the stairs. "Sergeant Phillips, I don't know what's happening here, but why are you standing and watching it?"

Yancey laughed nervously. "Didn't know quite how to break it up. If they were men I would have just knocked their heads together and put them on picket duty. But I wouldn't trust either of these two with a gun, would you?"

Lila, pushing her hair out of her face, was surprised to see that Sander was shaking with barely suppressed fury. He turned from Yancey to glare at the two women. "I do not know why this occurred. But if there is ever another incident like this between the two of you, I will personally put both of you off this property. Understood?"

"Plain as day," Fay said. She flipped her skirts and sauntered into the house.

HALF THE BATTLE

Lila merely nodded and slipped through the door to her room as the knot of men and boys dispersed. She looked in the mirror, wincing. Her hair was tangled, and there was a scratch on one cheek, several drops of bright blood dotting its length.

She half-expected to hear a knock on the door once the men had gone. But there was none. Instead she could hear Sander and Yancey, in intense conversation, going into the house. The same house where Fay was, who had threatened to tell them that Lila was hiding someone. She looked around the room. There was no sanctuary here at all.

Five

By the time he'd had a talk with Yancey and Fay Culpepper, Sander was ready to find his jug out of sheer frustration. Fay said about six words, leaving him angrier than when he'd started to talk to her. Usually a drink calmed him down after an encounter with Fay, but he could tell from the first sip that it would not soothe the raw places tonight. He tossed off one glass of the burning liquid and walked outside.

The grove was quiet, filled only with fireflies. He walked around the house, listening to men settling down for sleep, hushed conversations going on in and near the tents.

He tried to tell himself that his real destination hadn't been Lila's room. But he couldn't convince himself. There was a light burning, and he knocked on the door. "Lila?"

"Yes?" She opened the door a crack. Lamplight shone through the opening.

Now that he was here, Sander hardly knew what to say to her. "I wanted to make sure you were all right."

Her shoulders stiffened. "I'll survive. I'm just not used to being attacked."

"For being unused to it, you put up a good show.

What was worth getting that involved with that woman, anyway? She sure wouldn't tell me."

Lila looked relieved. "There's nothing much to tell. We argued. It was stupid." She wasn't saying much more than Fay.

"I can't afford to have my authority undermined that way, Lila."

She took a step back from the doorway, her gray eyes wide. She had a long scratch down one pale cheek, with two or three other places where Fay had drawn blood. It made him hurt to look at her. "Your authority? What does this have to do with you?"

Anger and aggravation flared in him. "I'm supposed to be in charge here. I can't have the people under my command having caterwauling fights in the yard."

Her chin tilted forward defiantly. "Let me remind you that neither Mrs. Culpepper nor I are under your command."

Sander stepped into the room so that he didn't have to shout. "You two may not be soldiers, but as long as you choose to stay here you are under my command. And you will act as if you are."

Lila looked around as if she were searching for something to throw at him. "Captain MacCormack, you are without a doubt the most aggravating man I have ever met." She paced the few steps that covered the room, then turned back to face him. "Your attitude is so rich. You are sitting in my home, using all the things in it, and you have the gall to tell me that I am under your command."

Sander closed the distance between them. "Under my command also means under my protection. There're people out beyond this farm that would be far less kind to you."

Lila went white and silent. Sander felt as if he'd just poured a bucket of cold water on her. If mentioning the bushwhackers made that sort of impression, she had seen them. Perhaps she had even been in contact with them. The thought chilled Sander.

He watched fear replace anger in her face. "I'm sorry. Perhaps you're right." Her voice was almost a whisper. Lila's hand rose slightly from her side, then fluttered down before she could move toward him. She seemed to be looking for comfort. He had precious little to give. His awareness of Lila, of the fears in her that he had awakened with his threat but could not still, hung in the atmosphere.

"You're all right then?" Her silent pleading engulfed him. Her eyes still told him that he was her enemy. But they also asked for comfort. He traced a path along her cheek, near the scratch. Her skin was too beautiful to be marred with the jagged line left by Fay's claws. "That's going to be a nasty scratch."

It took her a while to answer. "It will heal." Sander withdrew his hand while he was still able to control the urge to pull her close.

So her wounds would heal. Good. He wished he could say the same about the throbbing ache she'd opened deep in him. "You're lucky." His hand dropped as he turned to go.

When he was almost at the door she spoke his name. "Sander, what do you look for? At night when you're out on the porch."

It could not be a secret he kept from her. There would be too many others. "Ghosts."

Lila shivered. "And do you find them?"

"Almost always." He turned and was gone.

* * *

HALF THE BATTLE 69

Lila ached in different places every night when she went to bed. There was a satisfaction in reclaiming a little bit of the house each day from the neglect and dirt the rebels had brought in. As the gray uniforms brushed past her a dozen times a day, Lila swore to herself that Ty would come back and find the place clean, well kept, whole and free of Confederates. She would see to it.

Still, each new day of cleaning, washing and scrubbing brought new blisters, different muscles protesting. The bright side was that none of the Rebs looked at her twice when she entered a room. No one, except Sander. Even if he didn't stop talking, the heat of his gaze bore through her.

Lila stole back a few of her own possessions. Fay never said a word. She hadn't spoken to Lila since the night they'd fought, and Lila wasn't about to change the situation. She was able to make away with a black silk skirt, left in a corner by Fay with its fastenings rent. Her crinoline had been pushed back into a corner too, apparently too constricting.

There was still the matter of a blouse. It wouldn't do to go into Ironton and board a train in a calico work dress. In the end it was a cotton nightdress that gave her the answer to her current puzzle. Getting it ready to launder, she spread it in her lap, looking at the wide ruffle that began just below the knees. There were yards and yards of fabric there. She got her seam ripper and started in.

Three days later she had a much shorter nightgown and a decent cotton blouse. The sleeves were narrow, and it wasn't fancy, but paired with the silk skirt it would do.

She folded the blouse carefully and put it in one of

the dresser drawers, under her one decent petticoat. Now all she needed was money. That was going to be a good deal harder to come by than the blouse.

The day she finished the blouse, Lila was dusting the best parlor. She got to the mantel, gently cleaning the figurines. The china shepherd and shepherdess had always been her favorites. Ty had always had a fondness for the awful Chinese dogs that squatted on the carpet, tongues lolling out. Lila stopped dusting, one hand hanging limp beside her with the rag trailing the floor. Of course. Ty had liked the dogs, and Ty had his own hiding places around the house. She had been looking in her most likely hiding places, not his.

As soon as the thought hit her, she knew where to go. But now there was no time. The house would be filling with soldiers at any moment, done drilling and practicing. A wave of frustration washed over her as she left the parlor.

Blainey Hoskins was her helper in the kitchen that night. Lila never knew whether to curse or to be glad over that. His familiar presence was a comfort, but he could talk the ears off a mule.

Tonight his first question surprised her so much she nearly dropped the bowl she was holding. "You think your brother will be mad, Miss Lila? At you turning Secesh and all?"

"Turning what?" she screeched.

Blainey gulped, his prominent Adam's apple bobbing. "Going Confederate."

"I didn't know I had," she choked out when she could find her tongue. Was the whole county discussing her apparent shift of allegiance?

Blainey peeled another potato, his brow wrinkling.

HALF THE BATTLE 71

"Well, you're feeding us and looking after everybody. Pa says you must have changed sides."

"Just feeding this tribe doesn't mean I agree with what you're doing. If I do the cooking and cleaning, I'm likely to have a home to keep when you're all gone. The night I got here, there was a pig in the kitchen." Lila stirred the contents of the bowl vigorously. "Besides, there're twenty armed men here, Blainey. What else am I likely to do?"

The boy looked at her as if trying to read something deep. "That's what Ma said. She said she feeds stray dogs, but that don't make them family."

"She's right," Lila said firmly, putting the bowl down on the worktable and dumping the potatoes in front of Blainey into a bubbling kettle on the stove. No, none of this crew of ragtag rebels were family. Unless, Lila thought, they were like particularly aggravating cousins who came too often and stayed too long, saying horrible things about your branch of the family.

It had never been that way with Evie. She and Lila had traded homes frequently, going from one place to another often until being on different sides of the war had pulled their fathers apart and into stiff politeness. Even then, Aunt Ruth had insisted that Lila needed a woman's guidance and had found reasons to have her come visit the dogtrot cabin, so Judge Fox had given in. That was family, and none of these rebels were anything like that.

Not even the tall man who had just stuck his head in the horse trough, Lila mused. Water streamed from Sander's dark hair as he stood, leaving a damp trail down his back. He sat on the edge of the trough, giving a short bark of laughter as several men followed his example, trying to cool off. The aggravation she felt around him wasn't the awful-cousin kind. It was more like having a burr under her chemise, pricking some tender spot.

Thursday morning, as soon as the rebels were all out of the house, Lila went to work. Sander was gone, and Yancey was conducting a fierce drill over the stubble of the hay fields. She went into Ty's room and locked the door. If Sander came back she would find some excuse for her behavior. With any luck, recruiting Blainey's two wavering cousins would take him most of the day.

Lila started at the doorway and searched the room with her eyes. The wardrobe was pathetically bare. One winter uniform, an extra pair of gray trousers and two shirts seemed to be all the spare clothing Sander possessed. A large black leather book with a clasp sat next to his second pair of boots. A family Bible, well thumbed with use. She unclasped it and leafed through the pages. Nothing was there between the leaves.

It had been his mother's, judging from the writing. Lydia McKenzie married to Andrew MacCormack. June 12, 1832. A son, Lysander. Lila looked at it twice. His name was Lysander Hugh MacCormack. Born August 17, 1833. Another son, Hector James in November of 1837. A rough scrawl noted Lydia's death three days after Hector's birth. Lila sat on the edge of the bed, the heavy volume in her hand. What must it have been like, a boy of four with a tiny new brother and no mother? Did the stern facade she saw every day start then?

A noise below made Lila close the Bible and put it back in its place. It was interesting, but it wasn't going to get her to St. Louis. She gave the desk one last look. It was the one that had been in Ty's room since he was eight. He had been so proud of it then, lording it over her that he had something of Grandpa Fox's.

It was at that age he began chasing Lila and Chloe through the grove, waving a wooden sword as they shrieked. He was the dread pirate Blackbeard or someone even more ferocious of his own making. As Lila saw the two little girls in her memory, running through the trees, she looked at the desk. Of course. Ty's pirate-treasure spot. Once he'd discovered the secret panel, he never hid any of his real treasures anywhere else.

Lila pried at the surface of the desk with her fingers until she found the grooves of a panel. It gave, sliding downward until it revealed the neat little hiding place where a small metal box rested. Lila slipped it out and dove down into the tiny watch pocket sewn into her dress. But there was no need for any of the tiny brass keys. The box swung open and money fell out onto the floor. Scrambling, she gathered it up. When she had finished counting the pile in her lap, there was thirty-two dollars.

Lila restrained the urge to giggle as she knotted the money up in a handkerchief and shoved the unwieldy bundle down the front of her dress, where it made a sweaty lump. There was really thirty-two dollars. Enough for a ticket to St. Louis and a room there when she got to town. She could see the Union commander and tell him about the rebel company, the raiders ranging between this county and the next.

As she put the desk back together, pushing it against the wall, her fingers got cold. She finally had the money to go to St. Louis. But if she did, well-armed soldiers in blue uniforms would come and attempt to annihilate Sander. And the Davis boys and Blainey Hoskins. The thought made Lila fight for breath. That wasn't what she wanted. She just wanted them to leave and give her home back to her.

She looked down at the bulging front of her dress. The packet was still too noticeable. She tied the money into the hem of her chemise and smoothed her skirt down over it. That was better.

Lila looked around the room one more time. Nothing looked too disturbed. She slipped down the stairs, thinking about what she should start for supper. She gave a bitter laugh. She was lovingly feeding men that tomorrow or the next day she would turn in to their enemies. It didn't make sense.

But then, neither did Ty and Marcus facing Cherokee warriors on the plains for Kansas nor Evie buried near the ruins of her home for some unknown offense. What could a nineteen-year-old girl do to make a soldier like Yancey kill her? Lila headed toward the hot kitchen to start cooking.

Once supper was over, with Sander and Blainey still not back, she tidied up and slipped away. Fay hadn't said anything to anyone, so Lila had started going back to Chloe when she could. "You still won't come with me?" Lila asked.

"Positive. I'm not going anywhere." Chloe looked down pointedly at her huge belly. It couldn't really have grown much in the three days since Lila had been to the cave, but the shadow it cast on the wall was enormous.

"I suppose you're right. Should we try to find a midwife?"

"Only one I can think of is Arlie Hoskins, and she's not real sympathetic."

"Not as the mother of Madison County's proudest

addition to The Cause," Lila said. "Try to hold off for a week or so then, all right?"

"I'm truly not due for weeks yet, Lila. It only feels that way," Chloe grumbled. "You go on and go to St. Louis. If anything happens, I can get to Sallie Rogers."

Lila kept her thoughts on what a twenty-year-old widow would know about childbirth to herself. "Should I bring back anything?"

"Ten or twelve yards of bird's-eye would be nice. And a cradle. And what about a dozen oranges? I sure have had a craving." Chloe's smile was wicked, and Lila stuck out her tongue. "Just come back safe yourself, all right?"

"All right. I may be coming back here to stay. I can't see going to Union headquarters and then marching back up to the house." It would be a wrench, never to see Sander again. Never to know how he fared, if he lived. Lila stared into the flickering fire.

"You do what you have to. I'll pray for you for a week or so, then expect you at the door," Chloe said, standing up to hug her.

"I'll be here." Lila picked up her towel and headed for the creek.

Lila was still tossing when she heard feet on the flagstones outside her room. Raiders. Bushwhackers. She reached down and grabbed the knife under her bed. Her fingers closed hard on its handle as she padded over to the door. She'd push the door open and scream at the same time, she decided. But the scream died in her throat at the sight of the man at the table eating blackberry pie.

"You're still here," Sander exclaimed. He looked at her, standing in her nightgown, knife raised.

"What do you mean, I'm still here?"

"The money's gone. I figured you'd be gone with it."

Her bewilderment turned to anger in a flash. "You knew Ty's money was there? And you've been waiting for me to take it?"

"It was inevitable. Now you're going to go to St. Louis for your little exercise in futility. Will you be back, Lila?"

"Futility? What do you mean?" She stood over him now, fuming.

"Informing the Union commander of our whereabouts. It will be about as useful as the citizens' reports that have already been made, but I can't stop you from adding yours to the list. Rosecrans doesn't believe in us, Lila. He's so full of himself that he thinks we don't exist."

Lila's heart was pounding too hard. "That can't be true."

Sander took a long draught of his buttermilk. "The worst part is that he's not even so sure scum like Hellfire and Vengeance exist. That's what they call themselves, you know. That bunch of bandits roaming around. I'd like to blow the heads off all of them, and they're supposed to be on my side. Rosecrans just wants to ignore them."

"You're wrong. You have to be."

"For your sake, sweet lady, I wish that I was. Your idealism is beautiful to watch." Sander looked up, and his eyes were filled with pain. Lila stepped closer to him. She had to say something, yet no words would come. She looked down at the table to his empty plate, an open book beside it.

"What are you reading?"

"Law. And I'm mired in Latin."

"Where?" She found herself drawn to the book and

the man. She was close enough now that she could feel the warmth of him. He pointed out his place and read the phrase to her. "Oh, that." The arguments and discussions Ty and her father had had on endless winter evenings sprang to mind. Lila found herself quoting effortlessly. "It means . . ."

She talked, and Sander quizzed her. It seemed natural to lean over the table and point out a bit of the document. She never knew the exact moment when his arm had slipped around her.

Sander's hand rested easily on her hipbone, all his concentration seemingly on the book in front of them, while her concentration was really fixed on what his idly circling fingers were doing to her skin under the thin cotton gown.

As they talked his hand stopped its gentle caress of her hipbone and slid down her leg. The contact of his warm, slightly callused fingers with the skin at her knee stopped them both. Their glances met, and Lila saw reflected in his dark eyes the same mixture of wonder and hunger she felt. Her mouth opened for a deep breath, but there wasn't enough air in the room to fill her lungs. They burned as his fingers stilled for a moment, then moved upward slowly.

This was the moment when she should give a cry of outrage and rush to the next room, find the wooden bar and put it up at the door. But instead she wanted to let her quaking legs collapse and just slide into his lap.

Sander groaned and pulled her to him, burying his face in the front of her thin cotton gown. His hands traced fiery twin paths up from her hips, pulling her even closer as his mouth woke a hunger in her everywhere it touched.

He rose from the chair slowly, still holding her tightly, his body sliding along hers, and found her mouth. The air around them seemed to be made of warm syrup. Everything was moving in a heavy, endless stream. Her hand tangled in Sander's hair, reveling in the thick curls. He responded with a low growl she could feel, and an even deeper slanting of his lips on hers. The syrup was moving through her veins now, making her slow and languid.

Lila made no protest when Sander picked her up. There seemed to be no effort involved as he bent, without ever breaking away from her lips, and slid one arm under her knees. With each passing moment, Lila was more aware of just how much fabric she had removed from her gown. He carried her, taking gentle care that her feet didn't brush the door frame. He spilled her onto the bed, following her down onto the crackly mattress. The moon had risen. There was enough light to see him slip off his shirt quickly before he joined her on the bed.

He kissed her again, claiming her mouth, using his tongue to search it with a deep sweetness. Lila's passion rose in a dark tide, making her tremble. Her gown was hitched up to her waist, exposing all of her hip and backside to his stroking. Her body had a will of its own, her hips rising to meet his. Her fingers brushed the dark expanse of hair that covered his chest and traveled down to a line that disappeared below the top button on his pants. She paused, wondering how to remove them. His skin was hot and smooth, and she could not get enough of it.

Lila found the first button and worked it with clumsy fingers until it released. As his kisses on her mouth and throat drove her further and further past the brink of sane thought, her fingers worked convulsively.

The second button freed a considerable amount of skin to her touch, and the action seemed to startle Sander. He drew back with a breath that expanded his chest. He shook his head almost imperceptibly as if to clear his senses. Lila realized with a jolt that his eyes were blank.

"What am I doing?" He spoke so softly Lila almost didn't hear. He stared down at the pillow not an inch from her head, but Lila knew he wasn't seeing her. With startling clarity, she knew what he was seeing. Her fingers left him. He stayed above her, his muscles tense.

His flexed arm began to tremble. Lila could see the drop of sweat that traced the outline of his jaw. She put a hand on his chest, easing him further from her body. "Sander," she began, trying to force words out of her throat. "That night we met. The first thing you said was 'You're not Evie.' I know we were both talking about my cousin, Evie Harvey."

He said nothing, but his features were losing the heated, blurry look they'd had before, hardening like candle wax after the flame has gone. Lila's throat hurt, strangling every word she forced out. "Folks used to say we looked alike. Some. She was my cousin and my dearest friend in the world, Sander." She had to stop, to catch her breath. "What was she to you?"

He pushed away from her and sat on the side of the bed. The last of the heat left Lila's body. His dark, lambent eyes met hers; then he drew a shuddering breath. Finally he spoke as if each word sent shards of glass through him. "She was my wife. Or at least my lover. And the mother of my son."

Lila seemed to hear him from a distance. She drew

herself up, away from his touch. Suddenly his flesh was alien to her. "You know how she died, don't you? Even if you didn't do it." Lila drew her knees up, covering as much of her with the gown as she could, moving against the rough wall and away from him.

His face was drawn with pain. "I do. And you won't ever get that part of the story from me, Lila. It wouldn't help. No more than I could help Evie." Sander wasn't looking at her anymore, lost in his story.

"If you weren't there, how do you know all this?" The words stung him, and Lila was glad. She wanted to see him flinch when he admitted he hadn't been there.

"Evie told me what I didn't see. She was outside on the ground. On the ground, in February . . ." A shudder went through the bunched muscles of his back. For a moment, before she remembered the gentle dexterity he'd shown laying her down and seducing her, Lila reached out. But Sander was turned away, and he never saw the aborted gesture. His voice was tight, painful to listen to. "Ruth and Ernest were dead, and Evie was having the baby much too soon by the time I got there. There wasn't any time for anything except a few words and trying to make her comfortable. The baby lived an hour. Evie lived two."

His voice was pure pain, but Lila couldn't feel sorry for him. She didn't wonder anymore about Evie. But if wondering had been bad, knowing was much worse. Sander, still sitting on the edge of the bed, hands hanging limp at his sides, stared at the floor. She could tell he was fighting back tears. There was no comfort rising in her. All she could feel was disgust making her gorge rise. She could see him, embracing Evie, making that poor ill-fated baby.

Then, when Evie had needed him, he had been somewhere else. From his story, her idea that his own men had had a hand in it was probably right. Instead of doing anything else, he'd tidied up the mess and come to her home to destroy it in turn.

Here, he'd landed in her bed, telling her he was the one that had killed her cousin, as sure as the hand that had shot Uncle Ernest had lit the fire. "Get out of here, and don't you ever come back." Sander looked at her, his eyes dark and shining as wet onyx. He walked out, staggering a little.

Only after the light was gone from the kitchen and the outside door had closed did Lila lay down. She noticed with a detached part of her that his shirt was still on the floor. Silent tears came as her fingers fumbled with the ribbons of her gown.

At two, John Reed went on watch. Lila waited half an hour, dressed and left. No one stopped her.

Six

Three days later, the train was almost back to Ironton, and Lila was so tired her hair hurt. Why did Sander have to be right? He was the enemy. He was a Confederate commander, invading her home and fighting for everything she thought wrong. And he was shielding the man who killed Evie.

He was also honest and caring, with a finely honed sense of the ironic and a smile that only she seemed to light. And Lila, leaning back against the seat and swallowing hard, had to admit that as much as she hated Sander MacCormack's ideals, she did not hate the man. The emotion she felt when she was near him wasn't hate. The thought that it might be the beginnings of love made her push her eyes shut tight in denial.

She should hate the man for all she was worth. Instead her hate, or at least anger, was reserved for General Rosecrans's blond lieutenant. He was the man who got to tell her that the Union, or at least the general, didn't believe in the gathering bands of rebel soldiers in mid-Missouri. That she should go home and be good and roll bandages for the cause.

But going home meant going back to Sander. His love for Evie was evident in his ravaged face when he told her how Evie had died. Lila wondered how Sander could bear to touch her. To be reminded, every time he looked at her, of the beautiful girl that he'd buried. Lila knew that his had been the hands that had dug the four graves, three large and one much too tiny. And then he had gone on to live in her house and drink her father's liquor on the front porch. No wonder he saw ghosts.

Lila got off the train at Ironton, hauling her heavy bag, and sat down on a bench. She had no idea what to do next. She was a Union supporter of the most loyal nature. The Confederate cause and all it stood for was repellent to her. She should let the house fall to pieces around the company of soldiers that occupied it if the army wasn't going to come chase them out.

She should. She ought to. Lila sat with her tired body and aching feet motionless while she thought. Her shoulder muscles were knotted in spasms from carrying the satchel full of things for herself and Chloe. Shopping in St. Louis had been the only worthwhile part of the trip. Her head throbbed from the effort of trying to sort out her thoughts. The *shoulds* and *ought tos* were wearing on her. They spoke of the right things to do, just like those mottoes Mama used to make her embroider. She had always hated them. The last one was still half-done in a chest somewhere, never to be finished.

The right thing to do didn't leave any room for what her heart was telling her. That her home was still a haven, a place of safety, even filled with rebel soldiers. She needed to keep it safe for Ty and Marcus when they came home. She needed it so for herself. And perhaps she even needed one of those blasted rebel soldiers. She might hate everything Sander MacCormack stood for in the way of politics, but he was an honorable man. A man she was growing to love against all reason. When she really thought about it, what to do next was easy. She would go to Chloe and share the bounty that St. Louis had offered. Then she would go home. Home to the little room that cradled her life now. Home to the man whose cause repelled her as much as his honor and his nature drew her closer. Home to Sander.

Getting there would present a problem. It would be dark before she could get herself and her bags across the miles to the cave or the farm. And the raw new town of Ironton, some of its buildings still oozing pinesap, didn't promise much in the way of shelter. While Lila pondered, a wagon pulled up beside her, mules raising a cloud of dust as their owner hauled them to a stop.

"Whoa there, Meshach, Shadrach. Hold on now." The voice was gruff, and the hands on the reins were rough with years of hard work. Lila was glad to see a familiar face, even if it was Arlie Hoskins's lined one. "You need a ride back, Lila?"

"I'd appreciate one, Mrs. Hoskins."

"Your place isn't that far out of the way," Arlie said simply, giving her a hand up into the high wagon bed as the springs protested. "All the blue uniforms I've seen today make me want to hurry home."

Arlie clicked a signal to the mules, flicked the reins and they started off. For the first mile and more, until they were well out of town, she said nothing, and Lila didn't disturb the silence. She could imagine few topics of conversation that would be comfortable.

"Homer and me, we don't get much time to talk these days. He's awful busy, being minus a boy in the fields," Arlie finally said, still looking over the dusty rumps of the mules while Lila clung to the swaying seat. "Not that I begrudge him or anything. No, sir, we're mighty proud of Blainey."

"I'm sure you are," Lila said. It was the least she could offer, even if she wished Blainey had jumped in the creek instead of signing up with the Confederate army.

"Anyhow, we still get a chance to talk, once the younguns are bedded down." It was a task that Lila could hardly imagine at the Hoskins household. Three boys and five girls, and only the eldest, Myrtle, gone from home for good, what with Blainey popping in and out. Where they all bedded down in that two-room cabin was beyond her imagination. She tried to pull her flagging concentration back to Arlie, who kept talking. "I told him last night that by my count that wench of yours, Chloe, should be about ready to drop a baby. You need me?"

Lila tried not to fall off the seat. "Chloe? I wouldn't know . . ." she sputtered.

Arlie's blue eyes glittered in their rings of wrinkles. "Hogwash. She didn't go anywhere after her man lit off with the army. So she's here somewhere, ready to have that baby, isn't she?" Her eyes narrowed. "I didn't tell Homer, but I bet I know where she is. There's a cave, a big one on your land. When we were all young and sparking, we used to have picnic parties and carry lanterns and go down there. It would be a good place to hide."

"Mrs. Hoskins, I just can't say."

Arlie flicked the reins and snorted. "You really are as stubborn as your pa, God rest him. Now look, Miss Lila, I know that wench is free. I don't agree with such things. But black or white, women have babies just the same, and you're going to need a midwife."

"You're right about that," Lila said, looking over the mules' backs.

"Nobody should have to do without. You're too

young to remember, but Homer and me, we lost our first three. Twins the first time, come too early. The second time it was the cord around his neck." Lila could hear old, womanly pain. "Your ma, she helped out after that. And after that we had eight that lived. Since your ma taught me, I've helped nearly two score of babies into the world. Another one, no matter what color, makes no difference."

Lila looked at the weathered hands holding the reins. She could see them holding Chloe's baby. Blainey's description of his mother's comments on Lila's "turning Secesh" came back to her, and she smiled. "I'll get you word if I can. Thank you, Mrs. Hoskins."

Arlie's answering smile was tight. "You'll have plenty of time to get me word, child. First babies, they give you plenty of time." She drove on, shaking her head. Finally she turned to Lila to look at her with frank blue eyes.

"They say your pa, he decided to free his slaves after a revelation in church. That really true?"

"He always said it was, Mrs. Hoskins," Lila managed to choke out.

"Well, if 'twere me, I'da changed churches." Clucking to the mules, she said not another word the whole trip home.

It took an hour for Lila to tell Chloe everything, punctuated with dinner and several rests. She sat in the cave in front of the flickering fire. It felt marvelous to be barefoot and rid of the hoop skirt for a while. She'd almost forgotten how to manage one. It was a blessing to get shed of it again.

Lila wiggled her toes and sighed comfortably. "Still, I'm glad about Arlie Hoskins. She's good, Chloe, even though we don't see eye to eye on most things. We can trust her."

"I know. I just hope we don't have to deal with any of the other Hoskinses. I'm not sure how far we can trust the whole tribe." Chloe's brow knit into a straight black line on her forehead.

"It will be all right. You'll see."

"I'll see, whether it's all right or not. In a few weeks, you're going to be a godmother."

Lila leaned over, reaching for the heavier of her bags. "I know. And wait until you see what I got for my godchild."

She started pulling things out of the bag, feeling like a magician conjuring tricks. There were yards of bird's-eye for diapers, several hanks of fine, smooth white yarn for knitting and crocheting little things, and a new crochet hook. Hers had disappeared in the melee.

"No oranges. I just couldn't fit them in," she said, smiling. She looked over at Chloe, expecting to see an answering grin. Instead, she had buried her head in her hands while her shoulders shook. Lila flew across the cold, pebbly floor, ignoring the stones under her feet. "Now what's the matter, Chloe? Don't cry about it, whatever it is."

"I'm just so tired of this, I guess. Living out here in a hole, waiting for this baby who keeps kicking me in the wrong side of my ribs. And now you bring me things."

Lila squeezed her hard. "It isn't much, Chloe. Not hardly enough. And the best thing I brought wasn't in the bag at all, was it?"

The self-important lieutenant in St. Louis had given Lila one piece of good news. Ty and the soldiers under his command were still in one piece, most of them.

Chloe shook her head. "Nope. At least we know they're alive." She wiped her face with the back of one slender hand. "You're going back, aren't you? Even after everything with Evie and all."

It was more statement than question. Lila nodded. "I am."

"Might as well go now. No sense sleeping here on the rock floor when you can at least have a shuck mattress. Get me word when you can, and I'll try to get word to you."

"All right." Lila put the rest of her own belongings back into her bag. She slipped her shoes and stockings back on. Chloe helped her get the hoop all arranged again, then laughed herself half-sick at Lila edging out of the entrance to the cave with it on.

She came out of the dark, all shadow and silhouette in the dark skirt and bonnet. This time Sander knew her for what she was. This was no ghost, but a real woman, and she was coming back to him against all his hopes. It made his chest ache. She crossed the grove while the sweet melancholy of a harmonica wailed behind the house. Lila came to him with music.

She went through the grove and up to the gate in the whitewashed fence. The heavy chain and weight squealed as she pulled it open. Sander raised his head off his chest and straightened to watch her. Tonight she *was* the picture lady, elegant in the moonlight.

She walked up the path. Still, he said nothing. She climbed the steps, and he noticed that the top one squeaked. "You're home awfully quickly, Lila. It didn't take any longer than that for the Yankees to burst your bubble?"

Her eyes were huge and liquid. "No time at all," she

said, putting down her bag. She looked pointedly at the tumbler in his hand, still half-full. "It won't make them go away, you know. The ghosts. You can drink yourself blind, Sander, but they're still going to be here."

His anger flared at her incredibly young view of it all. "Can you make them go away?" he barked out, his breathing ragged.

"I could try." She pushed back her bonnet until it hung down her back by the strings and moved closer, her skirt bowing out behind her. He had meant the kiss to punish her, to be hard and angry. But the touch of her soft, giving warmth changed the anger in him. The contents of the tumbler hit the porch floor as his arms went around her.

Still she clung to him, giving, promising. When his chest was on fire he pulled back, gasping, out of breath. He shuddered once with the need of her, and she kissed him again softly, briefly, before she drew back to look at him.

"Does that make them go away?"

"Not all of them," he answered honestly. "But some."

One in particular. His memories of Evie were fading, no competition for the determined fire of the young woman who gave him one last sad look and walked through the house with her bag. He heard the back door open and close behind her as he looked out once more on the grove. There were only fireflies there now, and the image of Lila. No ghosts. He went in to find his place in the large black leather book on the desk.

Lila kept telling herself that soon it would be cooler. Soon her life would not consist of a hot, sweaty round of preserving garden truck, drying fruit as it ripened, making jam and getting ready for a winter that seemed impossible in the steamy heat of August.

If standing over a kettle and stirring bubbling contents was hideous, doing laundry was abominable. Not doing it would have been worse, what with the layers of sweat and dirt the men raised drilling. She shuddered to watch them, turned away from the sight whenever possible. Sander, running with a saber in his hand, made her stomach turn. How the gentle hands that had stroked her skin so knowingly could so casually hold an instrument of destruction was beyond her understanding.

The paradox of Sander, that he led his troops so effectively and led her heart where he wanted, filled her with confusion. The same man that was capable of bringing her to passion she could barely control was capable of killing. She wanted to deny that he could kill. But when she looked at him panting from a mock charge, she knew.

Each time she looked at him, Lila saw less of Evie haunting him. Sorrow and pain still crept in with the evening shadows. Both of them got deeper when he insisted on finding his jug and retreating to the front porch. On those nights Lila went to her room and found other things to do.

One of those things was working on his scanty wardrobe. He came down the stairs protesting when she'd turned the collar and cuffs of two of his shirts. All she could say was that she couldn't have him looking like a scarecrow.

"Why not? Yancey looks like a scarecrow continually. Want me to tell him what a good job you did?" The gleam in his dark eyes made dancing copper sparks.

She brandished a serving fork at him. "Do that,

Lysander, and I'll turn the cuffs and collar back the way they were."

His grin faded to puzzlement. "How did you know that? No one has called me Lysander in twenty-five years."

"I looked in your Bible. It didn't have Ty's money in it, so I didn't look long."

Instead of being outraged, Sander laughed. "Anyone else would have had another answer. No, there's no treasure to be found there, to be certain."

"Why did they stop? Calling you Lysander, I mean."

Furrows grew in his forehead. He turned away to button his shirt. "It was too big a mouthful for my little brother. And since he was always the last word in the MacCormack household, whatever he called me was what I answered to."

There was a chill in his voice that stopped Lila where she stood. "Would you rather be called something else?"

"Not anymore. Sander sounds natural now. The other sounds . . . affected. I'm no hero, Greek or otherwise." He continued to look out the window, and Lila went back to the kitchen to get the coffeepot. During the day, the image came back to her, several times, of a little boy who couldn't even keep his own name if his brother said otherwise. It was a thought that disturbed her work.

Two days later a rider came before the biscuits were out of the oven. It was a young boy, riding a tired horse. He flung himself off it and sprinted into the house. The urgency about him said only one thing to Lila. Bushwhackers. In a few moments Sander came out behind him, calling over his shoulder to someone. He stuck his head in two tents, then hurried on to the barn.

By the time he had his horse saddled and was leading him out, Lila had made a few sandwiches from the bread on hand and had wrapped them in a cloth. She went out to the yard and handed the packet up to Sander, who had swung up in the saddle.

"I don't know what this is about, but you'll need food," she said.

He nodded, looking past her. "They're back again. Burned a farmhouse down by the Castor River."

He didn't need to say more. Lila knew who "they" were by the look on his face. Raiders, again. And with the fire he was reliving the one that had taken everything he cared for. Lila grasped his hand. "Be careful."

"As careful as I can." He looked away, over the neck of the anxious horse. "I've heard these fools actually have a commission from Price. How he can do that with heathens who scalp people and burn their houses is beyond me."

Sander looked around. "Reed. Saddle this man your horse and see that he follows me. Henry, George, go with him. Have Sergeant Phillips issue you weapons."

He took off riding then, and Lila looked at the "man" who was to get Reed's horse while his own rested. It was Johann Grebe, maybe fourteen. His pale face was streaked with dirt and either tears or sweat. Lila walked over to where he leaned against the back porch.

"Your family? Are they . . . ?"

"Papa, he went to St. Louis. The raiders, they came before the light. Wanted our cow—and money. Mama didn't want to let them have either. They wouldn't believe there wasn't any money. And they took the cow . . ."

"She's all right? And your brother and sister?"

"Not hurt. But the raiders burned the house and the barn. When Papa comes back, he will find nothing. And he told me to take care of everything."

She shook him gently. "This was not your fault. Those men are evil and greedy, and they would have taken the cow even if your papa were there, Johann. You saved his treasures."

The boy looked at her, bewildered. "No, Miss Lila. All is gone. The barn, the hay, the house . . ."

"Johann. Your father will be unhappy about that. You're unhappy about that. But that is not his treasure. Your mother, you, Fritz, little Anna." She looked at him, watching some of the clouded sorrow clear into resolve.

"*Ja.* And tonight they need a roof. The kitchen shed didn't burn. We can clear a space there, and there is still the stove and the plow. I must go."

Lila pushed the light hair back from his suddenly older face. She knew the raiders had made another enemy, a dangerous one. "Be careful. And trust these two riding with you. They're rebels, but they are honest. They don't burn people's homes."

Johann nodded and walked to where Reed's horse was standing between the mounted Davis brothers. They rode off, and Lila went to rescue her biscuits before they burned black.

It was almost dawn again before Sander came back to the farm. He turned his horse over to the private who took it after he slid from the saddle. The raiders had vanished like smoke. Why did Price keep them on payroll? To burn out a woman and three half-grown kids over a cow. And the only weapon on any of the Germans had been a pitchfork. It was easy to see why the locals called them Hellfire and Vengeance. At least, for a change, there had been no bodies.

The nagging dread hadn't stopped since he'd talked to the woman the bushwhackers had burned out. He'd wondered more than once if the one they called Hellfire could be the man he thought he was. Mrs. Grebe's description had made him surer of it than ever. And even more determined to shoot when he found him, Price be damned.

Normally, the raiders didn't kill women. Not the honest ones, anyway. There had been that whore strung up two counties over, with the bizarre sign scrawled on a shingle below her feet: Fornikater. Even if they couldn't spell, their meaning had been clear enough. The thought that Evie had met her fate from the same hands made him shudder.

Sander needed something to wash away the bitterness that crept up the back of his throat. His stomach was so empty it was rumbling. He opened the door to the kitchen softly and looked around. There was just enough light from the coming dawn to find part of a loaf of bread wrapped in a towel.

"There's one jar of blackberry jam that I didn't seal. It's in that larder cabinet." Lila stood in the doorway. Her hair was in a coming-apart braid, and her abbreviated nightgown gave him a view of her legs that almost made Sander forget his hunger for food for another even more basic one.

She walked past him, passing the back of her hand over her eyes to rub the sleep out, lifting the heavy braid off her shoulder. "There. Can't have you eating nothing but bread. If you want, I'll get something else."

Sander shook his head. "You'll have breakfast to see to in another hour. Don't start now just for me."

"You didn't find them." It was a statement, not a question, and Lila had stepped behind him, using firm hands to knead the shoulder muscles that Sander felt loosen at her touch.

The slow, sure pull of her hands felt so good he was nearly undone. It was hard to concentrate on eating, even as hungry and tired as he was. The room was beginning to blur every time he blinked. All he wanted was to lean back and rest his head in the welcome pillow of the breasts behind him. "We didn't find them. Didn't even find the cow."

"Perhaps next time." Her voice seemed soft and slow. Sander wondered at her lack of emotion. "Can you do anything about them, if you catch them?"

Sander finished half of his bread, then grimaced. "We could make them return civilian property, I expect. But if they're really commissioned like I've heard, even that would be difficult. I just want to see these heathens face-to-face, and threaten to shoot them on sight if I find them harming any more civilians."

There was a raw ache in his throat from the pictures swimming in front of him. A burning cabin, a screaming baby whose thin screaming stopped all too quickly. His son was just one of the many civilians this raider band had killed. He felt himself slumping in the chair, and Lila moved forward, stroking his arms with her warm fingers.

He let his head fall backward to the comforting beat of her heart. The scent of roses welled up in his nostrils as he turned his head into the soft fabric of her gown. The close air of the kitchen got even closer as he took in the heat of her skin. He nuzzled his cheek to where the ribbons parted slightly down the front of her gown.

When his lips touched her flesh he stopped. Even for a summer morning, she was extremely warm. He stood, putting a hand on her forehead. It was hot too. Her gray eyes were bright, her cheeks flushed red. "You all right?"

She waved away his concern. "A little summer fever, I think. Hobbs and Sutherland were both complaining of it yesterday." Sander felt a cold chill run through him. He hated human sickness, knew nothing about it. The thought of Lila being sick made his insides lurch.

On top of a day around the clock with no sleep, this new worry made him unsteady. He grasped the chair behind him to keep from wavering. Once the blurring of his vision cleared, he let go. Dry-mouthed, he led Lila to the door of her room. "You go back to bed. I'll have some of the men see to breakfast and make sure that Fay checks on you plenty."

She seemed to smile at his concern. "If it will make you feel better. Go to bed yourself, Sander, before we have to pick you up off the floor."

"I will." He saw her sit down on the bed. Then, fighting his exhaustion as he would a living enemy, he closed the door. The stairs to the house had never seemed this steeply pitched before.

Inside, Yancey sat up on the chaise in the parlor, rubbing his neck to ease out the kinks from having slept on the too-short furniture.

"Glad you're back. I was getting concerned. No luck, huh?" Sander was tired of his face showing his business to everybody. Yancey filled him in on everything that had happened in the past day. "Got two on sick call, Hobbs and Sutherland. Fever, but not cholera or any-

HALF THE BATTLE

thing else serious. I've got them upstairs dosing them. Should be all right tomorrow, I think."

"Miss Fox has the same, I believe. See that Fay looks after her," Sander managed to get out. He was taking off his clothes as he went up the stairs, his tunic and shirt landing in a pile just inside the door, his boots jettisoned at the side of the bed. He was asleep before his head hit the pillow.

He came to in the hottest part of the afternoon, drenched in sweat and feeling muzzy from the heat. He padded across the floor and looked out the window. A faint breeze, hot as an oven, flowed through the opening, making the room no more bearable.

Sander went down the stairs and out into the sun, squinting. The water in the horse trough was warmer than spit. He headed back to his room, pulled on boots and grabbed the necessary supplies for a trip to the creek.

There the water was little cooler than the horse trough, but it at least cleared his head. He toweled off and dressed, feeling human again. In the yard, he stopped. Lila's room was closed up, the door shut and the window only opened a crack. It would be an oven in there now. He wondered where Fay had put Lila, and if she was feeling better. Henry Davis sat on the kitchen stoop, snapping beans into a bowl between his knees. He looked up when he saw Sander cross the yard.

"Captain, Miss Lila's not doing so good. I thought to wake you, but I didn't dare."

Sander felt his chest tighten. "Next time do. Where's Mrs. Culpepper, then?"

Davis looked confused. "Up in her room, I expect."

Sander went up the stairs, wondering why he hadn't heard anything when he'd gotten up. He pushed the door to Fay's room open, expecting to see a chair drawn up to the bed and the other trappings of a sickroom.

Instead Fay sprawled on the bed in her underclothes, a loose wrapper gaping open. "Where's Lila?"

Fay looked up slowly, her eyes flat and uninterested. "In her room, I expect. Why?"

It was almost impossible to keep from shaking her. "Why? You're supposed to be taking care of her."

Fay shrugged. "Nothing to do. Fever either goes or it doesn't. I'm no nursemaid." She went back to her book, trying to find the place where she'd left off.

Sander wheeled and strode out, trailing curses behind him all the way past a startled Henry Davis and into Lila's room, where he flung open the door and window before heading toward the bed.

She was there, her breathing harsh and shallow. Her undone hair tangled with the bedclothes flung around. One bare foot was near the floor. "Hot. Too hot," she murmured through cracked lips. Sander went back to the kitchen doorway.

"There's a tin tub upstairs in my room, Davis. Get it—and towels. Now."

Sander had never bathed a woman before, and he had no desire to do so. But Lila was so hot she nearly glittered. Fay was useless. Yancey was the only one in the company with any real skills toward doctoring, but the thought of his big paws on Lila was intolerable. This time, the job was all his.

Henry came back with the washtub. "Find buckets, and detail somebody to help you fill them at the creek," Sander said, looking around the room. "When the tub is full of creek water, get me a bucket from the spring for her to drink." Davis nodded and took off like a rabbit.

There was a little water in the pitcher on the dresser. Sander dampened a towel with it and wiped Lila's face. She raised a hand in an irritated gesture to push him away. But he continued to stroke the wet towel over her face, and her protesting hand fell onto the bed.

He eased her gown down to the most decent level possible before the goggling Henry and his brother dumped their first buckets into the tub. When they were gone again, Sander eased the connecting door to the kitchen closed and bolted it. He'd have to wet a sheet and hang it in the outside doorway to take advantage of any breeze, but still give Lila some privacy.

He looked back to where she was muttering on the bed, oblivious. Sander left her long enough to get more linens. She was going to skin him for that later. "Can't be helped," he said. He grabbed a sheet, dampened it in the tub, and stretched it in the doorway. Henry Davis was coming across the yard with another full bucket. Sander crossed the distance between them and took it.

Inside the warm room again, he filled a tumbler with spring water. Raising Lila into a sitting position so she wouldn't choke, he tried to coax the cool liquid down her throat. He bobbled the first sip, and it splashed down her front as she gasped. Soon half the water was inside her and the other half dampened both of them.

He stripped off his clammy shirt and went over to remove her nightdress. It was hard not to notice the smooth, creamy skin beneath. But any pleasure Sander might have taken from it faded before the heat that seemed to rise like a presence from her flesh. As he eased the damp cloth away from her, Lila protested with a whimper.

"Now, just hold on, sugar. We're just trying to get you cooled down," Sander said in what he hoped was a soothing voice. He picked her up, leaving the nightdress a wadded mess on the bed.

Lila shivered when he eased her into the tepid water, and her arms splayed out in shock, then went limp again. He wet a cloth and sponged her chest, watching little rivulets of water run down in the hollow between her breasts. Lila's head lolled back against the high back rim of the tub, and Sander nearly panicked. How did a person with a high fever act? Was her plucking at the towel on the floor normal? Did this glassy look mean he was going to lose her before he ever had a chance to tell Lila how precious she was? He laved water over her shoulders as she tried to bat his hand away. "Want Chloe," she said disjointedly.

"Whoever she is, I wish you had her, Lila." He kept the water dampening her hot flesh as every inch of it became imprinted on his memory. It was painful to see the calluses on her palms.

Sander's arm, behind Lila's back, began to fall asleep, but he didn't dare change his hold on her increasingly slippery body. At least she'd stopped struggling. She lay against the back of the tub letting him splash water over her body. When he dampened the rag and sponged her face, her eyes opened and she looked up at him. "You shouldn't be doing this, Sander. It's not decent."

"You're right," he agreed. It was perfectly indecent and harder than leading an infantry charge. Once Lila's fever broke, he never intended to do it for anyone again unless it was for pleasure. That thought snapped his head up and had him staring into the crazily tilted mirror over the dresser across the room. What would it feel like to bathe Lila like this with scented soap and a fluffy sponge, her giggling in assent?

Perhaps someday he would find out. But for now he

HALF THE BATTLE

would sponge off her skin and do anything to take his mind off the wonderful way her flesh arranged itself over her slender frame.

He gritted his teeth, conscious now of the sweat rolling down his face. Keeping his body in check and his hands doing just what they should was murderously difficult. Out of his struggles to master his body came a thought from long ago.

He'd been standing in a classroom at the military academy. The arm that was now nearly asleep between Lila and the metal rim of the tub had held a pointer as he'd lectured on tactics. One skinny, pale cadet had asked him how they were supposed to take their minds off their anxieties while waiting for a battle to begin.

"Distract your mind," he'd told them. "Recall something you've learned, something hard you've memorized perhaps, and make your mind concentrate on recalling it. Use something inspiring, like Plato. Not this lecture."

There had been laughter in the room, and he'd gone on. Now it was time to put his own tactics into practice. This qualified as the most difficult battle he'd ever fought, a battle over his raging will. He struggled to remember what he could of Blackstone's *Commentaries* to keep his mind off the perfection below his fingers.

He cast about mentally, wondering what he could recall. "Let's try the foundation of human law," he told Lila. She seemed calmed by the sound of his voice. He laved the rag over her again, pushing away his conscious thoughts of her body. "Upon these two foundations, the law of nature and the law of revelation, depend all human laws, i.e., no human laws should contradict them."

She stared up at him, eyes childlike in her confusion.

The contrast with the perfect, mature body that he was trying to ease out of the tub nearly broke Sander. He continued between gritted teeth. "Let's see. Where were we, sweetheart? Something about indifferent points . . . the divine and natural law leave a man at his own liberty, subject for the benefit of society to restraint within certain limits."

Sander eased Lila, covered only by a sheet, onto the bed. He suspected that this was beyond the certain limits Mr. Blackstone had in mind for natural law. It was beyond the limits he could set on himself.

Seven

When Lila opened her eyes and knew where she was, it was evening. But she suspected it was evening *again* somehow. She remembered too many fragments of strange happenings for only one day to have passed. At least two days were mired in this fever that was gone now, leaving her limp and languid on a disordered bed.

She looked down, suddenly conscious of how much skin the breeze was able to meet. She seemed to be wearing a man's shirt, open almost all the way to the hem. It was indecent, but delightfully cool.

Even better, it smelled like Sander. She settled against the pillows taking everything in. She was in bed in her own room, wearing his shirt. Fay had had no part in taking care of her. Listening she could hear heavy, regular breathing. She propped herself up on one elbow, slowly. The motion made her dizzy. Behind her, Sander dozed in the rocking chair. One hand trailed the ground as he slumped to the side, his legs sprawled out in front of the rocker.

He stirred slightly, but didn't wake. Lila resettled her pillows so she could watch him sleep. His lips were parted slightly and moved with each breath. She thought of what it had tasted like to kiss him with mint on his already sweet breath. She shivered in remembrance, and the movement made the shuck mattress crackle.

The noise stirred Sander. He sat straight up. Lila wondered, watching him come alert so fast, how many times a noise had roused him from deep sleep into battle readiness. "You're awake. And the fever really did break then, an hour or so ago. Hope you don't mind wearing my shirt. We, um, ran out of nightdresses."

"Who has been changing them?" Lila asked, unable to meet his dark, steady gaze.

"I have. Fay was never meant to be a nurse, and Yancey usually does the doctoring among the men, but . . ." His words trailed off.

Lila was embarrassed and gratified at the same time. "I hope I wasn't too awful. I've seen folks in a fever do some terrible things, say terrible things."

"You were a model patient. But who's Chloe?"

"A friend. Why?" Lila blurted out, hoping she hadn't betrayed her.

"She's apparently got a better bedside manner than I do," Sander said with a chuckle, not noticing her slump of relief into the pillows. "According to you, she gives a better bath."

"You bathed me?" It was all she could do not to squirm from embarrassment.

"Three times." The flush, growing from his collar upward, belied his solemn tone.

"Oh."

"Yes, three times." His voice was more spirited. "That certainly is an interesting birthmark you have on your . . ."

"Sander!" She clutched the shirt around her, scrambling to do up the buttons. It was hard to make her fingers work, and finally he leaned over and helped,

HALF THE BATTLE

buttoning the last three. His fingers were warm and sure, and Lila found herself shivering again.

"Are you cool? Should we find some clean sheets?"

"I'm not that cool. And you've done enough. You look as though you haven't slept in a bed in quite a while. What day is it?"

Sander smiled from one corner of his mouth. "What day do you think it is?"

"If I had to guess, I'd say Thursday."

"Very good. I wasn't sure you'd know."

Lila looked down at the foot of the rocker. There was a large pile of books, most of which she recognized from her father's desk. And, predictably, there was a large jug.

"Well, at least I know you weren't bored," she said, thinning her lips to a line.

Sander looked down. "What, the books? No, I read when I could, when you slept. Oh, you mean that." He looked up at her, quite serious. "It isn't what you think, you know. You've been drinking that."

"Me?" Lila squeaked. "I know enough about fever to know that you don't feed the patient liquor, Sander."

His answering smile was wry. "Even I knew that much. It was an empty one. Yancey mixed up some of the stuff he's been giving Sutherland and Hobbs. Haying switchel, he called it."

Lila nodded. "Quenches the thirst better than plain water if it's made right."

Sander leaned down, picking up a tumbler and hoisting the jug. "Judge for yourself. You've had plenty of it in two days."

The liquid was still cool in the heavy stoneware. Someone had gone all the way to the spring for the water, then searched for vinegar and honey. It tasted good, and went a long way toward explaining why her throat didn't ache and her mouth didn't have the cottony feel she would have expected.

"Yancey's better at this than I would have thought," she said, handing back the half-full tumbler. Sander took it with a practiced motion and set it down without looking. The action made her wonder how many times he'd done that in the last two days.

"Better than I am," he said with a grimace. "This nearly killed me. You are not allowed to get sick again, understand?" He said it in a light tone, but there was something behind the words that Lila felt more than heard.

"Understood. You have much too much on your mind to worry about this." Her thoughts were beginning to come back to things around her. "Has there been any more word of the raiders?"

"Nothing." Sander stared off into the cold fireplace. "They haven't shown up anyplace else." Lila looked at him, slumped in the chair.

"You really ought to get some sleep," she said softly. "We don't want you getting this fever."

He stood up, shaking himself like a dog. "I never get anything. It's a benefit of many campaigns and sleeping in ruts in the ground. If you can survive a few years of that, fevers are child's play. The only men who've gotten this one are the ones who haven't been on a real campaign yet. I expect Hoskins will show up with it next."

"I expect he won't," Lila said with a chuckle. "Not with the asafetida bag he's wearing around his neck. Arlie Hoskins has the healthiest ten people in that cabin you'd ever want to see."

"No doubt. No one wants to get within yards of them," Sander said grimly.

Lila laughed at the wrinkling of his nose. "It works. Perhaps I ought to fashion you one when I'm up to it."

"Don't count on me wearing it," Sander said, stretching. He rolled his shoulders, arching his neck. "It does feel good to get out of that chair. Should I see if there's anything like supper ready?"

"I don't know. Who's been doing the cooking?"

Sander laughed. "Yesterday it was hardscrabble stuff. Today the Davis boys had caught up on their sleep and they took turns. Rabbit stew. It looked fairly edible."

"I'll take a bowl, but go walk around for a bit first and get some yourself. Take a swim if you want."

Sander's eyes darkened in concern. "You're sure you'll be all right?"

"I'll be fine," Lila said. She watched him take the sheet from the doorway and close the door, fuss with the curtains at the open window until he was satisfied she would neither become chilled nor swelter after he left.

It put a lump in her throat to see him like this. No one usually cared for her when she was sick. With her family, it had always been her job to look after someone else. It was a new experience to be sick and have someone worry. Lila decided it was touching to see Sander worried, but she'd rather be well.

When she woke again, it was to the smell of rabbit stew, and the awareness that Sander was there beside her. But something wasn't quite right. She sat up, looking at him. There was a narrow strip of bandage around his right forearm. "You're hurt." It was surprising how seeing the blood spotting the white bandage made her light-headed because it was his.

He waved away her concern with his spoon, not bothering to stop eating. "For the first time in his life, John

Reed made a feint with the speed of a normal man. I just wasn't ready. It's only a scratch."

"How did you have the time to do that?"

Sander's laugh was sharp and dry as he shook his head. "I took your advice and went toward the creek. Yancey was just finishing up drill. I decided to join in and loosen up for a few minutes. Guess I wasn't quite loose enough."

"How does Sergeant Reed feel?"

Sander looked up toward the ceiling. "To see him, you'd think the firing squad was convening in the morning. I told him it was nothing, but he wouldn't listen."

Lila could imagine that to draw blood on his commanding officer probably made Reed sick. Sander stood up, putting his bowl on the bureau. "You ready for something to eat?"

Lila nodded. Her empty stomach was reacting to the smell of food with unladylike noises. Sander padded to the door, and she noticed for the first time that he was barefooted, an unusual condition for him. Normally he went nowhere without his boots.

At her giggle he looked down. "Figured I wasn't going anywhere tonight, and this feels good. That rain you slept through this morning is giving us a right cool spell." They could be old married people discussing the state of things, Lila decided. Gone was all the tension that had marked most of their knowing each other. Sander came back with a steaming bowl of stew and watched while she ate, sopping up the last of the broth with one of Henry's rolls. "More?"

"No," she said, feeling conscious that there was nothing between her and the bed but Sander's shirt, and it was covering precious little. "Go into the nursery and open the low chest by the window. There ought to be

HALF THE BATTLE 109

at least one spare gown under the blankets." Sander nodded and left.

Lila swung her feet over the edge of the bed, testing her reaction. Her knees felt wobbly, but they would hold her. She should be embarrassed by asking a man to go and sift through a chest of linens, folded and with lavender added. Instead she could imagine his hands touching the cloth, lifting it up out of the chest. Lila got up, going slowly so that she wouldn't tremble, and went to the bureau.

The cracked mirror showed a pale face and eyes that looked huge, hair that was as tangled and rumpled as her bedsheets. She got her comb and brush and started working through the tangles.

She'd gotten the worst of them out and had started on a braid when Sander came back with an armful of linens. "I found two, so I brought them both."

In the mirror she could see him stop, his arms full. Her own reflection, arms up behind her head to plait her hair, his shirt gapping where buttons had come undone and showing the swell of her breast told Lila why he swallowed convulsively.

A heat that had nothing to do with her fever rose in her at the thought of his arousal. To know that she was capable of stopping Sander in his tracks made her smile as she turned to him. "My hair looked like a rat's nest."

"And now it doesn't," he said, putting the linens down on the bed and coming to her. "Should you be up?"

"I feel all right," she said, conscious of the nearness of him. She looked down at his forearms flecked with dark hair, unable to meet his gaze. "You've pulled that cut open again," she said. "Stop worrying about me and come sit over here while I do something about that."

There were still scraps from her sewing in her workbag. Lila got them. Sander had already taken off his shirt and now sat on the edge of the bed, looking surprisingly vulnerable.

As she got her scissors to snip off the old bandage Lila saw his pale face. "If the blood bothers you, don't look."

She sat next to him, humming to distract him as she snipped. She eased the shredded cloth away from the wound where dried blood held it to the hair on his forearm. He flinched almost imperceptibly. "Almost done," she said, trying to sound soothing.

It didn't take long to clean the cut again. For once she was glad there were spiderwebs in the corner, as she swept a mass of them down, free of any denizens, and pressed them, with the wad of cloth, into the trickle of blood. "It stanches the bleeding. Honestly," she said, aware of the doubt in his eyes.

She knelt above him, watching the edges of the cloth where he held them, for seeping. When there was none, she moved his hand gently and put a bit of folded cotton over the cut, then bound it up quickly. "There. It's done." Sander was still holding the bit of rag and he looked pale. Seeing the signs, Lila took the cloth and gently pushed him forward.

"Blood does that to some people. Helping my mother made me used to it, I guess. She doctored everybody around when she could, and a fair lot of them bled at some time," Lila said. "But Ty's like you. He and Papa stayed far away from it. Couldn't even butcher a hog. Marcus, our hired man, always did that."

She was prattling on and knew it. But prattling kept

HALF THE BATTLE 111

Sander distracted so he didn't lose consciousness. Prattling also made her forget for a moment that she was kneeling close to him, her bare knees touching his leg, her fingers stroking his naked back.

Then Sander sat up and she could not forget any longer. Raw hunger was in his eyes as his hand came up and buried itself in her hair, undoing the half-braid she had never fastened.

His eyes were so dark they seemed black, and his tongue came out from between his lips as he drew in a slow breath. Then his hand was on her shoulder, drawing her down from her posture on her knees and into his lap, and he was kissing her in a way that made Lila lose track of time.

In an hour, or perhaps just a few minutes that felt like an hour, he pulled away from her swollen lips. Still silent, he got up, bolting the door that led to the kitchen, making sure the curtains were closed where the breeze pulled at them. Then he lit the lamp.

When he came back to the bed, Lila reached out eagerly and traced his cheek, his forehead, back down to his mouth until he bent and kissed her palm convulsively. He kissed her wrist, nuzzling the cuff of the shirt she wore, tracing a hot line up the inside of her arm.

"We have to stop now or not at all," he said, still holding her arm. She put a hand on his chest, and through the dark thicket of hair she could feel the thudding of his heart.

"If you were thinking of stopping, why did you lock the door?" she asked.

"Would you want company now?"

"None but yours," she admitted, keeping her hand tangled where she could feel his heartbeat. The moan that started deep in his chest vibrated under her fingertips before he came to cover her mouth with his.

When he raised up to unbutton the shirt that was the only thing between them, Lila wondered at his trembling hands. "You've been bathing me for two days, Sander. What's different now?"

"You. Now you know I'm looking at you," he said with a slow smile.

"And I'm glad," she said softly, gasping as his large hand caressed her in a slow circle that destroyed her reason. She sat up halfway and shrugged off the shirt, letting it drop behind her.

There was only one more barrier to the warm skin that Lila longed to feel next to hers, and something in her eyes must have asked Sander to remove it. He stood, his eyes never leaving hers, and what was left of his clothing dropped to the floor.

His hips were narrow, and there was a sweet spot on each high crest of bone where Lila's hands fit naturally as she drew him down to her, matching the hard length of him with her welcoming softness. He murmured her name into her hair as his hands traced fiery paths down each side of her, making her shiver in delight.

His skin was satin under her fingers, rippling with muscles, and patches of crisp hair teased her flesh where they touched her. She wondered if her need for him was as evident to him as his was to her. His need was obvious, not just in its physical presence but in the fevered urgency of his fingers as they stroked her flank. "Ah, sweet, what you do to me," he said, burying his face in her hair, enveloping her with the sharp, masculine scent of him. Lila wrapped her arms around him, found her body answering his need by rocking upward to meet him.

HALF THE BATTLE 113

Their mouths met again, merging them into a liquid desire that was so intense Lila stifled a sob. He drew away from her slowly, smoothing her hair away from her face. "Oh, please don't stop," she said, still on the verge of tears from the strength of the hunger within her.

"I couldn't if I wanted to," Sander said. It was almost more than she could bear, having him so far away.

"Please," she whispered, "Oh, please," not at all sure what it was she was asking for, but knowing with a certainty born of a some ancient knowledge that she needed it desperately.

And then he was back to join her, eyes dark with concern at her gasp but unable to draw away. She wrapped herself around him, savoring the length of him in a haze of sensation that drove them both to the edge of reason and then beyond. Lila grasped his strong shoulders, clinging to him through the storm that burst around her and inside her.

There was pain, but it was washed away almost as soon as it began. So this was what her body wanted so fiercely from him. Later, when he lay beside her, his eyes were darker than ever before. Sander traced a callused thumb across her cheek. "I've hurt you, I know I have," he said, drying a tear.

"No, you haven't. This is just from being sick and still a little tired," Lila said. *And from being so very much in love with you,* she wanted to say, but the uniform pants crumpled on the floor beside the bed kept that from being said. It was enough that he was here tonight beside her. When it got light she would face all the unpleasant facts about the morning, like the tents outside the window and the inevitable removal of those tents that would come someday soon.

Tonight her love held her in his arms, idly twisting a strand of her hair in his fingers, and for the first time Lila heard him humming as she drifted off to sleep.

The morning light was every bit as harsh as Lila knew it would be. She woke to the novel sensation of sharing her bed. Behind her, instead of the rough log wall, was Sander's body, curved to fit hers. Lila savored his easy, regular breathing tickling the back of her neck.

When she opened her eyes fully, shock made her raise and turn. Light streamed through the window, and outside were sounds of the camp coming awake. And Sander wasn't asleep. He stared back at her, frank humor sparkling in his eyes.

"Morning, sleepyhead. I was beginning to think you were going to sleep until noon."

"And I'm surprised you're still here. I thought, once it got light . . ." Lila found herself blushing.

"I couldn't leave you. Everytime I even shifted you'd roll over and curl up next to me," Sander said.

Lila had to move away from him, scooting to the foot of the bed. His naked masculinity should be embarrassing her. She knew she should be recoiling with horror, but instead she could only think how beautiful he was and how she regretted not one thing that had occurred last night. Her only regrets were that they were so unsuited in the daylight.

Her thoughts shocked her, and the shock must have shown in her face, making Sander react. "I suppose we need to discuss a few things." He rolled up to a sitting position, swinging his feet over the side of the bed.

"Quite a few things," Lila agreed. But none of them seemed as important as her need to stroke the smooth skin of his back as she sat up behind him. On impulse she leaned over and kissed the back of his neck.

He made an inarticulate, happy sound deep in his throat. "That is not discussion. But at least I don't have to ask if you slept well."

"Very well, thank you," she said, continuing to drop little kisses on the back of his neck and on his shoulders as she twined her arms around him, savoring the warm, male feel and smell of him.

"Now, look, I have to get up and start working on some dispatches, and there's drill. Lila, everyone will be up and around by now."

"And I suppose they'll be hungry, too. We can't expect George and Henry to cook forever." Lila let him go with a sigh, watching the way his muscles flexed when he stood. She felt so ridiculously happy. "Sander?"

"What?" He started collecting his clothing from the floor and sorting it out, hanging things over the back of the rocker and smoothing them a little.

"Will we be able to . . . I mean, tonight . . ." She found no way to ask him what she wanted to know. It sounded so wanton in the daylight. She started looking for something that resembled her clothing. She remembered dimly that last night he had brought her two clean nightgowns, and they had to be there somewhere. She leaned over the bed, seeing a swatch of white on the floor.

Still putting on his pants, he stopped with one leg balanced on the rocker. "I don't imagine so. Every man out there has a damn good idea of what went on by now, I expect. Until we're married I'm going to have to give this room a wide berth."

"Married!" Lila nearly fell off the bed in her surprise and confusion.

"Well, yes." Sander sounded as if he were explaining things to a very dull child. "After last night, you can hardly expect to do anything else, can you? I've been drilling respect for civilians into their skulls for weeks and months. And besides, I do not want my bastards populating the county."

"Oh, well, no, I expect not." Lila fought back tears. Anger welled up from the tightness in her chest. "What if I say no?"

"Say no? It's a little late for that, isn't it?" Sander's face twisted into a wry grimace. "If you wanted to say no, it should have been said last night." He finished buttoning his shirt, then looked at her, his lips compressed, before he spoke. "Is there someone you can ask. To marry us, I mean?"

"I still don't see . . ." Lila began. The knocking on the outside door cut into her angry speech.

"Captain?" The call through the door unmistakably came from George Davis. "I'm ready to mount up to post dispatches, sir. You have anything else for me to take?"

Sander moved to the door. He opened it a crack, blocking any view of her with his body. As he said a few terse words to George, all the fight went out of Lila.

He was right. All those men out there knew exactly what had happened last night. It was common enough knowledge that George Davis had knocked on her door when he needed to find Sander. And if they knew this morning, anybody in a ten-mile radius might know by dark.

Sander closed the door and stood facing her. Lila could hardly look at him. "I suppose I could find someone." Playing any part in this scene mortified her. She wished fervently that he would leave.

Sander didn't hear the hurt in her voice. "It's the one thing I regretted with Evie, that we never actually stood in front of a preacher. But her father said he'd rather we just held hands over the family Bible than go to the Baptist preacher that was the only one in the neighborhood."

Lila nodded. "Reverend Pond is a decided Republican." As was Reverend Davies at the Methodist church two miles away. Even though she'd gone to his church all her life, even sung in the choir, Lila couldn't quite see herself going now and telling him that she wished to be married to keep from producing Confederate bastards for an honorable, if obtuse, officer. Her lips felt wooden as she continued to talk while she went to the dresser to find some clothing to put on. "When do you want to do this?"

"It will have to be soon. What about Sunday?"

Lila forgot to be concerned anymore about being naked under the sheet she clutched for modesty's sake. She whirled to face him, the sheet cascading to the floor. "I cannot arrange a wedding ceremony, get a suitable dress and have food ready in three days, Sander."

He looked at her, his brows knitting together. "We will be married by Sunday, Lila. I can't let you out of my sight until we are."

"Why not?" This would be the moment she wanted more than anything. The moment he would tell her that he loved her so much that they must marry, immediately.

Instead, his face paled and he turned away from her. "I just can't. But it's got to happen and happen very soon. All right?"

"All right," she said, feeling as subdued as if she were laying somebody out instead of planning a wedding. All the girlish dreams that Lila had cherished for years about her marriage had evaporated in the last few moments. Being a realist, she had to tell herself that she'd done away with them last night when she'd welcomed this stubborn rebel into her bed.

Still, it made her throat tighten into a knot to hear this mundane planning of something that was obviously going to be just another irritation to the man standing in front of her. She grabbed a nightgown from the floor and struggled into it, tired of being naked before him without it being noticed.

"Good," Sander said, going to unbolt the door to the kitchen. "And Lila . . ."

"Yes?" She turned to see what expression went with the fervor when he called her name.

His look was intense and earnest. "We won't be here much longer. And depending on what happens, if you want to pretend none of this ever happened afterward, well, it's all right with me. I wouldn't expect anything more."

The tears flooded her so quickly that she was almost unable to answer. "You're much too gracious," she said, turning her face to the wall as she tore through her hair with a brush. Sander left without another word.

Eight

Lila sat on the floor of the cave, feeling like a sulky schoolgirl instead of a blushing bride. Chloe clucked and shook her head. "Anybody looking at you would think you were planning a funeral, Lila, not a wedding."

She poked crossly at the fire with the end of a stick. "It's not a wedding." Lila thrust the stick in front of her again, making a shower of sparks. "Weddings are things that people in love with each other have to start some wonderful new life together. This is something else all together."

"Then why are you going along with it?" Chloe prodded. "Why not just up and leave again?"

"Because I want to stay here and help you have that baby. Because Sander's right, and I don't want to populate the county with his bastards. And because I love him even if he doesn't love me," she concluded glumly, pushing the stick in her hand into the flames.

"There could be worse ways of starting out," Chloe said softly.

"I expect there could. But there could be many that were better, too," Lila said. She pushed herself up and started for the door. "I have to go home. There's still plenty to do."

"What are you wearing?" Chloe said. "I wish I could come, but there's no way you could explain me."

Lila smiled sadly. "I wish there was. It would help to have a friendly face around. I'm wearing my white muslin. I found some fresh ribbons in the blanket chest to trim it with."

"It was mighty decent of Fay Culpepper to give it back to you in wearable condition," Chloe said agreeably. "Is she standing up for you, then?"

Lila snorted. "Not likely. I don't have anybody standing up for me. There's nobody left except you."

Planning a wedding by herself had pointed up the holes in the fabric of her life worse than usual. Doing everything herself, or scrapping many of her plans because there was no help and no time for her to realize them, reminded her of how things really were. She had no mother, no aunt and no cousin to come and help decorate the house or make food for the guests, even if they did consist of a company of soldiers and one ancient circuit-riding parson, courtesy of his Hoskins cousins. Tyson had always said half the county was Hoskinses, and Lila was beginning to believe him.

"Oh, my," she burst out, startling Chloe. "Ty. I haven't even written to tell him."

Chloe winced. "Now there's a letter I'm glad it's you writing instead of me. Tell him to give my love to Marcus. Tell him that before you tell him about the wedding, in case he stops reading suddenly."

Lila grimaced and nodded, fighting back a sudden burst of tears.

"I'm sorry. I shouldn't have said that," Chloe said. She stood up and walked over to the entrance of the cave, reminding Lila of pictures she'd seen of a ship under full sail. Still, she managed to give Lila a hard, comforting squeeze. "I'll be there, if only in spirit. My body would take up too much room in the parlor right now anyway."

Lila walked back to the house slowly, swinging the basket she'd taken with her to gather glossy green leaves to float in the bowl in the dining room along with some roses for a centerpiece. She thought about all the family stories she'd heard about weddings, about her parents' simple ceremony at the Methodist church, the only thing the struggling young lawyer could afford, and the wedding breakfast afterward.

Lila thought of Sallie Rogers, so pale and proud three years ago when standing at the altar with her Bart and three weeks later sitting in the same church to hear his funeral sermon when he was the county's first war casualty. No, perhaps weddings weren't always perfect and happy. So maybe there was something she could do to make a good life out of this less than perfect start. She looked up at the stars above her, glittering impassively down. "So it won't be a perfect wedding," she said softly, with only those stars to hear. "It will be a good marriage." She'd see to it, with the same determination she used now to make her lists and tick off every little item. It would be a good marriage.

Saturday night Lila sat in the family parlor, watching Sander leaf idly through his law book, listening to the inevitable poker game going on. When she stood up from the chaise, he gave her a questioning look.

"I don't have to be bored stupid listening to this," she said with a wave toward the cardplayers. "If I'm moving back into the house, I'm moving all the way back in."

She went to the best parlor and got the lamp and lit

it. Setting down the light on the piano, she lifted the lid that protected the keys. She sat and ran a finger up the keyboard, not sure now that she was here whether she really wanted to play or not. The tone was tinny and out of key, but reassuring.

She found the music book and opened it, started working her way choppily through all her favorites. Her fingers were stiff, and there were more times that she stopped, trying to play a passage right, than there were smooth stretches of music.

Still, it felt homey and natural to be playing, listening to the talk across the hall and smelling the smoke that surrounded the card game. It wasn't the same as Ty and Papa's jovial arguments over the cases on the county docket, but it was company.

After a while the Mozart and Bach felt too heavy, and Lila got out the lighter things, finally settling on the Stephen Foster book that had been Papa's last Christmas present to her. There was sadness to the songs for her now, but she still enjoyed them, even managed to lose herself in them.

She was only a little aware of the first few men that drifted into the room and sat softly on the furniture, newly uncovered that day and brushed off. Then, in the middle of "Old Dog Tray," Sander came in, standing behind her and putting his hands on her shoulders as she played. His warm, sure touch through her dress made her skin tingle. When she finished the piece and turned the page, one of the boys called out shyly. "Do you know 'Lorena,' Miss Fox?"

"I'll play anything but 'Dixie,' " she said, trying to sound light and launching into the request. John Reed was in the room somewhere, and was persuaded to use

HALF THE BATTLE

his fine tenor. Some of the others sang along on choruses, but Reed was usually alone on the verse.

After five or six more tunes, Lila finally turned, laughing, to see the troop she'd collected on the chairs and the floors. "I didn't realize I had this large an audience. Should we take up a collection?"

"Not if you're particular," Sander said, squeezing her shoulder. "If there's more than twenty dollars in scrip among this whole crowd, I'm not aware of it."

"One more song," someone piped up, and was joined in the plea.

"One more. We'll let you pick it out," Lila said, looking up at Sander, feeling impish. He shook his head with a grimace.

"You would have to say that. I'm the most unmusical one of the lot here. Sure you don't want Reed to do this? He might come up with something more pleasant."

"Your turn," she said, smiling, watching the answering light in his eyes.

He leafed through the book, finally stopping. "This one."

Lila looked, nodded and began to play. As John Reed stood again and launched into Foster's lament about the folks waiting at home in Kentucky, Lila started to wonder as she played.

She could hardly wait to finish and bid the men good night as they trooped out of the room. When only she and Sander remained, she turned to him. " 'Old Folks at Home,' hmm? Are there any folks somewhere you should have written about tomorrow? I finished that little chore last night before I went to bed."

Sander gave a short, mirthless laugh. "I suppose I

should, eventually, just to let them know. But no one will care, Lila."

"Not even your father?"

"Especially not my father. I haven't spent more than two or three nights under his roof since I was six years old," Sander said, the light leaving his eyes. "It isn't likely that he will care one way or another that I've found yet another reason to keep from going back. I suspect he would welcome it."

Lila heard the edge in his voice. "You're going to find that jug, aren't you?"

He looked back at her, solemnly. "I suppose I should say no. Would you believe me?"

She sighed. "Not at all." She watched while he went to the dining room for a tumbler and poured a measure into it, then walked out the door. He sat on the front porch, leaning on the post, and splayed his legs, motioning Lila to sit in front of him on the step.

She lowered herself to the wooden step, arranging her skirts and leaning into his chest. Sander's arm went around her the moment she settled. His shoulder made a comfortable resting place for her head. Lila could feel him lift the tumbler, swallow, could hear the dull noise of the glass as he set it down.

Once he started talking, it was the longest she'd heard him hold forth on anything. She kept holding her breath, wondering if he was going to stop suddenly and turn back into the house for the security of the poker game in the pool of golden light, the jug that was in there. But Sander kept talking about his life while he buried the fingers of one hand in her hair and toyed with the curls she'd tied back.

She could feel the pain in his voice as he described watching his father pack his few belongings when he was six and hand them to his aunt, a tall, silent figure he hadn't ever spoken to before.

"She put me into a rattletrap wagon, and we went the ten miles or so to her farm, near Palmyra. It was a pretty poor place. My uncle did some hunting and trapping, and plenty of drinking, and she had a brood of little children to raise. So she was happy to have a hand besides the two field hands. I worked just as hard as they did, but I got to sleep in the house, even if it was up in the attic."

"How long did you stay there?" Lila asked softly.

His hand slipped out of her hair and roamed down to her shoulder, then her arm. "Years. She sent me to school in the winter when the ground was frozen too hard to work. And she kept me fed and clothed. I can't say I honestly ever remember her talking to me except to tell me to do something or answer a question if she thought it merited an answer. My father wrote once a month, giving us all the news from home."

He lifted the tumbler again, and Lila could feel the muscles in his chest tighten. "That way I found out what kind of pony Hector was riding and how he was doing with his tutor," Sander said, not disguising the edge to his voice. "And I expect Aunt wrote back so that my father could find out how many acres of corn I'd hoed."

Lila felt tears sting her eyes as the stars blurred above them. In the fingers that stroked her hair and the taut muscles in Sander's chest behind her, she felt the pain that a child had buried so long ago. And again she swore that somehow in the little time they were going to have together, she would erase as much of it as possible.

* * *

Sunday morning was clear and hot, but not terrible. Lila opened the windows in the best parlor to air it out some, then made sure everything was done that was going to get done. She set out bread and jam and boiled eggs. That was all the breakfast anybody was going to get. She left the house before anyone else was downstairs.

She went back to the kitchen, to check and see that the cake was still untouched under its towel wrapping and the cold tea for the punch was still covered with gauze. Everything was undisturbed, and in her bedroom her gown, hanging against one wall, floated a little on the bit of a breeze that came through the window.

No matter whether she was standing or sitting, Lila had the intense desire to fidget. The rocker squeaked as she pushed herself backward. There was just nothing to do right at the minute. It was too early to get dressed, the preacher wasn't here yet, and no one was really even up for breakfast.

She looked around the room; glad that it was the last time she'd have to wake up in it. Of course it would be terribly odd to wake up tomorrow morning beside Sander. The rocker lurched violently as she pushed harder than before. What if he snored? It was possible. Uncle Ernest had always fairly erupted at night. Sometimes she and Evie had giggled so hard when listening to him that they'd shaken the bed up in the loft.

She drew one foot up on the seat of the rocker, considering. No, it would still be odd and wonderful to sleep next to Sander, even if he snored. There were many things to make up for any strange noises he might make, such as the long, warm length of him lying next to her.

Lila stretched both legs, settling into the seat of the

rocker again and drawing one bare foot along the stone floor. By the time it got dark tonight, this would all be over. The men would be polishing off the last of the food, and Sander would probably be complaining that his collar was too tight. She would be writing a new entry in his family Bible.

She put both feet flat on the floor. That Bible. There was something in it she should be remembering. She thought for a moment, closing her eyes to see the pages in her mind. Then she counted for a minute. She was right, she knew it. For as much as he vowed not to care when they married, as long as it was soon, Sander had chosen a day he could remember. Today was his birthday.

She looked around the room, trying to decide if what she was about to do was foolhardy. She had intended to hand the parcel she'd done up in brown paper to Yancey when he came down the stairs and have him carry it up with coffee. But no, she would take it up herself.

There was still no movement in the house when Lila entered. She could hear some noises in the room that housed Yancey and Fay, but from the sound of things they weren't likely to be appearing anytime soon. She tiptoed up the stairs noiselessly, wondering if she should knock. No, that would only give Sander the chance to tell her to go away.

She slipped the door open and stopped on the threshold. The bed was empty, still rumpled but unoccupied. Sander stood by the dresser mirror with his toilet kit spread out before him and a scissors in hand. He smiled when he saw her standing at the door.

"Thought it was bad luck, seeing the bride on the wedding day. What are you doing up here?" He went back to trimming his beard, and Lila grinned, remembering all the times she'd sniped at him for its straggliness. Today he was taking no chances.

"Wedding day, yes. But it's another day altogether," she stated.

She wasn't prepared for Sander's reaction. He paled visibly, setting down the scissors. "You've changed your mind. You're not going through with it."

"Of course I am." She crossed the room to him, wanting to find a way to put her arms around him, even though he was shirtless and she had an armful of package. "It's just that we have other business to take care of first. A birthday, I do believe."

He looked at her strangely. "Birthday? How did you know?"

"I snooped, remember? Looking through your family Bible. It is August the seventeenth, isn't it?"

His dark eyes were grave. "It is."

She handed him the package. "It's my wedding present to you, and now birthday too."

He took the package, but made no move to open it until she urged him over to the bed and pushed on his shoulders, sitting him down and plopping down next to him, aware of how indecorous it all was and not caring a bit. The mystified expression he held was enough to make her happy.

His eyes clouded. "I didn't get you anything. I suppose it is traditional, isn't it?"

"I expect. But we haven't done any of this very traditionally so far," Lila said, watching him toy with the string, a thought occurring to her. "You did get a ring, didn't you?"

His eyes were huge. "Oh, Lord. Lila, I didn't even do that."

HALF THE BATTLE

Her annoyance held a flash of pain, but she tried to show neither. "I suppose it doesn't matter, Sander. We'll still be just as married without one. Open your present."

He looked down again at the parcel, pushing it around on his lap before he went to work on the string. Lila was leaning on his shoulder with impatience by the time he got all the folds undone and shook out the smooth white shirt.

"I hope it fits," she said, fretting now as she hadn't all the time she'd been working on it at odd hours in the last week. "I took the measurements from one of your old ones. The one that's frayed in the collar."

He held it out before him, the raised white stripes in the even whiter cambric catching the light. "It will be fine, I'm sure. It's beautiful. Thank you." His shoulders were stiff, and he put the shirt down gently beside him on the bed.

Lila didn't know what she had expected, but this wasn't quite it. "You're welcome," she said quickly, rising to leave the room before she sputtered at him.

His words, spoken from where he sat, stopped her two steps from the door. "Nobody's ever made me a birthday present before. My aunt got me one, once. A store-bought pair of boots when I turned twelve and was getting ready to leave for military school. She said I'd be an embarrassment without them. And once some of the cadets I taught bought me a book, when they'd found out it was my birthday. But no one's ever made me one."

She whirled around to face him, pretending not to see the suspicious glitter in his eyes. "Well, someone has now. Get used to it, Sander MacCormack, because

I believe in birthday presents and Christmas presents and 'just because' presents."

"You would, rich lady like you, with a piano and everything," he said, catching her around the waist as she advanced on him. He drew her into his lap and kissed her soundly, taking advantage of the mouth that she'd opened to protest his last remark.

The kiss was deep and thorough, and Sander's hand tangled in her hair as he searched her mouth. Lila shivered a little as she caressed the warm velvet skin of his shoulders and back, deliciously naked under her fingers. He finished the kiss and drew back a little. "There now. You'd better go, or I'll do all sorts of things a groom isn't supposed to do before the wedding."

Lila hopped off his lap and headed for the door. "I will, before I do anything unbridelike to match you." She skittered to the stairs, heart pounding, and paused halfway down. The man was actually whistling! It was tuneless and oddly cadenced, but Sander was whistling. It gave her hope.

Sander decided much later that accepting the wedding present from the men had been the first pebble in the landslide of his wedding day. Uncorking it in front of the parson before the ceremony had been the first good-sized rock in the downhill slide.

Lila was beautiful in the white muslin dress, all sprigged with lavender ribbons. And the tiny pink roses from the garden out back made a perfect trim for her veil. She looked so fragile and beautiful with her hair curling around her. When the swaybacked mule that held the ancient preacher in his rusty black coat came ambling into the yard, Sander could tell that she was near tears. But before he could say anything she'd straightened her shoulders and marched up to greet the man.

Sander had never held much store by preachers, and the right Reverend Obadiah Stevens did not increase his confidence in them. He was mostly toothless, and his sunken cheeks gave the illusion of great age under the battered black felt hat covering most of his wispy white hair. Sander came out on the porch to greet the man, slipping an arm around Lila for comfort as he shook the old parson's hand.

"My grandniece, Arlie Hoskins, told me all about y'all," he said in a creaky voice, then hawked and spat over the rail to clear some of the dust of his journey. "Where we doing this?"

It was then that the men had come up next to the raddled old mule. John Reed, as befitted his lofty position as corporal, held the jug.

"Captain, we'd like to give you this. A wedding present. T'ain't much, but not just everybody will take scrip around here." He went up the stairs and handed him the jug.

Sander thanked him, feeling Lila's muscles tighten beneath his hand. Still, she was gracious, even though he knew she'd rather pour the offending liquid into the azaleas below.

The speculative gleam in the parson's eyes was impossible to miss. "Wedding present, hmmm?"

Before Sander could apologize for waving spirits in front of a man of the cloth, the man of the cloth had nimbly popped the cork on the jug and taken a sniff. "Say, you boys bought this from Josh Perkins, I'll wager."

Reed had blushed. "That we did, sir."

The parson's nose had fairly quivered as he'd snuffled

the aroma coming from the jug. "I knew it, just by smelling. He makes the stiffest panther's breath for twenty miles." He looked inquisitively at Sander. "You don't mind, do you? Just to clear the road dust?"

Sander could hardly refuse. The old man hefted the sturdy jug with a strength one wouldn't have thought he possessed, while Lila sputtered beside him. "I really think perhaps a glass of lemonade, Reverend." She exited the porch to get the offered liquid, and Sander could hear her muttering.

In a moment he took back the jug and corked it as the old man passed a hand over his lips. "That does right pert," Reverend Stevens said, his eyes glittering. "Now, we going to tie the bonds of holy matrimony for you under the arbor here, Captain, or in the dwelling?"

"In the dwelling. Let me show you the way," Sander said, ushering him in while keeping the jug away from his grasp. He made a note to stow it someplace out of sight until after the ceremony. Lila would have his hide if the old coot was any tipsier than he was going to be with the pull he'd already taken.

It hadn't helped. He'd put the jug on the far side of the piano, with a shawl draped in front of it for camouflage. Still, the parson had found it before the ceremony. There was an aroma of still around him, and he was dreadfully unsteady on his feet as he opened the book as rusty black as his battered coat.

Lila was so stiff as she stood beside Sander that she might have been carved out of wood. He felt sweat trickle down his neck. He'd agreed to this, and wanted it for her sake. And now it was all going wrong.

There was no music. No flowers except those she'd picked herself. The witnesses were a bunch of soldiers who shuffled and coughed behind them. Or beside them, in the case of Yancey who was standing up for him. Seeing the solid presence of the man who'd stood beside him in situations only slightly more perilous on battlefields, Sander was struck by something. There was no one beside Lila.

Of course, her kin were all either dead or hundreds of miles from here. But surely there was some friend among the neighborhood women. Sander was opening his mouth to ask about it when he heard a wagon creak to a stop out front, then the protestation of the porch steps under a solid figure.

"I didn't miss it, did I?" called out Arlie Hoskins.

"No, ma'am, haven't missed a thing," Yancey called out amiably. "C'mon right in."

The parson attempted to straighten up at her entrance. "Arletta," he said in a clipped voice, with a nod.

"Uncle Obadiah." Her answer was just as clipped, and Sander got the feeling that this was not the first time she'd seen the old man three sheets to the wind. She breezed into the room and gave one pointed look to her offspring, who leaped off his chair without a word and ushered her into it. "Now don't wait any on my account." She settled her voluminous brown taffeta skirts on the parlor chair and nodded a few times at the old man.

"We shan't." The parson looked down at his book again. "Dearly beloved . . ."

Sander heard most of the ceremony through a haze. Mostly he just watched Lila beside him, looking a bit scared and very serious. He could not believe that she had not bolted at the last minute. When he woke this morning, the first thing he'd done was check the kitchen. From there, he could hear the gentle, even breathing in the dark that told him she had stayed.

It was a wonder. What someone like her wanted with a fool of his caliber was beyond him. With any luck she wouldn't have to put up with him long, anyway. Then she could pretend he never existed, if she wished.

Of course she wished, he told himself while he watched the old parson's badly shaven chin bob up and down. She'd been madder than a wet hen when he'd insisted on this wedding. But there was no way he was going to go away this time without one. He'd left one woman to swell with his bastard, and to die because of it. It wasn't going to happen again.

"The ring, young man," the parson said pointedly. His sharp, birdlike gaze told Sander it wasn't the first time he'd made the demand.

"Uh, well, there isn't . . ." he began before he felt a sharp jab in the back of his ribs. Mrs. Hoskins was behind him, rummaging in her reticule.

"I thought as much," she huffed, finally extracting something she put in his hand. "It was my ma's. I'm the only daughter, and I can't give it to any of mine. They'd squabble over it from day one." Her speech was delivered to Lila, whose eyes were filling with tears. "Now don't you say no, child. It probably won't fit anyway."

Sander looked down at the delicate gold band, set with tiny pearls. He slid it onto the cool finger of the woman beside him, repeating the parson's words with fervor.

The old man made his pronouncements, and Sander kissed his bride chastely, promising her more at a time when soldiers didn't surround them. And the look she gave him in return told him without a doubt that she understood.

It was over so quickly, that communion. Yancey was

there, whooping and pounding his shoulder, and then Arlie Hoskins came up, arranging Lila's veil and clucking over her a little while she embraced her. "Now don't you say nothin' about that ring, I mean it. Those gals have already driven me nearly insane over Mama's good dishes and the side combs. I'm not about to give them anything else to squabble over. Sometimes I wish they were all boys. Sons make a goshawful mess, but they sure are easier to raise."

The older woman then stood in front of Sander, face serious but eyes twinkling. "Now you, Captain, can say all you want about the ring. I figured you wouldn't have thought about it. Nobody who could have sat at my table five times and eaten chicken and dumplings and never noticed those three pretty girls would know anything about wedding rings."

Sander's collar grew another notch tighter. "I do appreciate it, ma'am. If there's anything I could do for you . . ."

The twinkle had dimmed. "You've got more precious jewels of mine than that, Captain. See you keep those treasures safe." She looked pointedly at her son and his gangly cousin standing in the corner joshing, and Sander felt his skin grow clammy.

"I'll try my best," he told her, fervently hoping that his best would be good enough.

It would never be good enough for the woman beside him, that he knew. She gladly accepted Mrs. Hoskins offer to pour punch, and bustled about herself to make sure everyone was fed in the next hour. And somehow the parson found that damned jug again. Sander wondered if he was ever going to get any of it himself. He'd sworn that this day, of all days, he would not drink a drop.

Not to steady the hands that were hard to keep from trembling when he watched his sparkling young wife see that all were served, even Yancey. Not to fuel his curiosity at the whereabouts of the widow Culpepper, who seemed to have vanished like smoke in the last few days, for which he was eternally thankful. And not even to bolster himself for the ribald suggestions that inevitably came out of having a troop of soldiers for a wedding party.

Still, that punch cried out for something with a bite to it to take the edge off its cold tea and grape juice sweetness. Even Lila's mint leaves floating in it didn't make it any more palatable. She'd worked so hard on all of this. The men ate like horses, complimenting her on everything. Sander wanted to do the same, but it would have sounded so silly. He knew how little this resembled the wedding she would have planned, given the resources. Compliments for the cake, cobbled together out of what was on hand, and the cold ham and biscuits, artfully arranged to hide the fact that there weren't many of them, stuck in his throat.

Watching her pass another tray around the room, and taking time to have a word with John Reed, made his heart ache. She was a true lady. This was not right, this farcical wedding with a bunch of boys in butternut-dyed trousers for witnesses and a tipsy old man weaving the words over them. But it was the best he could give her.

When Yancey put another cup of punch in his hand with a broad wink, Sander took a sip quickly. Spiked. If he broke this promise, it would only be the first of many. If Lila didn't know what manner of man she was marrying, she'd find out soon enough. He drained the cup.

The angle of the sun through the parlor windows caught him by surprise when he next looked. Mrs.

Hoskins was adjusting her hat and arguing with the reverend. "Now Uncle Obadiah, you know you ought to go home with me. I've got evening milking to attend to, so you just hurry on up and get ready."

"No, Arletta, you go on," Reverend Stevens finally pushed out. "There's a big tent meeting down to Patterson at week's end, and I need to get a start on going."

Sander heard Mrs. Hoskins mutter a most unladylike phrase as she turned from the swaying figure in black. "Suit yourself. I need to get on back to the cabin."

She stuck out a hand to him that was as plain as any man's and as strong. "I wish you well, Captain." She had a few words with her son that Sander couldn't hear, and then she was gone.

Once she was gone from the yard, leaving dust behind her, Lila came out on the porch. She blew air out in an aggravated puff. "Now what are we going to do, Sander? That old man is still in there, and he's drunk. I don't think he can even sign the marriage certificate."

"That wouldn't break your heart, now would it?" Sander heard himself saying. The shock in Lila's gray eyes just made him more voluble. "I mean, it would be much easier to pretend this whole wretched day never existed that way, wouldn't it?"

"Wretched?" The landslide that had been building all day poured down on Sander and engulfed him along with Lila's trembling contempt. "Why don't you just try awful? Or hideous?"

He turned on his heel. "I might at that. I'll get Yancey to see the old man on his way."

Nine

Lila sat on the bed in Sander's room. She still thought of the pale walls and dark furniture as belonging to Tyson, and it felt odd to be contemplating sleeping here. Even without the ever-present shadow of Ty in the room, it would feel odd sleeping here. The thought of Sander walking in was even more disconcerting than thinking about Ty right now.

She unfastened her shoes and took them off. Without them and the veil, she felt almost normal again. The veil had been jettisoned hours ago in the heat when it was just too difficult to keep the blasted thing from dragging through food on the table. She expected it was still hanging from the corner of her great-grandfather's picture frame in the best parlor.

She smiled, thinking about any of the rough soldiers, standing stiffly in the parlor, touching that veil. They'd as lief have touched a water moccasin.

The men had treated her so differently all day. They'd been hushed and respectful, and tremendously uncomfortable. She could hear them outside, where they'd gathered after they'd shed their dress uniforms.

She looked around the room, growing dim in the twilight. It was really too early to be in her bedroom. She should be doing something downstairs, but the pointed looks of the few men not outside and the smiles when they'd thought she wasn't looking had driven her to refuge. Yet there was nothing in her refuge to keep her busy. Her workbasket was still in the family parlor, and there were no books here either.

There *was* Sander's Bible. She opened the wardrobe, still not full even with their combined garments. The book was heavy in a comforting way, and she paged through it. She marveled again at his mother's beautiful handwriting, stroking one page.

Impulsively, she sprang from the bed and went to the desk. There was a pen and ink. Carefully she brought the Bible over and opened it to the right page. The roughness of her hands made her grimace as she carefully inked the pen and got it ready. She knew her writing was not nearly as neat as what had been put there before. Still, it wasn't as awful as his father's slashing scrawl.

Lila concentrated on forming each word, each letter, as beautifully as she knew how. When she was finished there were no blots. She stood back a little to judge her handiwork. It would do. " 'Married, this seventeenth day of August, 1864,' " she read to herself softly. " 'Lila Claire Fox to Lysander Hugh MacCormack.' " Good heavens. That made her a MacCormack now. The thought made her sit down hard in the chair beside the desk.

A week was too short a time to absorb all these changes. Lila fanned her flushed skin in an irritated manner. Sander shouldn't have rushed this like he did. She needed more time to get used to the idea of being Mrs. MacCormack.

Being Mrs. Sander MacCormack meant an evening of waiting for her new husband to return from his tasks, but since it had gotten quiet, she went back downstairs. Even then, her happiness at his weary presence was cut short by Yancey's return. Having been entrusted with seeing the parson home, Yancey stomped into the house, announcing that in the middle of one of his hymn-singing hollers, the drunken old man had slid off his mule, possibly into a ditch. Yancey wasn't sure—because he couldn't find him. Lila contained her anger until the sergeant left, but just barely; the idea of the parson passed out in the damp until morning made her blood boil. And the fact that Sander denied responsibility for the man's well-being was the last straw.

"There's nothing to do," Sander said, shrugging. "He'll sleep it off and go home in the morning."

Lila's wordless frustration carried her out of the parlor and up the stairs, coldly aware that she and her husband had waited only hours before their first argument.

An hour later Sander still hadn't made it upstairs. At first Lila had thought he'd follow her. He hadn't, not then or later when she'd undressed in a flurry of wardrobe-door banging.

This was not the way she'd thought her wedding night would end. Of course, she hadn't counted on Yancey losing the parson. Still, she had dreamed about a slow, lengthy retiring. Of finally teaching Sander some of the mysteries of corset strings and such.

Instead she sat bolt upright in the dark, propped against one of the sturdy feather pillows she'd aired just the day before. If she wasn't so angry with the man, she'd be in heaven, Lila decided. Sleeping on a real bed with clean sheets around her would be glorious.

It wouldn't be glorious alone—not now. Alone it

would still be cool and crisp, the linen teasing her toes. It would also be incredibly humiliating.

Tiny fingers of panic rose in Lila's throat. Maybe he wasn't coming to bed. Maybe he was so disgusted with the whole marriage that he was just going to sleep downstairs. As unhappy as she was, that was the last thing she wanted for Sander. She could imagine the faces of the men on the drill field in the morning if word got around that their beloved captain had slept in the parlor on his wedding night. Ye gods, maybe he was out in one of the tents. The men would never forgive her.

The floor was cool under Lila's feet as she felt her way to the door and opened it. From the top of the stairs she could see the glow of lamplight in the parlor. She leaned against the wall, a wave of relief washing over her. Frugal, careful Sander wouldn't have gone out and left the lamp burning. She got all the way down the stairs and to the doorway of the parlor without Sander saying anything, and she wondered again if he was determined to ignore her.

Her hand flew to her mouth to stifle nervous laughter when she saw him. His head was pillowed comfortably on his open book, and one arm drooped over the side of the chair toward the floor.

She came to him gently, not wanting to startle him. She'd seen before how Sander came awake, and she didn't want to be in the middle of that. She called his name softly, fingers brushing the soft curls on his forehead. His head lifted immediately, and he sat blinking owlishly.

In a moment recognition cleared his dark eyes. "Oh, damnation. I fell asleep over Blackstone on my wedding night. How late is it?"

"Late. Come upstairs," Lila said.

"Are you sure?" His question and the look that he gave her sent prickles racing up her spine.

"I'm sure," she said, going to the lamp beside him and picking it up.

Sander was forced to follow her, with her pool of light, or sit in the dark. He followed. When Lila got back to the bedroom, she suddenly became aware of the quiet in the house. It struck her, then, that none of the other men were in their beds. Apparently they had all opted for space in the tents.

The thought made Lila even more fluttery inside than she had been before, and she set the lamp down on the desk and scooted into bed and under the sheets in one motion.

They were alone, truly alone, in this big house. Sander was methodically removing his tunic and pants, smoothing his new shirt as he put it over the back of the desk chair. He stood still for a moment and looked at Lila. "I don't own a nightshirt. I know it flies in the face of convention, but I don't. Shall I stop now?"

Lila forced herself to look straight back at him. "Is that how you usually sleep?"

Even in the dim light she could see his white grin. "Not in a bed during calmer times. Now, out in a bedroll on campaign, I would have kept the shirt and pants on. Here . . ." He lifted his palms and smiled ruefully.

Lila couldn't hold onto her anger any longer, no matter how pure and righteous it was. His smile, and the little bit of discomfort that she could feel in his waiting stance, melted her reservation. "Then take off the rest and come to bed. And Sander?" She found herself smiling. "Don't douse the lamp just yet."

* * *

Sander gave silent thanks that, if she were determined to go through with this, Lila was in her nightgown. That pile of female rubbish in the corner would have defeated him for certain. One of these days he was going to have to start learning.

The thought made it even harder for him to unfasten his drawers calmly, step out of them and lay them aside. It took every ounce of his concentration to act calm and controlled while his nerves screamed.

It was a good thing he hadn't had any more punch, not the way Yancey had been pouring it. No, this time he was terribly sober. Of course, being sober had its pitfalls too. He was alert enough to see the soft gleam in Lila's eyes, her moist lips shining as she pressed them together and fiddled with the embroidered edge of the bedsheet.

When he turned to put the room in darkness, she finally spoke. "Not just yet."

"Are we going to sleep with a light on?" Sander fought with a smile and lost.

She suddenly looked prim in her white gown, a froth of ruffles rising high on her neck. The color rose in her cheeks, and she was having trouble meeting his gaze. "No, I like it dark when I sleep."

Her expression when she looked back up made Sander tongue-tied. "Ah. Good." He walked over to the bed and sat, suddenly excruciatingly aware of being naked.

His doubts evaporated as Lila dropped the sheet and leaned over, smiling. Her hand brushed his cheek, the fingers soft and smelling of roses. Without thinking, Sander turned his face into the caress, brushing his lips against her palm. Her answering groan of delight made him forget his anxiety.

His hands sought her narrow waist, pulling her close to him. "This is not going to do," he murmured. "If I'm going to sit here naked as a plucked chicken, you are joining me."

He pulled at one end of the creamy ribbon at her neck. It unfurled, leaving a sweet spot that he could kiss right at the hollow. Before undressing her further he paid attention to that spot, slowly and thoroughly. As he kissed and nibbled there, Lila's hand slid down his spine, tracing a path that made it hard to concentrate on slowly plundering her skin.

The second ribbon uncovered the round, pale globes of her breasts almost to the nipples. Her body moved closer to his, was almost in his lap as Sander kissed first one, then the other. As he dallied in the hollow between, her fingers tangled in his hair and Sander could hear her breath catch in her throat.

Pulling the third ribbon opened so much to his view that Sander could hardly decide where to travel next, a decision made much more difficult by his own body's singing demand for attention.

His deliberation made Lila blush, and she looked down modestly to hide her confusion. The gesture would have been much more effective if looking down hadn't given her direct evidence of how she was affecting him. Her eyes held the most delightful mixture of surprise and triumph when she looked up again. "Oh," was all she said. She slid out of the top of her gown with a little shrug Sander wasn't sure how to describe, except that the one fluid motion left her with frothy white cotton around her hips and nothing above.

The gown tangled around her knees, and she pulled free of him momentarily to slip it away and drop it off the bed. As she came back to him, Sander lowered her to the bed, her hair spreading out on the pillow.

There was so much in her eyes. Fortunately, with all the emotions that glowed lambent in that gray gaze, fear was absent. But so was what he wanted to see the most. He lowered his body beside her, kissing her. At first he was gentle; then he delved deeper with his tongue, his mouth covering hers, as her fingers played up and down his spine in sweet torture.

Finally, when he thought he would drown in her if he didn't stop, Sander pulled away. Lila clutched at his back, her eyes wide. "Tell me what you want," he said, watching her pretty confusion.

"I don't know the words." She certainly knew the actions, as the hand that slipped between them proved, nearly taking away his resolve.

"All right, then, I'll tell you what I want." It was agony to keep his breathing regular, to keep from exploding. "Tell me that you trust me. We made a lot of promises in front of that old reprobate this morning, Lila. I don't respect him, but I respect the promises we made. Tell me you trust me."

Her eyes, already cloudy with passion, clouded further. "I trust you."

"Even when I say the old man isn't dead?"

Her simplicity broke his heart. "Even then. I'm your wife, Sander. I have to trust you."

Sander felt a burning tightness in his chest. He hadn't realized until now that he'd been holding his breath, waiting for her answer. It wasn't love, but it would have to serve. He gave in to the leading grasp of her hands on his buttocks, covering her with his body, finding a home in her embrace.

* * *

Lila realized later that neither of them had ever doused the lamp. It had sputtered out on its own sometime between the bouts that left her body sweetly sore and her lips feeling swollen. But the moon had risen to give them a little light. It was all the illumination they needed. Her light came from looking at the dark, serious eyes of the man beside her.

Those eyes had finally closed in sleep. Sander's fingers were clutching her hair, as a child's might in slumber clutch a favorite "lovey." She fervently hoped he didn't roll over still holding the substantial hank twined in his hand. He looked so comfortable she didn't want to disturb him. His breath came sweetly, soft and even as he settled in beside her.

Lila knew that many a woman said her man looked just like a little boy when asleep. She couldn't imagine Sander's cares ever drifting far enough away for him to look like a child again. She pulled the sheet up slightly over both of them, making her movements slow and soft so that he would not stir.

What a puzzle he was. In the height of passion he asked, not for love undying, but for trust. Perhaps he knew it was harder for her to give. Lila closed her eyes, willing her body to let her sleep. In the morning those dark eyes would be alert again, and there would still be no one in the house. She smiled. Better rest up.

Ten

Lila looked at the pitiful little pile of linens laid out in front of her. "Chloe, this is pathetic. No infant should start life with this little bit and in a cave."

Chloe shrugged her shoulders. "I am not going to give birth surrounded by Confederate soldiers. This cave is mostly dry and very comfortable."

Lila turned to face Chloe, hands on her hips, in a battle stance that she knew wouldn't win her friend over. "You'd be so much more comfortable in a bed, in the daylight."

"Alone, or with you, I would. Not with those yahoos up there. No disrespect to your husband. I'm sure he commands the finest company of Confederates in Missouri. But they're still rebels and I'm having no part of them. And neither is my son."

Lila sagged. "All right, have it your way. But we need to get some things from the house. What are you going to use for a cradle and clothing?"

"I have blankets. And I hadn't planned on a cradle. I want to be able to move quickly if I have to." Lila searched her friend's face. The last statement belied anxiety she'd never admit to. Lila could see it in the slightly gray cast to her skin, the busy movement of her hand along the skirt of her gown.

"All right. I'll look around the nursery and see what I can bring. I'll be back tomorrow."

Chloe nodded, then frowned. "Are you sure no one misses you? It's a little risky coming in broad daylight, isn't it?"

"It would be riskier coming in the evening. Sander would notice if I were gone long."

Chloe made a face that was half-grin, half-grimace. "He's keeping close track of you, is he?"

Lila fought a blush. "You might say that." The silence stayed between them for a moment, Chloe's bright brown eyes searching her face. "All right, I'd miss him too. I don't know what I'll do when he leaves. And he will, soon." It was all too plain. There were so many dispatches, so many drills of increasing ferocity. The men spent fewer evenings playing cards and more inventorying packs, cleaning weapons, telling stories. Last night as she'd walked in the yard she'd seen Blainey Hoskins and his cousin listening to one of the battle tales, eyes big as saucers.

"He hasn't said when?"

Lila shook her head. "And I haven't asked, either. I'm afraid to, I expect."

Chloe stood in front of her, putting hands on her shoulders. A hug was out of the question; her bulky middle burgeoned between them. "He'll tell you soon enough. Now scoot home before you're missed."

Lila gave her shoulders a quick squeeze and left. No one was around to notice her exit from the cave. The men were on another of Yancey's marches. They wouldn't be back for hours, and even then they'd all hurl themselves in the creek before expecting supper. She headed for the kitchen to make sure everything would be ready for them.

When she pushed the door open, a movement made her stand stock-still in the doorway. Fay was in the middle of the stone floor. As the door was pushed open she yelped like a singed cat. She glared at Lila. "You could make more noise, not sneak up on a body like that."

Lila hid a smile. "I didn't expect anyone to be in here."

"Especially not me," Fay added with a sneer. "Well, even I get hungry between meals once in a while."

"Then have an apple," Lila said.

Fay took one without enthusiasm. "Don't mind if I do." She sidled toward the door and left. What had Fay been scouting for? The odds that she was in there merely for a snack were next to none. If Fay was in the kitchen she was looking for something to steal. Or to take with her.

Thinking of Fay made Lila compare her to the animals that never came closer to man than the edge of a campfire's light. Fay had an uncanny sense of self-preservation. She'd waited until three days after the wedding before she'd slunk back to the house. And now she was getting ready to leave again. This time, it would be for good.

Up on the highest shelves there were a few dry supplies, and high in the pantry was some of the jam Lila had put up. Lila looked at those jam jars. They would make good barter or keep a body well with a little bread and some dried meat. Hastily she pulled over a chair, plucked up two pots of blackberry and scooted down.

The movement made her a little dizzy. She leaned against the wall for a moment to steady herself. That had been happening in the last few weeks. One moment she'd be fine, the next dizzy and swallowing past nausea. In a moment she was fine again. She wiped at the light sweat that had broken out on her forehead and moved out of the kitchen.

When she stood outside Fay's door, she knocked before she went in. She put the pots of jam on the dresser. "Here," she said brusquely. "I can't spare much, but you'll need them, wherever you're going."

Fay eyed her suspiciously. "What makes you think I'm going anywhere?"

"Right before they leave, you'll be gone."

The older woman sighed and pushed a hank of limp red hair out of her eyes. "Didn't know you were smart enough to know. Why are you giving me the food?"

"You'd take it if I didn't. This way it makes me feel better."

Fay's thin upper lip drew back in a little snarl. "I'll just bet it does. Lady Bountiful. Better hang onto plenty yourself, missy. You'll need it when the bushwhackers come, if you're still here."

"Oh, I'll be here. I'm not leaving again." Lila's voice sounded firmer than she felt inside.

Fay's chuckle was ugly. "Oh, you'll leave. When the place is burned and everything's gone, you won't be so proud. You'll go where you have to and do what you have to just to keep body and soul alive." Her pale eyes seemed to see something faraway before she stared at Lila. "Think I was always like this? Some old bag trading my body for booze and a bed? Well, I wasn't. I was a respectable widow, back in Tennessee. That was before my boy Billy went off and joined. They brought him home in a box. Then the damned Union trash burned the cabin." Her eyes glazed over again. "You'll leave."

Lila fought the urge to put an arm around her bony shoulders. "I'll stay. Nobody would dare burn this house, not while they know Ty's coming back. Nobody that had to keep living in this county would, anyway."

Fay didn't answer with words, just gave her a pitying look and shook her head. "My Billy was young too. He believed in all that sort of thing. And they killed him just as dead as if he'd believed in nothing."

Lila went out, closing the door behind her.

That evening started as usual. They sat in the family parlor, Sander reading his law book at her father's big walnut secretary, Lila rummaging in her workbasket. She found a linen handkerchief with ripped lace that she'd been meaning to salvage when the endless supply of socks to darn and collars to turn ran out. Absently, she ran her fingers over the smooth fabric, then went digging in the bottom of her workbasket. There was a bit of cotton batting there, and some lace that almost matched the hanky trim. She threaded a needle and set to work.

In less than an hour, she spread out her finished creation on her lap. It was darling. The batting had been stuffed in one edge of the handkerchief, and a little knotting and tying had made a round, featureless face and a bonnet out of the stuffed edge. Two knots, and there were little hands reaching up next to the face, the rest of the material trailing down like a christening gown. Chloe's baby had a toy. Once he could get his hand to his mouth, he could chew on the soft little poppet. Lila's eyes misted, thinking of tiny, chubby fingers.

Sander's oath, coming from behind her, made her nearly rise from her chair. "Lord, woman. That your way of telling me things?"

She stared down into her lap, bewildered, then

looked up where he stood behind her chair. His face was pale, with a deep crease across the forehead. And he was unmistakably angry. Lila couldn't imagine what had brought on the storm in his expression. "What do you mean?"

"That baby doll. You need to be making baby dolls, Lila?"

So that was it. She snorted softly in relief. "Not for me. There are other women in the world, and I happen to know a few of them. Just because I don't get off the place much—"

"Much!" Sander exclaimed. "Once that I can think of since I've been here. Oh, well, no matter. I'm sorry I startled you. Thinking of turning in yet?"

He seemed to be sagging in relief, and Lila felt a bitter anger because the thought of her carrying his child had made him so disturbed. Normally this was her favorite time of day, when Sander changed from being a commander and coaxed her up the stairs. His anger and his obvious relief afterward had taken all the pleasure out of her anticipation of the evening. "Not yet. Are you, Captain?"

"Oh, no. I've offended you. And now you'll snap at me even harder when I ask if there're any of those molasses cookies left."

"They're in the crock in the pantry. Eat them before they get stale." Lila went back to the work in her lap.

"Ah, married bliss. I'm going to take a turn around the yard." Sander went out, the back door banging closed behind him.

Lila sat staring down at the handkerchief baby. Sander's words had stirred something in her that had been on the edge of her thoughts. Like so much that bothered her, she'd been pushing it away. The dizziness, the nausea. The effort it took to push herself out of bed in the morning. A mental count confirmed things. It must have happened that first night when her fever had broken, or perhaps on their wedding night the week after.

Not even nearly starving at Evie's or hiding from the raiders in constant fear had disturbed her body enough for it to deny its monthly cycle. She really *should* be making two handkerchief babies, one for Chloe and one for herself.

If it hadn't been dark already, and Sander somewhere right outside the door, Lila would have entertained thoughts of going directly to Chloe. She could ask her if being pregnant felt this way, if one became all jumpy and teary and tired most of the time. They could giggle together about what they'd share.

Then Lila's thrill at that first thought plummeted. Chloe at least was carrying a baby both of its parents wanted. Once Marcus got back, God willing, he'd be the proudest daddy in the county. Sander had turned pale at the mere *thought* of her bringing a child into the world. Given the nervous way he'd contemplated the possibility of fatherhood, she'd make her own handkerchief baby quietly. "No sense getting him more disturbed than he already is," she muttered. "We'll just keep this a secret." As she spoke she tucked the doll into her workbasket and unconsciously stroked her abdomen softly, caressing the faraway person she spoke to; just beginning to believe it was real.

Her secret made Lila even more jumpy than she'd been. She and Sander were a pair, she thought in irritation as she closed the lid on the workbasket and got up. Neither of them could sit still for ten minutes. When the back door slammed and she could hear his measured tread in the hall, she was up and straightening the room, humming a little. "Now, Lila, can we go upstairs?"

The light that was normally in his eyes as he teased her to their room was missing. Lila wondered what other guilts were preying on him, other than snapping at her earlier. "Certainly, sir, if you're that tired. Just let me set this to rights." She twitched at the curtains until they hung right and refolded the throw over the chaise. "All right. You may take the lamp."

Sander smiled slightly and did as she asked. They mounted the stairs in silence. Force of habit kept them from talking until the door of their room was shut. It was too obvious from the scuttling noises behind the door that Fay had, as usual, paid attention to their ascent.

Sander set the lamp down on the broad desk and sat in the chair to ease off his boots. He watched as she deftly undid the buttons down her back. "I never did learn, did I?"

Lila froze, hearing the past tense in his statement. "Learn what?"

"To serve as a lady's maid. I'm still just as clumsy at it as when I started, weeks ago. Don't know a corset lace from 'Yankee Doodle.' "

Lila made her hands work, slid the gown off and hung it up, trying to talk while she moved. "See, you're proving yourself wrong already. Two months ago you wouldn't have even known what a corset lace was. Now you even know what it's called."

"And still hate them just as much." He was out of his tunic and his shirt now, standing behind her. "Let me attempt to divest you of the wretched thing, madam."

His fingers were more practiced than he'd let on.

The hated corset was gone in a moment. As she put it aside, Lila realized that she would have to start lacing it much looser soon. That would make Sander happy, even if the cause would appall him. His hands still roamed her waist as she slid off her petticoat and stood facing the wardrobe doors.

"Are you going to let go of me long enough so that I can take down my hair and get into my nightgown?"

"I don't know. Are you going to complain if I watch?" He dropped a nuzzling kiss on the back of her neck, making the hairs there rise.

"I always let you watch Sander." At first it had seemed scandalous, even not removing that last layer of underclothing beneath the protection of her nightdress. Lila had been sure that was the way things should be done among proper married folks. But Sander had coaxed and tempted, those dark eyes sparkling, until she no longer blushed as she disrobed.

"You do." He stepped back, and Lila could hear him easing off the rest of his clothing while she held her nightgown in her hand. She walked across the room and laid it on the chair.

In a moment she was slipping into it, conscious of him watching her. She perched on the edge of the chair, not disturbing his tunic hanging over the back. Idly, she promised, as she did every night, that soon she would say something about his habit of leaving clothing everywhere. Then a pang of fear rose, choking her, at the thought that soon the room would be perfectly neat because his clothing would be strewn around some battlefield instead. The tunic hanging across the back of the chair looked like a friend.

Lila forced trembling fingers into her hair, taking away the pins. When it was all free, she shook her head once before she found her hairbrush, half-buried under a pile of papers Sander had strewn on the desk, and worked on the heavy mass over one shoulder. Then she braided it in one heavy, loose braid and turned to the bed where Sander sat, the sheet decorously pulled up to his middle, a soft smile on his face. "Should I?" she gestured toward the lamp.

"There's a moon," he said in a voice as soft as his smile. "It's plenty light." He was gentle and thorough, almost as if he were memorizing her body, and Lila wanted to shriek with the pain he was causing her. Not with his mouth, which was warm and pliant on her willing flesh. His long fingers were gentle as they grasped and probed and stroked. But there was a sweet sadness to his every gesture that made Lila tense and wary. The spiral of sensations he awoke in her made Lila's throat tighten, and she pushed back tears. This she would remember, this she would take with her next week or next month when her bed was empty. Not some peaceful, calm drifting into lovemaking, but a hailstorm of feelings that pelted both of them, made her stifle a sob.

When they had both slumped onto the bed and she lay with one leg still thrown brazenly over him, Sander's hand combing through the loosed hair falling down her back, Lila finally spoke. "You're leaving." The stiffening of his entire body under her didn't stop her words. "When were you planning to tell me, Sander? Ten minutes before you got on your horse and rode away?"

His voice held pain. "I was going to tell you in the morning, once it got light."

"And when are you leaving?" Lila wondered at her own voice, as hard as that of a stranger.

At first Sander said nothing, just sighed. "The day

after, before noon. Whenever the column gets to us. We're marching on St. Louis."

She slipped out of his arms and sat up, binding up her hair. The knowledge left her cold, but didn't give her the immediate desire to try to make it to the railroad station. If Rosecrans was as dim as his lieutenant had painted him, it was no use anyway. She finished braiding her hair. "Do you think you'll be successful?"

Sander gave a short, bitter laugh. "I honestly can't say. Wouldn't tell the men that, but with you I must tell the truth. If Shelby were leading, maybe. But with Price calling the moves . . ." He said no more, turning over to face the wall and the wardrobe. For the first time in weeks Lila didn't touch him as she drifted into uneasy slumber.

In the morning it would have seemed like a bad dream. The sun was shining, and there was a coolness to the late September wind that teased tendrils of hair across her face as Lila walked to the kitchen. But two more jars of jam were gone from the open pantry.

And when she went upstairs the nursery door was open and her chest of goods had been rifled. A quick look told her she was missing a quantity of hunter green ribbon and some lace. All compact goods that would fetch a price from someone starved for little luxuries. At breakfast Sander gave Yancey a silent, questioning look. The red-haired giant nodded mournfully. "Gone. Slipped out sometime in the night, while Reed was on watch."

Lila nearly dropped the coffeepot she was heaving onto the table. It was really true. If Fay was gone, the men would leave as well. Sander couldn't meet her gaze and only toyed with his breakfast. Lila couldn't eat at all.

Eleven

Lila stared at the ceiling, listening to Sander's ragged breathing as he came from deep sleep into wakefulness. It made her want to reach out and touch him, feel the smoothness and warmth of him under her fingers. It made her want to change her mind about staying silent. He'd roll over, smile at her with the hazy smile he had when he was first waking up and she'd tell him that he was going to be a father.

Then, outside the open window, a horse whinnied and Sander came awake, not hazy and warm but instantly alert, the soldier in him responding to the sound. He got up and padded to the window and opened the sash, leaning his head out. "Hobbs, Sutherland," he called. "See those tents are struck now that it's light."

There was an answer below and he withdrew, closing the window. "And good morning to you, too," Lila said tartly, sitting up in bed.

"Sorry. I know I should be more solicitous, but there's so much to do," Sander said.

"And so little time for all of it," Lila said, moving toward the wardrobe. Sander came behind her and put his hands on her shoulders.

"You're right. And we have the least time of all." He

didn't sound unhappy, just matter-of-fact. The kiss he planted on the back of her neck seemed dry and far away, as if he were already gone somehow. Lila wondered how she would get through this day.

She would just have to try. She shrugged her shoulders gently, and Sander's hands slipped off. "I'll get dressed and start breakfast," she said, trying to sound as everyday as he had. "No sense in making the men wait when heaven knows what they'll get tomorrow."

They dressed in silence and Sander was out of the room quickly. Moments later Lila was out too. As she went through the hall she noticed how empty the rooms all looked without any trace of their inhabitants. Many of the men had moved out to the tents permanently when she had taken up residence in the house.

Lila wondered whether she could sleep tonight in this place, alone, if they all left. She wouldn't be able to sleep in the same bed she'd shared all these nights with Sander, that she knew. Perhaps she could move back into her old room if Fay and Yancey hadn't destroyed it.

Before she thought of sleep, she had so much to do that she pushed the thought from her mind. She went to the kitchen and began making biscuits. Blainey Hoskins wandered in. "You need eggs this morning?"

"Might as well, Blainey. And some bacon if you'd get it on your way back." He took a basket and was gone.

By the time the biscuits were in the oven and several skillets were heating on the stove, he was back, helping her slice bacon and crack eggs. "How's your mother taking all this?" she asked him.

"She cried," he said solemnly. "I haven't seen Ma cry since I've been taller than she is." His wide eyes attested to how long that had been.

She patted his hand. "Can't be helped. It hurts, sending you off like this, all of you."

"Yes, ma'am," he answered. Since her marriage to Sander, she had become a mature woman in his eyes instead of the girl he'd grown up with.

"Why don't you turn that bacon while I carry in the coffee," she said, handing him a long-handled fork. "Mind that grease doesn't splatter on you. I'll not have the captain think I'm wounding you before you even march off."

The coffeepot seemed heavier than usual as she lugged it into the dining room and set it down, getting cups out of the corner cabinet. Yancey walked in as she set down the last cup and took one, pouring himself coffee. He took a scalding sip and sat down, sighing with pleasure.

"I still don't like you much," he said without preamble. "Can't understand what was going on in your mind when you convinced the captain to marry you. But, Mrs. MacCormack, I am going to miss your coffee."

It was as close to a compliment as she was ever going to get from him, and Lila almost smiled. "I'm sure you are, Sergeant," she said as she turned back to the kitchen.

As she passed the porch she looked out in the distance toward the main road. The sky was clear and blue, yet on the horizon there was darkness. For a moment Lila thought it was a storm. Then she realized that it wasn't a rain cloud. It was a cloud of dust raised by hundreds of feet and hooves. The Confederate column.

"Probably another two hours before they get here," Sander said behind her, making her jump. "Better keep going." He disappeared into the kitchen, then came back in a moment, a rough sandwich made from bacon

HALF THE BATTLE

and biscuit in one hand. He headed toward the barn, never seeing Lila's eyes glaze with tears as she watched the approaching cloud.

Sander tightened the girth on his saddle, checked all the harness. It shouldn't be this hard. He had been waiting for this time for months. He'd gathered a company of soldiers, trained them, supplied them, and even gathered some extra supplies for the column that was now strung out along the road. Many of the men and boys sat along the sides, eating a quick cold meal.

There were men from the suttlers' company up in the barn loft, tossing down the hay he'd helped bring in himself, sweating like a mule to get it collected for just this reason. His heart should be singing as they stacked it in the wagon. Instead it was hard to put one foot in front of the other to make sure everything was done.

He would have given his Enfield for just one jug, but he hadn't touched a drop since his wedding day. He didn't think Lila even noticed. Some days he didn't notice himself, he'd been so busy, in the days readying the company for this and in the nights with Lila.

Why was leaving so hard? She wasn't going to care when he was gone, wasn't even down here watching. He went into the house, determined to have some last word with her if he could find her. It wouldn't do to just leave without saying anything at all. Not when he didn't know when, or if, he'd ever be back.

She wasn't on the first floor of the house, but standing in the dining room, he could hear noises overhead. All the windows, from the landing on, were open as if she was giving the place a good airing. Probably trying to get rid of the odor of rebels.

She was in the bedroom Fay and Yancey had shared, the one he knew to be hers before they'd come. So she couldn't even wait until he was gone to take it back, to move out of the one they'd shared as if it were repellent.

Sander stood watching a minute before she noticed him. Her hair was tied up in a loose knot on the back of her head, some bright strands already straggling out across her back. She still looked almost as scrawny as she had when she'd haunted the house in the moonlight. In any case, she seemed too small to turn the bulky mattress by herself as she was trying to do.

"Here, let me," Sander said, striding across the room. Her eyes widened as she looked at him, and he realized she probably hadn't seen him before with saber and holster over his tunic like this.

"You don't have to," she began, but let him help turn the mattress. She stood silently for a minute when they were done, then looked at him again. "Thank you," she said. "Were you up here for something? I don't think you've left anything behind."

Not likely. In the mood she seemed to be in, she'd probably burn any memories of him.

"I don't think so. I'll look," he said, going into the room that seemed barren without the sweet clutter of his papers strewn across the desk and her clothing mixing with them. He flung open the doors to the wardrobe and looked in. Nothing. "No, I don't see anything." He started to close the doors when Lila, behind him, gave a cry.

"Oh, no, look. We can't have you leave that." She pushed beside him and knelt, reaching into the bottom of the piece of furniture. She came out holding his mother's Bible; the dark leather had blended with the floor of the wardrobe. "Let me find something to wrap

HALF THE BATTLE

it in." She looked around before he took it from her, holding out his other hand.

"No need. I'll just put it in my saddlebag."

It fell open in his hand and Sander looked at the page, confusion growing as he read. "You entered our marriage in here," he said, aware of how stupid the statement sounded, almost like an accusation.

"I did. We can't pretend it didn't happen, Sander. Even though there weren't many guests, people will know."

"Of course," he said, forcing words through the bitterness that threatened to choke him. "And if people know, much better to think you were married."

She opened her mouth to answer, but no sounds came out. Through the open window came louder sounds of horses and men. Sander walked over to look out.

"I have to be going." He turned to face her, to take a last look. She seemed to be pleating a little bit of her skirt in both hands. "The Vikings and the crusaders said a very thorough farewell to their women about this time, but I suppose there's no need for that, is there, Lila?"

She colored and backed away, looking down at the floor. "No, I suppose not. How—"

"Did I know you wouldn't want to? Easy," he said, walking to the doorway. "It's my Bible you've written the marriage records in. It goes with me; and, like me, it may never be back. Once I'm half an hour from here you can take off that band and pretend all this never happened. But don't do it, understand? Don't do it for at least a month."

"Never," she echoed. "If we're not to have any Viking good-bye, then we might have a normal one, at least," she said, sounding so practical. "So you don't believe you'll be back? This war has to end someday, Sander. Don't you think I'd want to know what happened to you, whatever the end?"

"Of course, madam. I believe the Confederacy still guarantees a pension to widows." She flinched, and for a moment Sander felt guilty about his words. As she came nearer the guilt trickled away, leaving all the feelings he could never tell her about. She stood in front of him, still marble pale, asking something with her eyes. "Good-bye, Lila."

"Good-bye, Sander." One pale arm lifted, came to rest on his shoulder, as she drew him down for a moment for a kiss that was brief, but drove all thoughts of anything else from his mind until a shouted order to the troop on the road drifted through the window. He straightened and pulled away from her, turned and walked into the hall.

It was all he could do not to rush back up the stairs and enfold her in his arms, plead with her to let him take words of love and prayers with him, anything.

Instead he went out and mounted his horse. He gave the order and the company fell in behind him to join the throng on the road. The house and property where he'd spent so many weeks screamed to be taken in one last time, but he kept his eye on the road in front. Yancey rode beside him on the big roan that looked as disreputable as he did. The sergeant turned and looked back at the house, shading his eyes and whistling tunelessly between his teeth.

When he turned back again, Sander stared at him. "Don't tell me. I can't bear knowing. If she's there on the porch or at a window it will tear me apart. And if she isn't it would be worse. Don't tell me."

"Fair enough," Yancey said. He went back to whistling.

By the time the parlor clock chimed two, there wasn't anything more than the dust cloud on the opposite horizon, the trampled grass, the horse dung and wagon ruts to tell anyone the column had passed through.

Lila had stood at the window in her parents' old bedroom watching. Blainey Hoskins waved. John Reed raised a hand in salute. Even Yancey had looked back in farewell, scowling. Sander had never turned back. Once he was set on the road, he never looked at the house, at her. They were already memories and apparently not pleasant ones.

When his back and his horse had blended in with all the others, becoming an indistinguishable speck, she finally let herself go. She sank down on the carpet and wept, still holding onto the windowsill. The rasp of her sobs was harsh and ugly, but she couldn't stop them, not until the column was far down the road and she could hear birds again.

When she was all cried out she rose from the floor, wiped her face on the sleeve of her dress and took a deep breath. Sander was gone. He could very well be dead in a week. If so, she'd probably hear of it eventually. But even if he lived, love for her would never bring him back here. Something else might, but his distant kiss and stilted good-bye had proved it wouldn't be her. She was left with some memories and perhaps a child. Pain in her hand made her look down to where she still grasped the windowsill.

She was holding on to a rough spot, and there were several large splinters pressing into her skin. She picked them out with unsteady fingers. That was it, the last cry she would have over Sander MacCormack. If he ever came back, they could start fresh somehow, but the tears were over. Picking out the last of the splinters made her concentrate so hard she didn't hear any of the noises downstairs until a light feminine voice called out in impatience, obviously not for the first time. "Lila Fox, are you in here? Lila?"

Even at that volume Lila knew who her caller was. For a moment she thought about staying where she was, slipping the door shut quietly and hoping Sallie went away. But Sallie Rogers, though she might have the mental acuity of a soap bubble, was determined. She'd go through every room in the house.

"I'm upstairs," Lila called, smoothing her skirts. "I'll be right down."

Sallie stood in the front hallway, the door still open behind her. "I came to find out if you were really here. I'd heard you were, but with all those Confederate soldiers around I thought surely you couldn't have stayed," she prattled. "I know I would have been scared out of my wits."

"Yes, I'm sure," Lila said, coming down the stairs to join her in the hall. "It was kind of you to be concerned."

Sallie reached out and took Lila's hands in hers. Lila knew that even through her thin white gloves Sallie was using the contact to gauge just how much manual labor she'd been doing in the middle of an army camp.

The gloves were just the finish to her costume. As she took in Lila's worn gray gown, Lila looked at her from her feathered hat to the tiny, unscuffed boots poking out of the last ruffled tier of the plaid taffeta.

With everything she had to do, entertaining Sallie Rogers was the last thing on her mind, but it couldn't

HALF THE BATTLE

be helped. If it had been someone of a more practical nature, Lila would have asked for help in hiding the flour barrel and Mama's good silver before the bushwhackers got wind of Sander's departure. But Sallie would just get in the way. "Would you like a cup of blackberry tea? I was thinking about stopping for a little while myself," Lila lied. Actually, if she'd stopped now when alone she might not have gotten up until it was dark.

Sallie tilted her head prettily in a way calculated to show off the huge bow in the ribbon that held her bonnet in place. "That would be nice. I can see why you'd like to rest a while, Lila. You look positively peaked."

And puffy and wretched, Lila added to herself as she looked at Sallie's sparkling blue eyes. "Why don't you make yourself comfortable in the parlor, and I'll put the water on," she said, leading Sallie into the company parlor. She winced inwardly when she noticed that her veil still hung from the corner of one gilt picture frame. She hadn't ever had the heart to take it down. Hanging there, it reminded her of the better parts of her wedding day. She'd even noticed Sander give it a surreptitious look and smile. Doubtless Sallie would notice it soon.

She went back to the kitchen and put a kettle on the stove, took the last few molasses cookies from the crock and set them on a plate. Her hands looked red and workworn, but that didn't bother Lila. It had been so long since her life had been like Sallie's, all needlework and gentility and calling on neighbors, that the thought of having smooth white hands sounded as unreal as wearing glass slippers.

After arranging the cookies on the plate Lila took a tray holding them and the cups and saucers into the parlor. When she got there she could see that Sallie was leaning forward out of her chair, examining the veil with her eyes. "Wasn't that your mother's wedding veil?"

"It certainly was." Lila put down the tray, taking special care not to smack it down and rattle the cups. "And it happens to be mine as well. Don't you think the lace did over well?" It was gratifying to see Sallie gaping like a fish as Lila breezed out of the room to get the teapot.

Sallie couldn't sit still after that parting shot. She actually followed Lila out the door and down the stairs to the kitchen. "Your veil? Does that mean you've married?"

"A wedding veil normally does." Lila fought to keep an unkind expression off her face. The water was boiling, and she poured a stream into the teapot, closing the lid on the cloud of steam that rose.

"Do you mean you came back here married, and lived among all these soldiers? How gallant of them to respect you," Sallie said with a sigh.

"No, actually I came back here and married one of them," Lila said, wrapping a towel around the warm teapot and leaving Sallie gasping like a carp again. It was becoming a habit, her trailing behind and making little chokey noises like a colicky infant's.

"But . . . you can't mean one of *them*."

"I can. I hadn't planned on it, but life does have a way of surprising us, doesn't it?" Lila said, settling the teapot and sitting down. She realized with a pang that she should be more circumspect around a woman who was the widow of a Union soldier.

Sallie seemed so flustered it was hard to tell what she was thinking. Her pale eyes roved around the room, apparently trying to find anything that would draw the conversation away from the topic of Lila's marriage. Failing in that, she looked Lila up and down. Under her assessment, Lila was glad she was still as slender as she'd been when she'd returned from Evie's. Having Sallie think the obvious was irritating.

In the silence Lila poured tea for them both and offered cookies to Sallie. "Would you care for one? They were Sander's favorite. Captain MacCormack, my husband." She held out the plate, refusing to let the subject die.

"I see." Sallie eyed the cookies as if they contained dead bugs. She looked past the plate to Lila's hand. "You're still wearing your wedding ring, even after they've gone?"

"Of course," Lila said, setting the plate down so hard one cookie slid over the edge. She picked it up and kept it, realizing suddenly that she hadn't eaten anything all day. "I intend to keep wearing it."

"Probably most feasible," Sallie said. "I mean, they could come back, and there're always those dreadful raiders. It can't hurt to be taken for one of their persuasion, I expect."

"I'm not of 'their' persuasion," Lila said. "I'm not of anybody's 'persuasion' anymore. I'm just ready for both of these armies of fools to stop killing each other." She hadn't said it out loud before, but it was exactly how she felt. How incredibly small this house would seem if Ty and Sander would both inhabit it, but how wonderful to be able to try. The tea service in front of her blurred with the tears caused by the thought.

Sallie was struck dumb again, and used the time to nibble cookies and sip her tea. She settled back in her chair, trying to look like a normal teatime visitor to a normal household. After half a cup of tea, she sighed and sat up, obviously ready to embark on another topic of conversation. "The column came right down your front road, did it not?"

"It did. I expect I will be chasing the dust for a month," Lila said, wrinkling her nose. Perhaps the cleaning would make the ache of missing Sander dull a little.

"Amazing what strange things they leave in their wake," Sallie said. "Just coming over here I saw some of the oddest things. They'd left blankets, and a huge empty crate that seemed to have held shells or something. And someone had even stopped to tie a rag on the bushes halfway between your house and ours."

Lila bolted upright. "A rag? Where? What color?"

Sallie looked amused. She stuck one tiny hand into one of the pockets of her skirt. "Bright red. It turned out to be a whole bandanna. I can't imagine even a rebel soldier wasteful enough to leave it behind," she said, pulling it out of her pocket.

Lila put her teacup down so swiftly that the brown liquid slopped over the edge onto the table. "How did you get here, Sallie?"

"I rode, of course. The carriage wouldn't take the tall grass, and my father-in-law simply forbade me to go by the road after all the commotion earlier."

Lila stood, trying to think where all her supplies were. "Good. Then ride over to Mrs. Hoskins' and tell her she's needed."

"What? The Hoskinses? I wouldn't be caught dead over there. That cabin is terrible, surrounded by those vicious hounds the man keeps, and no one would ever call them off for me," Sallie said, her eyes wide with genuine fright.

Lila stood close to her, fighting the urge to shake her.

"You'll go, and you'll tell Mrs. Hoskins we need her here, that it's Chloe's time. Or you can lend me your horse and go help deliver Chloe's baby if Mrs. Hoskins doesn't get back in time."

Sallie's eyes were so wide that they reminded Lila of a horse's in a thunderstorm. "I'll ride over to the cabin," she said quickly. Lila crossed the fields quickly. There were shreds of red on several of the blackberry bushes, and she broke into a fast trot. She couldn't manage a run without picking up her skirts, and there was no way to do that with the bag she carried. Out of breath when she reached the cave, she leaned there panting for a moment before she went in. "Chloe?" she called.

"Back here." Even with the lamp lit it took her a moment to find her friend among the jumble of furniture and logs piled around the makeshift bed she'd made. "When all those soldiers started passing by I was afraid you'd never see the signal." Chloe's eyes pinched closed while the skin around her mouth went tight and gray.

"That one was the worst yet," she said, after a few panting breaths. "How come nobody tells you it feels like this?"

"Mama always said nobody remembers long enough to tell anybody else," Lila said, looking around for ways to make Chloe more comfortable.

"I'll remember this until I'm eighty," Chloe said, her eyes dark and sweat pouring off her forehead. "That is, if I live to see tomorrow." She puffed out another breath.

Lila opened her bag and started pulling things out. "I brought a clean nightgown. You'll be more comfortable in it. Why don't we get you changed?" She smoothed it out. It was the short one she'd worn herself the night she and Sander had made love the first time. It seemed the ideal thing for Chloe to wear for the moment.

"I'll probably ruin it," Chloe said wryly.

"It will wash," Lila said, kneeling down to where her friend half-lay, half-sat on the pile of quilts. "I sent Sallie Rogers for Arlie. They should be back in a while."

"Good," Chloe said. "Seeing her sounds pretty good right now." Her eyes darkened and she reached out for the quilt under her. "Oh, Lord, here it comes again. If Marcus comes home whole, I'm going to kill the man."

Lila was so shocked, she didn't know whether to laugh or cry. "Why, Chloe, what a thing to say!"

"It's true. He got as much pleasure as I did making this baby, and not a lick of the pain. Soldiering has to be easy compared to this."

Looking at her friend's drawn face, Lila wasn't about to argue. She wondered how much time had passed, where Sallie was by now. She got Chloe into the clean gown. Tying the last ribbon, she sat back on her heels. "I'm going to go get some water from the spring. Want to walk along or stay here? There's no one around to see us either way," she said.

"Walk along," Chloe said. "This child seems to be sitting on my spine and grinding his heels into it. Walking can't feel any worse."

She got up, her belly a low and sharply defined mound. Chloe ground her fists into her backbone as she walked toward the entrance to the cave. When Chloe got to the doorway, she groaned. "What's the matter," Lila asked. "Another pain?"

Chloe peered out and shook her head. "No, not yet.

It's still the middle of the afternoon." She looked at Lila with sober eyes.

"Well, yes. Probably not later than four," she said gently, wondering why that made tears start in Chloe's eyes.

"In here, the pains lasted so long, I figured it had to be dark now. Girl, we've got a long way to go."

"We surely do," Lila said, pushing a branch aside. Arlie had better come soon.

Twelve

It was just before dawn when a newborn's thin wail pierced the cave. Lila wrapped him in a piece of the clean linen they'd saved and handed him to Chloe.

"Hello, Freeman," Chloe said softly. Then she grimaced. "Feels like there's more to this."

"Afterbirth," Arlie said succinctly. She had arrived hours before, but even after the long night she was as brisk and efficient as ever.

Suddenly the air in the cave was filled with the coppery smell of blood. Lila's head swam.

"It's getting light out," Arlie said. "Why don't you get a breath of air?" Lila nodded at the message in Arlie's eyes and started gratefully for the entrance to the cave.

The day was clear and cloudless. She couldn't help wondering what Sander was seeing, where he was. A day's march for that size column couldn't have gotten them much farther than Ironton. Any assault on St. Louis was still a day or two away.

She straightened, stretching all the muscles that had cramped while she was tugging on the sheet or crouching to help Arlie. It felt so good to work the kinks out of her shoulders. She rolled each one backward, hearing one of them crackle in response.

HALF THE BATTLE

The growing light made her look toward the house. There were chickens that would need to be fed and a cow to milk. It would be strange, doing everything herself. She reached around her back, kneading away the tightness just below her waist. Maybe she could still talk Chloe into coming back to the house with her in a few days when she could travel. For now, she and Freeman deserved to stay where they were and get to know each other, not be dragged around. But soon she would fix up the nursery at the house and insist that Chloe use it. She scanned the horizon again in the direction of the house and stopped dead. There was a tiny plume of smoke, and unless Lila's tired eyes were playing tricks, it was coming from a spot inside the fence on her property. She bolted back into the cave to tell Arlie, intending to head back there.

At first, the realization that the smoke was coming from the kitchen chimney was comforting. But fast on the heels of that knowledge came the admission that there should still be no one there. For one crazy moment she convinced herself that it was probably just Fay, sneaking back to cook herself breakfast.

That was before she saw the horses. Nearly a dozen of them, and a couple of mules as well. They pawed at the ground inside the yard, and Lila could hear their riders calling to each other from various spots on the property. The thought made her so mad she didn't consider anything else as she pushed open the back gate.

Once the cold reality of who these men were had struck her, she was already facing several of them, slouching and dirty in worn clothes, clustered on the kitchen stoop. "Where's your leader," she asked, making the nearest two jump. "I want to know just what's going on here."

One of them laughed, showing sparse yellow teeth. "Not likely cookin' his own breakfast. Up to the house yonder, if you really want to talk to him. But he don't take kindly to interruption, missy, not before he's fed."

One of the scragglier-looking bushwhackers nodded. "Likely to carve out yer liver for breakfast if you bother them."

Lila turned away from them and walked up the flagstones to the house. Inside she could hear creaks and small crashes, as if drawers were being pulled out and dropped.

She flung open the back door, ignoring the bang it made when it hit the plaster wall behind. Let them jump. She barged into the dining room, wishing fervently that the only gun still in the house wasn't in the back half of the cellar. Her whole body was trembling, but that didn't stop her from calling out loudly. "What is going on in here? Where are you and who are you?"

An ugly snicker much too close to her in the dining-room doorway made her jump, which was apparently just what the man standing there intended. "Virgil Pearson, ma'am. 'Course, most folks don't call me Virgil anymore. Most times I go by Vengeance."

He lounged in the doorway, cleaning his filthy fingernails with an evil blade. He snapped it into the case for emphasis, and Lila made herself not flinch, even when he leaned in close to her. He had dull brown hair, parted down the middle under the greasy hat pushed back on his head. His small eyes reminded Lila of those of the wild hogs that roamed the country, the kind they put fences around cemeteries to keep out.

"Pap Price, see, he thought Virgil was too tame.

Thought Vengeance suited better." There was unholy glee in his gapped grin. "It's from the Bible, like 'Vengeance is mine, saith the Lord.' "

"Now had I known there were going to be formal introductions I'd have stayed around instead of going through the silver," drawled a second voice from the family parlor. Lila whirled to face this softer, but more menacing voice, uncomfortable with turning her back on the grinning young man beside her.

The figure in the other doorway was taller and almost courtly, even in his worn and faded clothing. Lila had heard Reverend Davies in church talk about fallen angels. At the time she'd found the phrase wonderfully poetic. Here, with one in front of her, it was just obscene.

"You, I suppose, are Hellfire, then," she spit out in a clipped tone that surprised her with its evenness. Inside she was jelly, wanting to scream or throw up. But these men were trashing her home in a way Sander and his troops had never even considered. Another crash upstairs made her wince.

"Correct. And you are?" His questioning eyes almost reminded her of Sander's in some uncanny way. But where Sander's eyes were always dark with concern or sparkling with humor, these were chocolate buttons, deadly flat.

"Lila Fox MacCormack," she added. It brought a hoot from the man behind her and raised eyebrows from the one across the room.

"MacCormack, you say? How novel." He seemed to be weighing his words. "Any relation to the Confederate captain that so recently vacated these parts?"

"His wife." Lila pushed her chin forward and stared at him.

"Wife. Shit. That means she's not a fornicator, doesn't it?"

"It certainly does, Virgil. She is definitely not a fornicator." The man's voice was icy calm.

Virgil sounded disappointed. "I could really use me another fornicator."

"Another day," his companion said.

Lila was mystified by the exchange, but somehow knew it had great significance for the two of them. "I would thank you to leave my house."

"Oh, we will," Hellfire said smoothly, crossing the room toward her. "As soon as everyone has breakfasted and found themselves a quilt or two. Damned little money around the place, Mrs. MacCormack. Don't suppose you know how we could remedy that?"

"If I did, do you think I'd tell you?"

"We've kilt better folks than you for talking to us like that," the man behind her said, ending with a giggle that made cold sweat run down Lila's back.

"Virgil, my friend, you're so dense at times. The lady is telling us, in her genteel way, that there is no money. If there had been, it would have gone with the company yesterday anyway." He took her elbow and guided her out the door. "I suggest we breakfast outside. Much more pleasant, don't you think?"

It was like looking into a snake's eyes. Lila had always heard that little animals did that and became frozen still until a copperhead killed them and ate them.

In a few minutes they were all seated on the grass eating bacon and eggs and the last of the Davis brothers' bread. Lila watched as the men scooped up their food, ate silently, then broke up again on Hellfire's orders to fill saddlebags with any leftover food and to forage in the barn for feed for the horses. Virgil strolled

HALF THE BATTLE

over to where the chickens scratched. They clustered around his legs, looking for a morning scattering of grain. Deftly he reached down, grabbed one and wrung its neck in one fluid motion, dropping it so it danced headless, and doing the same to another.

When they'd both flopped over, he took a piece of twine out of one pocket and picked up the floppy corpses, tying their feet together and walking over to his horse, which moved sideways a little, eyes wide and nostrils flaring at the fresh blood.

"Don't you fuss now," he crooned, stroking its neck, and it settled. Lila thought wildly, still sitting on the ground beside the raider chief, that the horse had borne worse burdens than two dead chickens.

There were other things hanging from the cavalry saddle. Other pelts, it looked like, skins from small animals of different colors, tied with rawhide thongs to hang around the edges of the saddle.

Lila was looking at the ragged edges of the little skins, wondering why they were there, when a coldness overtook her that started in her belly and moved out to her motionless arms and legs. They weren't animal pelts at all. They were human scalps.

The man beside her followed her gaze. "Don't worry. I don't let him do that often. And never to ladies. Only the fornicators, as he calls them. Our Virgil is terribly religious. It's his greatest asset. He's almost harmless, most of the time. I'm sure he would care for you much more deeply though, Mrs. MacCormack, if you were able to give him a little present." The voice was so smooth, so compelling, that Lila's nausea faded to be replaced with a terror much stronger.

"I wouldn't let him touch me even to scalp me," she said in a low voice.

Hellfire laughed, a disconcerting sound for its detachment. "I had nothing of the kind in mind, I assure you. I was thinking more of money or jewels. Our Virgil sets more store in either of those than in companionship."

"I told you before, there's nothing," Lila said dully. Perhaps this was the end of her life.

"Then we shall have to settle for your excellent provisions and the blankets," he said, rising. After he stood he leaned over and cupped her elbows in his hands, making her stand before she could protest. He reached out and stroked her cheek with the back of one hand. His flesh was warm but not pleasant, and Lila felt her gorge rise again. "But I warn you, we will be back."

She said nothing, watching him tip his hat and swing up onto a tall gray. One shout sent men running. In a moment all were mounted.

Virgil ambled his mount as close to Lila as he could without touching her. She could see the gruesome display around the saddle clearly now, and part of her mind became detached as she looked at it, noticing each little clump of dark hair or fair, some curly, some mousy-looking with wear from rubbing against other portions of his gear. His voice seemed to come from a distance. "Like he said, we sure will be back. Count on it. We'll have us a tea party next time." His giggle was even more jarring as a background for what Lila saw hanging from the pommel of the saddle next to the flopping chicken corpses. A fresh scalp with hanks of long, pale red hair. In it were twined hunter green ribbons, just the color of those she'd missed after Fay vanished. Fay, whose hair unbound would have reached as

HALF THE BATTLE

long as that horror trailed over the saddle, its strands blowing in the breeze.

Lila pushed blindly away from the horses and stumbled halfway across the yard to a clump of hydrangea bushes before she fell to her knees and was violently sick, the laughter of the departing horsemen ringing in her ears.

Lila waited an hour before she went back to the cave. Arlie Hoskins listened gravely to her tale when she told it, still shaking. "That's a bad bunch. You got any weapons?"

"One rifle, down in the cellar."

"That husband of yours make sure you knew how to shoot it before he left?"

Lila shook her head. "He never even knew it was there. It's Ty's old hunting piece. I could fire it if I had to, but I'm no shot worth speaking of."

Arlie sighed. "I'll send one of the boys over tomorrow with ammunition, and he'll clean it for you and make sure it's loaded. Those fools come back; I want you to take a shot at them even if they are Secesh. Devil's spawn is more like it."

She looked around the cave, satisfied that her patient was still sleeping, one arm crooked around the babe. Lila looked at both of them, then back at Arlie. "Mrs. Hoskins . . . ?" she began.

Arlie gave a short, soft bark of laughter. "Child, I can tell from your face what you're going to ask. All babies look like that. There's nothing wrong with young Freeman there. His mother thinks he's beautiful. You will too in a day or two. Being birthed is a hard thing on a new life. You'll think yours is just as beautiful, and he won't be any prettier."

Lila found herself wrinkling her nose in dismay. Arlie had seen almost immediately that she was seven or eight weeks along. "If you say so."

Arlie patted her shoulder with a broad hand, walking her to the doorway. "Trust me. Blainey, he looked like he'd been squashed for a week, but then he was the prettiest baby of the whole lot."

If Blainey, with his jug ears, had been the prettiest, Lila wondered about the rest. Freeman woke his mother a time or two during the day, and Lila helped change him and get the two of them comfortable in the brief interludes of wakefulness that always ended with mother and babe dozing back off together. She busied herself with little chores, wishing again she'd had the foresight after the raiders rode off to gather more supplies so that she wouldn't have to think about going back to the house again any time soon.

That saddle full of its macabre trophies came back whenever she thought of standing in her own yard again. When dark came she built a much bigger fire than she needed near the entrance of the cave, between the three of them and the world. It was there, sitting at the edge, feeding tiny sticks into the blaze, that Chloe found her when she finally woke to real consciousness for the first time since Freeman's birth. She walked over and put a hand on Lila's shoulder, making her stop the gentle rocking she hadn't even been aware of.

Her questioning eyes made Lila start the entire story, words pouring out in a terrorized flood. The two women built the fire up again, gathered all of Chloe's knives and sharpened sticks, and made a tangled nest of blankets.

Then, finally, Lila slept, one hand touching Chloe,

Freeman between them, as the dark shadows of fear bounced along the walls of the cave to weave their way into her tortured dreams.

Thirteen

Lila hid with Chloe in the cave. Just thinking of the raiders destroyed her. Creeping into the cellar to get the gun had given her nightmares for two nights. She wasn't sure which frightened her more: Vengeance, with his inhuman edge, or Hellfire, cool, suave and distressingly familiar in some uncanny way. Thoughts of either made her hands shake so that she was afraid to hold Freeman.

The baby did get much better looking in a few days. His dark eyes opened for longer periods, and his brown skin was softer than anything Lila had ever felt. She and Chloe exclaimed over him by the hour, counting his toes and fingers, clucking over his navel stump.

When he was four days old, Lila made it to the house and got one bedroom tidied. She congratulated herself for bravery as she crossed the threshold of the room she'd shared with Sander, but the spilled ink from the desk, with one footprint tracked across the rug, undid her.

It was Hellfire's, she was sure. His boots had been distinctive, almost like moccasins, and the soft edges of the print ground into the carpet brought back all the glittering menace that went with thinking of the man. She barely made it to the basin on the washstand.

After she'd cleaned up she left the house quickly, carrying her bag of fresh clothing and supplies and trembling, not with fear, but with anger. "We're taking back the house," she told Chloe. "I don't care how much you like this damp, nasty hole in the ground. If we leave the house vacant they'll be back, and they'll try to burn it this time. I won't have it."

"Fine," Chloe said simply, stopping Lila two steps inside the cave entrance.

"Fine?" Lila echoed.

"Fine," Chloe said. "Freeman can't stay underground like this. He needs sunshine and things to look at besides these dripping gray walls. And I need to be someplace where my breathing doesn't echo when you're gone. We'll move tomorrow. It's too late in the day to do it now."

"All right," Lila said, busying herself by putting the contents of the sack away. The insanity of that gesture struck her after she'd smoothed several pieces of underwear in her pile. She was unpacking things that she needed to start gathering to move back to the house.

She pushed stray hair away from her forehead and straightened up. Her body was beginning to feel slightly alien to her. It was thickening in some places, and her breasts were heavy and tender. There was a spot in the small of her back that seemed continually achy.

A whimper from Freeman pulled her from her reverie. Chloe got up, clucking, and picked him up, talking nonsense to him. She changed him deftly and settled back down to feed him. Without being asked, Lila dipped spring water out of the bucket and brought a mug of it to her. "Thank you. I'm sure I'll do the same for you."

"I'm sure you will," Lila said, trying not to sound

tart. "You're the only one likely to know I'll need the help." Even if Ty and Marcus came home, neither of them was likely to pay any attention to the babe she would have. And the babe's father would never know he existed.

He. She was as bad as Chloe, Lila decided, calling this little alien "he." But now she understood Chloe's surety that the person she'd been carrying was male even before Freeman had proved her right. This little stranger expanding her waistline was so alien it had to be male. No female presence would do this to her.

Lila blew out air in a mirthless laugh. It didn't matter anyway. Male or female, she had to protect this little soul because no one else would. She got herself a drink from the bucket and sat down to fold clothes while she watched Freeman and Chloe. They were oblivious to her, and she envied them.

When she went out the next morning, Lila said a word she'd learned from the soldiers in the yard. Chloe, hearing her, gave a surprised laugh. "Of all the people I know, you would be the least likely to say that," she said, still laughing.

"I can't help it," Lila said, beating her hand against her skirts in anger and agitation. "It's going to rain, and it's gray and nasty out here. We're going to be up to our ankles in mud the whole time we're moving and . . ."

Her words drifted away as she and Chloe both saw the glow at the same time. If it had been from a different direction it could have been sunrise. From where it peaked, over the rise between the cave and the house, it could only be fire.

Lila whirled inside the cave and came back with the gun. It felt heavy and awkward, but comforting. She had no doubt she could use it. Her only concern was staying upright during the report.

Chloe clutched Freeman so hard he began whimpering. "I'm going with you."

"Oh, no you're not," Lila said. "I don't want Freeman anywhere near those ghouls. I don't want you near them either, for that matter. Go over to the Rogerses' and tell them what's happening. Even if they don't send anybody, stay there."

"And leave you here to go up that hill by yourself?" Freeman was howling now.

"Yes. And I have to go soon before whatever they've set on fire gets the house to burning." She made herself walk quickly instead of running, terrified that she would stumble with the gun and blow herself to pieces. Over the hill she could see the raiders. Some of them were loading a wagon with bales of hay, furniture, sacks and barrels.

A few more leaped around a huge bonfire. As she went down the hill one of them heaved the load in his arms on top of the fire, and Lila watched in horror as one of the delicate caned chairs from the parlor caught fire on top of the pile.

The front gate was gone, torn off and flung aside in pieces, and the front door hung from one hinge. Two of the panes of the window in the front parlor were missing. But, mercifully, there was no smoke coming out of the house yet.

In among the smells of burning wood and scorched varnish came a more savory smell, and Lila cursed to herself as she strode nearer the fire. Roasting pig. They'd found at least one of the shoats she'd turned loose when the troops left. It disgusted her to think that

Hellfire and Vengeance would eat meat that would have kept them going all winter.

Vengeance looked like a demon, leaping jerkily around the flames. When he moved away, Lila gasped. The middle of the fire was not just old dead timber, as she had believed. The shell of her piano blazed up, taking with it the last of her reserve.

She charged closer to the fire, screaming, "Get off my property. Now! Just take what you have and go, or I'll shoot you!"

A roar of laughter erupted around the bonfire. Lila dug her heels into the soft ground and raised the shotgun. "I mean it."

When no one moved she squeezed the trigger, shutting her eyes at the same time. The load of buckshot missed every raider, and she landed on her backside in the mud. The laughter from the fire was even harder than before. One man pounded his neighbor on the back, both laughing so hard they wheezed.

Lila pulled herself up out of the mud and grabbed the barrel of the gun. She could use the heavy oak stock for a club. They would understand that she wanted them gone.

As she charged, swinging, Hellfire appeared before her. The ranks of his men parted for him, and he stood there, oblivious to the gun she swung. He lifted one hand and caught the stock.

"Ah, Mrs. MacCormack. Virgil promised you we'd be back. I can't understand why you're so disturbed."

"Get off my land and away from my house," Lila said. Inwardly, she cursed her own stupidity for bringing no weapon but the gun.

"Can I have her?" Vengeance crooned from the

other side of the shadows. "I bet she'd squeal just like that shoat."

"No, Virgil, we shan't touch this one. Remember, our commission from General Price does specify that our targets are to be military."

Virgil's snort showed how much he thought of that. "She'll only go on bothering us."

"I think not." Hellfire's odd smile was lit on one side by the bonfire. "There's nothing left to bother us over. We have anything worth having that we can transport. And if we don't move today, we're going to miss out on all the fun anyhow."

"Then go, damn you, and be gone," Lila said.

"Ah, sweet lady, we shall," the raider called Hellfire said. "But first you will accompany me through the house to make sure we have all that we came for."

He grasped her arm at the elbow and pulled high and hard so that she had two choices: follow him swiftly or have her arm jerked out of the socket.

There was little in the house except furniture too large to move. Even the crystal pendants off the chandelier and the lamps in the parlor were gone. The smaller rugs had vanished, and the calfskin-bound books in Papa's secretary had been ravaged.

Lila tried to look into the dining room without moving her head and telling the robber what she was looking for. "Oh, yes, the silver is gone," he said with a wolfish grin. "That largest platter, the Blue Willow too. I'm told that Quantrill has a lady who values the finer things. Presenting that to her should make me a favorite."

She said nothing, even when he walked her through the parlor. The wallpaper was a different color behind where the piano had stood. And crumpled in one corner was her wedding veil, the picture it had been draped over missing. She tried to give it nothing more than a flick of her eyes, sensing that anything she would exclaim over would be seized.

Upstairs the beds had been tossed about, and this time the feather beds and the quilts were gone. Ty's desk was pulled out into the middle of the room, the panels ravaged, the empty strongbox on the floor.

"Why are you doing this?" Lila asked, looking down at the rug. The inky footprint was still there, and his boots did match it, making anger blaze up to replace her despair.

"Just making sure we haven't missed anything," he said. "I truly thought, despite what our sources had said, there would be more here."

He let go of her, and Lila resisted the urge to rub her arm. No sense giving him the knowledge he'd caused her pain. Outside, the cellar doors squealed open, and her head turned.

"Is it there, then, your treasure?" he asked in a voice soft as a caress.

His words teased at her. She could not fly at him, screeching. It would only mean death. "Treasure? Only if you call the peaches and the beans treasure. I suppose we would have, along about December, if you'd left them to us," Lila said, alarmed by the light that flashed in his eyes.

"We? Now that is fascinating, madam. You are the only human soul I've ever seen around the place, and yet you speak of 'we.' Quite interesting."

Lila could hear every sound around her as she watched the malice glitter in the raider's eyes as he stepped closer to her. There were men in the cellar now, and several raiders called to each other across the yard. Then there seemed to be another, sharper note to the conversations outside. Lila couldn't pay attention to the difference because suddenly Hellfire was there, as close as breath. He was wearing black gloves that felt butter soft when he grasped her chin and pulled her face up sharply to meet his. His fingers bit into the sides of her face as his cold eyes stared into hers.

"Who is this we? Where are they?"

The roof of her mouth hurt from the force she was using to press her tongue there to keep from crying out.

The commotion had spilled from the yard into the house now, and there was someone coming up the stairs. That someone was hurrying, and Lila prayed it was not Virgil. The thought of being between the two bushwhackers, with her back to the door, put tears in her eyes.

The door banged open. "Let her go now. This pistol is loaded, and Confederate or no . . ." Lila could barely keep herself upright as the surprise of hearing Sander's voice washed through her. He stopped in the doorway, and his next words came out strangled. "I mean it, Hector. For her, I'd shoot you." The raider's hand had dropped, and Lila, still facing him, saw him smile.

"I'm sure you would, brother." Lila backed away from him and turned. Poised between the two of them, she could see it now herself. One dark, haggard, dressed in gray. One beautiful, light, the only uniform piece the belt from which his saber hung. But both had the same eyes, the same deep hollows to their cheekbones, an unconscious stance that hitched one hip higher as they stood like fighting cocks sizing each other up.

"This is beyond even you, Hector. Leave before I kill you." Suddenly Sander's eyes were as flat as his brother's, and Hector was laughing as he pushed past both of them and walked down the stairs.

Lila wanted to fall into Sander's arms and sob. She wanted to feel his long fingers tangled in her hair while he whispered promises to her that no one would attack her again. But one look at his grim face as his eyes followed Hector down the stairs told her that wasn't going to happen, at least not now.

"Go on and follow him," she said, stiffening her spine. "I'm all right."

"You're sure. He didn't hurt you?" Sander's eyes were bottomless with pain.

Hector stopped halfway down the stairs. "Now, Sander, from what I hear that seems to be your specialty, not mine. We leave the women we've visited untouched. Or at least as untouched as we found them. You, however, seem to be leaving a trail across the county," he said, then went on down the stairs.

Sander was behind him in a flash, landing halfway down the stairway, almost on his brother's back. They tussled their way down to the foot of the stairs while Lila stood at the head, sick and dizzy.

"Stop it. Just stop it," she screeched, gripping the stair rail. They separated, panting. Hector broke the silence first, laughing.

"The lady seems to care for your sorry hide. Or perhaps she's just tired of the abuse of her home," he said with a sneer. "I've got business elsewhere anyway. Price will welcome the supplies."

"He sure will," Sander said, advancing on him again. "That's why we're back here, to load the last of them up and get them back to the lines."

"So I've saved you the trouble," Hector said, turning his back and striding out the front door. Sander followed him out, and Lila went down the stairs after the two of them as fast as she could.

She stood on the porch, watching. Yancey was in the yard, holding the harness of a restive mule hitched to one of the supply wagons and hollering at the driver. "Leave him be," Sander said, and Yancey scowled.

"But they've got our load of hay and the food. And every damned blanket out of the house."

"Leave them be," he said again, watching Hector cross the yard and jam his plumed hat on his head. "We'd have to kill them to get it back, and it's a waste of ammunition. He says he's taking it to Price anyway."

Hector cantered up close to the porch on his horse. Lila made herself stand still and stare him down, even when she could feel his horse's breath on her arm. "Do you know where you're going?" Sander's voice sounded tired and defeated.

"I thought you could offer us a scout to lead the way back," Hector said.

"It won't be that simple. The whole line is probably halfway to Jefferson City, with a couple of thousand Yankees behind them. Good luck catching up," Sander said, his shoulders sagging.

"So the assault is a rout. What happened to the victorious march on St. Louis?" Hector seemed genuinely interested.

"We got waylaid at Fort Davidson. They blew up the fort," Sander explained.

"Price didn't catch on until daylight, and then we had the whole Union army on our tail," Yancey added.

"Well, he'll still welcome sustenance for the fleeing masses." Hector spurred his horse, which danced sideways as he tipped his hat toward Lila on the porch.

Before he could get farther, John Reed walked

around the corner of the house toward Sander. "Captain, they will need a scout," he said. To Lila, he looked battered, and his wire-framed spectacles were askew. He also looked as if he had aged a decade from the boy he'd been a week ago. "I'm no use here, and I do know the way back. I'll go with them."

"I'm not comfortable with that, Corporal," Sander said, and Lila could see his lips whiten as he pressed them together.

"I insist, Sander," Hector said. "Or don't you trust me?"

"I trust you as much today as I ever have, Hector," Sander said, his gaze level.

Hector turned to Reed. "Saddle up the best nag this sorry outfit has so that you can keep up if you're going to be a scout, son." He laughed and edged the horse back close to the porch, trampling the bushes close to the railing.

"Madam, your hospitality is unequaled," he said, tipping his hat.

Lila's loathing overwhelmed her. "Come back again and I'll kill you myself," she said, gripping the porch rail. He roared with laughter as he jammed his hat on, and with a whoop that sounded like a bobcat's, started the train of wagons, mules and horses moving. Virgil gave an answering screech and thundered across the yard to join him.

As they left by the entrance where the gate had been, headed for the road, a buggy careened around a curve in the road. An older man leaped out as he reined to a halt, and Lila recognized Ed Rogers. He and Chloe, clutching Freeman, were the sole occupants of the buggy.

"Let them go," Yancey called. "Get out of their way. They aren't worth the effort to try and stop, sir."

"That's easy to say," the old man roared. "You're on their side."

"Oh, no, I ain't claiming 'em," Yancey said. He spat on the ground. "But I'm not going to waste ammunition on them either, because then I'd have to bury them."

Rogers looked at the receding column. "Have it your way. Couldn't stop them alone, anyway." He got back in the buggy and clucked the horse into action, pulling through the gap in the fence before the dust from the retreating column settled.

Chloe got out of the wagon, trying to settle the squalling Freeman. She looked at Lila, questioning her without words.

"Come in the house," Lila said, daring anyone to tell her different. "We'll see what we have left. Thank you, Mr. Rogers, for trying to help. I appreciate it."

Mr. Rogers looked like he didn't appreciate it at all. He nodded and turned the buggy around, leaving before either Sander or Yancey could say anything.

Lila watched Sander's back, slumped now in a defeated stance. His shoulders drooped, his holster was empty and his uniform was filthy from patches of red mud and rusty brown that looked like dirt. She knew he had to be swaying with exhaustion, but if he wasn't ready to admit it yet, she would never get him to do so. She went into the house with Chloe, surveying the damage.

"That bunch as ugly from the front as they looked from the back?" Chloe asked, glancing over her shoulder at the retreating column of raiders.

"Worse. I think I would have been dead if Sander

hadn't come back," Lila admitted. "They burned the piano."

"We're lucky they didn't burn the house," Chloe said, bouncing Freeman on one shoulder. She looked around for a place to set him, but there were no chairs with whole seats. She walked over to the nursery window. "Didn't all make it back, did they?"

Lila pushed her hair away from her face, conscious that the trembling was receding from her fingers. "I expect this is just a detail to get the supplies."

Chloe peered out the window and shook her head. "It's more than that. I know enough about shapes under blankets to know they were bringing something back in that wagon, not just getting ready to take something away."

Lila went cold again. Looking out from this height, the outline under the gray blanket was painfully obvious. She and Chloe looked at each other, mirroring distress. "Blainey," she said softly.

The stairs seemed unbelievably long and steep. Lila forced herself down them, clinging to the rail. Over and over, she could see Arlie at the wedding, telling Sander to take good care of her boy. By the time she got down to the yard, Sander was sitting stiffly on his horse. He looked down when she approached. "I'm leaving for a while, but I'm leaving Yancey and Hobbs and Sutherland. You won't be alone." New lines were etched around his mouth.

"It's Blainey, isn't it?" Lila was surprised at how sharp her voice was in the wind that blew ashes across the yard. "You took him away, and now he's dead. Sander, he was just a boy."

"He was a soldier," he said simply, and spurred his

horse into a walk. The wagon driver followed him, and Lila watched them leave the yard.

She didn't hear Yancey come up behind her until he was close enough that he could have touched her. "Don't you think he doesn't know that kid was green?" he said, a snarl in his voice. "The man can hardly sit that horse for the blood he's lost, and you light into him first moment you can."

"Blood?" Lila said, knowing she sounded stupid.

"Took a hit in the shoulder. Don't tell me you couldn't see that either?" He said, acid in his voice. "Some soldier's wife you make. Thank God we ain't staying long."

Lila was inclined to agree with him as she watched the wagon bouncing on the ruts toward the Hoskins' cabin.

Fourteen

When all the men were gone, Lila went into the bedroom to start sorting through Sander's things. The shirt she'd made him was stuffed down in the bottom of one bag, bloody and with a jagged hole in the left shoulder.

She called softly to Chloe. "I'm going down to the kitchen to see what state it's in."

"I could probably tell you from here," Chloe said with a grimace, standing in the doorway. "But I expect everyone's going to want to eat tonight."

"Oh, I imagine they are," Lila said with some surprise. "I was going down to start steeping some herbs for a poultice, but I'd better put on a pot of soup or something too, hadn't I?"

"Hard as they're all working, they'll need it," Chloe said. "I'll stay up here and try to straighten up."

Lila nodded. "Don't tire yourself out too much. And don't take any guff off any of these men, not even that big one who was up here earlier. He's mostly bluster anyway."

"Until today you thought he was a killer." Chloe's frown was doubtful.

"Until today I didn't know that raider was Sander's brother," Lila countered. That had changed everything.

The kitchen was a shambles. Almost everything worth having was gone. There were a few potatoes left in the bin and one sorry onion. The kitchen garden was horse-trampled, but at least one cabbage had survived. It wouldn't be the best soup she'd ever made, but no one would go hungry.

Once the soup was simmering, she set her mind to getting another pot of water boiling while she searched for the right herbs for the poultice. It was pushed back, steaming, to stay warm when Sander filled the doorway.

He managed a weak grin. "At least this time there wasn't any pig in the kitchen."

She scowled. "I'd rather have the pig. He was better company than those raiders. And prettier." He sat down at the table and tipped his head back. Lila was shocked at the gray tone of the skin stretched tight against his cheekbones.

"The soup isn't ready yet, and I'm afraid there isn't much of anything else," she said, drying her hands on a towel and going to him. "Take off that tunic and let me see the shoulder."

He frowned. "Yancey told you, didn't he?"

"Of course." She stood in front of him, edging his knee aside and working the fastenings of the tunic. She tried to work with fingers feather-light, unwilling to cause him pain. When the tunic was open, she let him ease out of the dusty garment with its one patch of blood. The shirt underneath stuck to the bandages.

"Oh, Sander," she said softly. She wasn't sure when his right arm had come up around her waist, but it felt wonderful to be held while she tried to pluck the material away. She bit her lip. "No matter how I do this, it's going to hurt."

"That's all right," he said. "I could stand a little pain. It will take my mind off going to the Hoskinses."

His eyes glittered. "How is she?" Lila asked, still trying to ease the stiff material away.

"Numb. She knew the minute she saw me in the doorway. At least I was able to tell her that it was quick—and clean as it ever gets."

Lila couldn't stand to pull the last bit of the shirt away, knowing the pain it would cause. A flash of inspiration came to her, and she found a clean rag in the stack in the pantry that no one had bothered. The jam they had taken, and all the dried apples. But clean rags had been left behind. She put one in the pot steaming with the poultice, then pulled it out with a long-handled spoon, waving the cloth. Sander's eyebrows raised. "That looks like it would take the bristles off a hog."

"We'll just let it cool down a minute, then I'll fold it up and put it on your shoulder. It will feel better than ripping that shirt off," she said.

The wet cloth was almost too hot to handle when she wrung the gray-green liquid out of it and carried it over. Sander winced silently as she eased it on.

"You look like you want to whistle, or swear," she said, trying to sound light while she watched him for signs that he was going to pass out on her. She didn't like the color of his skin.

He pulled her close and buried his face in her middle. Feeling him nuzzle there made her draw back quickly in alarm. She told herself it was impossible for him to feel the changes she could barely see herself, but at this moment the last thing she needed was Sander knowing she was pregnant.

His look of hurt and shock brought tears to her eyes. For a moment she wanted to break down and tell him everything. Before she could say anything Yancey strode through the door and banged a jug down on the table.

"Damned heathens didn't get everything worth stealing," he said. "Look what I found in the parlor."

"Pour it quick before this woman takes off any more of my skin," Sander said. Lila let go of him and turned away, unwilling to let either of them see her tears.

Fire. Sander felt it everywhere. In his throbbing shoulder covered with the scalding cloth, little rivulets of fire traced down to the ugly furrow where the ball had opened his flesh. Behind his eyes were all the tears he'd choked back, tears for Blainey, for himself, for Lila. They burned into the surface of his brain like acid.

And now the fire from the panther's breath Yancey had poured into the glass in front of him joined the others, igniting a course clear down to his belly. If he poured enough of the fire in that jug down his throat, would he stop seeing Blainey lying in the field and staring up at him? Sander knew one thing for certain. There wasn't enough oblivion in that jug to do away with the thing that hurt the most.

He'd been a mile away from the house when something had told him things were happening there. Yancey had called him a fool when he'd spurred his horse and taken off ahead of everyone. But the panic had been real, as if Lila had been calling in a voice only he could hear. To his dying day, he'd wonder what he'd interrupted upstairs. He would never know whether his brother had been about to kill Lila or kiss her, or if he'd already kissed her and was about to do it again. There wasn't enough fire on earth to blot out that doubt.

Especially when Lila wouldn't look him in the face

anymore. She jumped like a singed cat when he touched her. What other proof did he need? Lila's voice was hard when she spoke to Yancey. "Get him upstairs. I don't want him passing out down here."

Yancey put a hand under his good shoulder. "She's right, Captain. Why don't we find you a place to roost?" The room reeled when he stood, and Sander had to stay unmoving for several long moments before his head cleared enough for him to take a step. Lila didn't even watch. She turned back to the stove again, bent on her work. Her indifference traced another molten track down Sander's soul.

Once Yancey had taken Sander out of the room, Lila gave way to the tears she'd held back. Any illusions of love with Sander were gone for good now, dissolved as he sat in the chair in front of her and was still a thousand miles away.

She took her supplies and trudged up the stairs. Sander lay on the bed, eyes closed, cloth still on his shoulder. The lamp by the bedside had been lit, showing his pale, still face. Lila set down her burdens and sat on the edge of the bed. He stirred, but didn't open his eyes. She eased the cloth off and unbuttoned his shirt all the way. There was an ugly bruise on the right side of his ribs.

She got his shirt off with a minimum of moving him. He grunted oddly when she pulled the left sleeve away, opened his eyes for a moment. They were glazed, either with pain or drink, and she stroked his hair. "Rest. I'll be done soon." His eyes closed, and she went about removing the bandage. The flesh underneath made her wince. There was a deep furrow in the skin, exposing tissue beneath. A flesh wound, and healing already. Still, it oozed, some of the seepage looking like pus, so she made a compress of the herbs and gently bound it to Sander's shoulder.

He grumbled a little, and his right hand came up as if to remove the aggravation, but Lila held it firm. "Oh, no," she said. "That stays on, even if I have to sit on you," she said.

"Just try that," he said softly.

"I will if you give me any trouble," she declared. His eyes stayed closed, but one corner of his mouth pulled upward for a moment. The movement made her brush the hair off his forehead in a caress. She took the lamp away from the bedside and put it on the desk.

Walking back across the room, she hit a stockinged toe on one of the items she'd taken out of Sander's packs.

It was his Bible. She took up the book to leaf through it while she sat. It would keep her from going to sleep, and heaven only knew she could use some of the good news in it tonight.

There was something between the pages. Lila found the yellow sheet of paper. It was a letter, smudged in places and smelling faintly of smoke. She smoothed it out, feeling guilty for reading it, but reading it nonetheless.

Her heart leaped like a startled rabbit's when she saw it was addressed to her.

September 26
Dearest Lila,

That looks odd even on paper, because I have never called you that in our life together, even though I hold it in my heart. Tomorrow we attack, and it is a foolish business. If you are reading this, then I will be dead. Yancey has promised to give you my things, so I trust this will reach you. He is an honorable man, though you do not like him.

Forgive me for insisting that you marry me. I could not bear to let this one last chance for happiness escape me, and so I insisted. Do know that I was, for a little while, happy. Being with you made me as contented as I have ever been on earth, and I am sorry that we will never share contentment.

Many others are around the fires tonight, fingering pictures, writing letters. Although I have no portrait, I carry your honeyed hair and gray eyes with me wherever I go. And even without letters, I know that you did all you could to make me happy. I will always regret that I cannot say the same.

My pitiful knowledge of the ways of women has certainly made me a terrible husband, I am sure. If I have not loved wisely, at least know that I have loved fervently even in my silence.

Yours,
Sander

Lila wasn't aware of the tears coursing down her cheeks until she finished reading the letter a second time and folded it back the way it had been. She slipped it between the pages of the Bible and put the book back where it had lain, pausing again to wipe more tears from her wet cheeks. Sander loved her. She tiptoed over to the bed and kissed him softly, first on the forehead, then on the bridge of his nose, then the mouth.

Exhaustion kept him from responding except for a low murmur that stilled quickly. She pulled a blanket over him, up to his bandages, and fed a few more sticks onto the fire. Then she settled back into the chair to watch in case he stirred.

Sometime later, Lila jerked awake, pitching forward

in the chair. The movement made her stiff neck muscles scream in protest, and her feet, which were prickly with lack of circulation, slid off the bed like parts of a wooden puppet.

Pale sunlight streamed in the windows, and Sander stood by the end of the bed, gripping one post. "What on earth are you doing up?" she asked.

"I have to get up some," he said, clenching his teeth. "If I don't this shoulder will get even stiffer than it already is and I'll be in a world of trouble."

"Oh, all right," she said, reaching out and feeling his forehead. It was cool and sweaty, not hot as she'd feared. "I'll go downstairs and find something for breakfast."

The door of the stove was open, and a few sticks of new wood had been laid on top of the dying embers. Upon those sticks curled and blazed a piece of paper.

Lila blinked in horror. Sander, his back to her, seemed to be using one foot to push something under the bed without drawing attention to it. His Bible disappeared. She looked back to the stove, to where the paper curled, blackened and fell to ash around the sticks.

He'd burned the letter, getting up off his sickbed to make sure she never saw it. Sander didn't ever intend for her to know what he'd written. Lila straightened and walked past him, her throat constricted at the loss of something that never saw the light of day.

Fifteen

It was all wrong, Lila thought. When she'd seen Sander return she'd been limp with relief. And when she'd read the letter he'd written, she knew that he really loved her after all. But then he'd burned it, and with it burned what was left of their marriage.

Now he stumped around the house, shoulders pulled in to protect his wound. Every time she wanted to begin again, he was drinking. When she couldn't find enough to feed everyone a hot meal once a day, he had money or barter to get liquor.

She'd stopped being surprised by the devastation the raiders had left. She'd never hoped a human being would die and rot in Hell before, but she wished that of Hector MacCormack. If he had the power to turn the man she loved into the blank-eyed tippler who existed now, no other fate was too good for him.

Lila cooked and cleaned and did as much as she could every daylight hour so that when it got dark she could fall on her bed and collapse, not stirring until it was light again and she could start over. She knew that in her own way she was using work the same way Sander was using liquor. "Neither of them is working," she said darkly.

The poker games had started up again, of an evening, in the parlor. Yancey's deck of cards was wearing thin, but there were no replacements so they made do. They gambled for spent matches, there not being enough scrip among the whole crew to make a decent game anymore.

Sander was poring over a law book at the secretary. It was the first time Lila had seen him do that since he'd come back, and without a drink at his side. It made her hope. She and Chloe sat on the chaise, side by side, talking softly and sewing.

Finally Sutherland stood up in disgust, throwing his cards on the table. "I give up. I couldn't get a good hand to save my soul."

"And wouldn't know what to do with one if it bit him on the ankle," Chloe said softly, making Lila hide her laughter.

"I heard that, gal," Yancey said, turning around. "Think you can do better, you come on over and try."

Lila straightened up. "Sergeant, if Mrs. Wayne wishes to join your game, I'm sure no one would have any objections. But in this house, she is to be addressed as you would any other married lady. Not as 'gal.'"

He rolled his eyes and looked over at Sander, then grimaced when he saw that his commanding officer wasn't defending him.

"Well, Miz Wayne?" he countered. "You play poker?"

"You may regret this, Sergeant," Lila said. "She was taught to play by my father and brother."

"Better take care, Yancey," Sander drawled. "Anybody taught to play poker by a couple of lawyers could be dangerous company."

"I'll take my chances," Yancey said. He looked around the table to make sure no one was arguing with him. Then he pushed Sutherland's empty chair with his boot tip. "Well?"

Chloe dusted off her hands on her skirt. "What's the game?" she asked, rising.

"Dealer calls, five-card draw, nothing wild."

"You're on," she said, settling into the chair with a fluid grace that made Lila grin into her sewing.

An hour later Yancey was trying mightily not to swear. The effort had made sweat bead on his forehead. Chloe kept the same impassive face she'd worn all the time she'd cleaned the rebels' clocks. As she dealt yet another hand, there was a thin wail from the basket in the corner.

"Gentleman, I'm afraid I'm done for the evening," she said, rising. "It wouldn't be fair for me to forfeit like this and keep all my winnings, so I'll just push them back into the center. It's been a pleasure." She swept up Freeman in his basket and disappeared up the stairs as Yancey muttered something inaudible.

When her door closed, Yancey shook his head. "Never again. Remind me boys, never again." The laughter that broke out was raucous.

In the noise Lila looked over at Sander. He was looking back, with a warm grin that took her in. The brightness of it jolted her so badly she nearly stuck her needle through her finger. Without even thinking, she returned his smile. He looked over at the cardplayers, then back at her and smiled again.

"Well, y'all can play the rest of the night if you want, now that you've gotten your winnings back. I'm going to bed. You ought to go too, Yancey."

"Why's that, Captain?" The big man had a scowl on his broad face.

"You'll need your rest to help load that wagon in the morning and take it back to General Price."

"I suspect I will." Yancey gathered all the matchsticks into the center of the table. "That's it, boys, we strike the game." He cast a speculative look at Sander. "You coming too?"

Sander shook his head. "Another week. The surgeon told me he wouldn't certify me for duty again until I could turn my arm all ways without this damned thing breaking open. And it still does, every time."

Lila's heart began to slow back to normal. She knew it was too soon, that the ugly scabbed scar wasn't ready for him to even wear his uniform. The relief that he knew it too was overwhelming. As he stood, she put aside her sewing. "I think I'll go upstairs as well. This light is beginning to hurt my eyes."

The lamplight cast a warm glow of familiarity over the room. Lila willed herself to breathe normally, taking off her petticoats and stockings, chemise and drawers, and reaching for her nightgown. It was gone. Lila stood, hair falling to the center of her back, and nothing on but her wedding ring. She looked up toward the shadowed ceiling, wondering what she'd do now.

"Looking for this?" Sander said. From one finger, extended over the side of the bed, was her nightgown. "I've been warming it up over here. Want it back?"

"Now what do you think?"

"I think I'd like it just fine if you didn't take it back. But come on to bed, Lila." His voice was husky, liquid with emotion, and it made her turn. She crossed the few steps to the bed, his eyes on her making her heart beat hard and fast. She sat on the edge of the bed gingerly, not wanting to jostle him against the headboard and disturb his shoulder. "I'm not made of glass." He drew her to him, covering her mouth with his.

This was different from the chicken pecks they'd been giving each other for a week. This was molten, his mouth slanting over hers in need, his right hand coiling through her hair to the back of her neck. Lila moaned deep in her throat without meaning to, savoring the liquid fire that Sander brought to life in her.

Her fingers curled into the crisp mat on his chest, feeling the thud of his heart. He leaned closer, enveloping her in an embrace, and she drew him closer to her. Without ever breaking the searching contact of his mouth on hers, Sander slid her onto his lap, then over, leaving her legs to trail over him as he settled her into a nest of pillows and quilts in the middle of the bed.

"I have missed you," she said softly. "Let me show you how much."

"I already know," he said, covering her mouth with his again and covering the length of her body with his. He crooned words that made little sense, but made a beautiful melody in the lamplight. Lila was struck with the perfection of him above her, with his earnest purity despite all the pain she knew was in him. It made her reach out, her whole body cupped upward to welcome him.

When she had settled him back into the bedcovers, clucking over the tiny pull in the healing of his shoulder, and getting a wolfish grin from him for her trouble, Lila sought the haven of his uninjured arm. The warm glow that sang in her blood denied any need for sleep. Instead, she needed to trace her fingers lightly over his skin and talk of all the things they'd hidden from each other since he'd come back.

The house was settling to bed around them. There

were little creaks and bumps from the other bedrooms. Somewhere outside a horse whickered. Then Freeman grizzled a little, and quite obviously found his fist in a wet slurp.

Sander seemed to listen to that sound, then laughed softly. "He was the one, wasn't he? The one you made the doll baby for. Lord, Lila, I was never so shocked in all my days as seeing you leaning over that thing. I thought . . ."

"I know what you thought," she said, dragging her finger down his chest. "Would it have been so terrible, Sander?"

"Yes. I can't think of bringing a baby into this world without seeing my mother and Evie . . ." His voice trailed off and Lila could see the pain. "Besides, I just wasn't put on this earth to be anybody's daddy."

"Oh." Now wasn't the time to tell him he was wrong. Not now when they had finally made their peace after this awful week. In the morning she would break the news, gently. Lila fell asleep in Sander's embrace, plotting ways to draw him gently into the mazes of fatherhood.

The noise exploded on her sleep all at once as Sander vaulted out of bed. There was the thumping of his finding his pants in the dark and the jingle of heavy harness outside combined with the calling of men and the strange, unearthly noise mixed with all of it.

"What's wrong? What's happening?" she asked.

"I'm about to find out," Sander said grabbing a gun from the desk.

Through the half-open door Lila could hear him hurry down the stairs with Yancey. The front door opened and Sander called out. "Who goes there?"

"It's us, Captain. We're back and you're needed. It's bad, I'll warn you." Corporal Reed. Lila's blood chilled. If he was back, then so were the raiders.

She closed the door to her room and pulled her chemise and dress on as quickly as she could. Chloe stuck her head through the door that connected their rooms. "What's going on, Lila?"

"The bushwhackers are back."

"Not all of them. I looked out, and there's only about four men out there besides Sander and Yancey. But someone's in the wagon bed, making a hellacious noise."

Lila jammed her shoes on, not bothering to fasten them, and twisted her hair into a loose knot as she went down the stairs. Standing at the doorway, she watched a strange tableaux. Sander leaned over the wagon bed, looking at whatever was inside. Whoever, Lila amended, as a hand rose from it, and the noise continued.

It was an unearthly moan. The misshapen wrappings around the hand that groped for Sander seemed to indicate that there were some fingers gone. Reed was beside Sander, speaking softly. "We caught up with Price, and he delivered the things that were left. What we didn't pass off to Quantrill a few nights before we met Price."

Sander scowled as he listened to the story, still looking down into the wagon bed at the man who lay in the straw, bunched up there. "How did this happen?"

"Price sent this mob off to burn a railway bridge the Yankees were going to have to cross to follow the main column. I went with them because it was on the way back. We'd gotten almost there when we ran into the Yankees. They were waiting for us."

"Shells?"

HALF THE BATTLE 213

Reed nodded. "Big ones. One of the first salvos sent most of the horses to hell and gone. Then Virgil decided he was going to charge the guns, said he'd slit some Yankee throats before he died. I'd never seen anything like it. Pieces of him just went everywhere. His head flew right into Heck's lap. He looked down and started gibbering like an idiot, and his horse went crazy. Then they fired again, and a shell tore into him too."

Lila fought nausea. The picture Corporal Reed had painted was vivid. Now she knew what was in the wagon and why it made the noises it did. And since it was her husband's brother, she was going to have to ask the men to take it into the parlor. "Sander?" she called. "Can he be moved?"

Sander looked up at her, seeming to be surprised that she was there. He shook the hand off his arm. "I don't think so. I'd be afraid of lifting him." He looked at Reed. "How long did it take you to get here?"

"Two days. We've been on the road since it happened. Once the shelling stopped, the Yankees weren't interested in what was left. We put Heck in the wagon and lit out. About ten miles later we stopped to bandage him up best we could. That was Tuesday, a little before dark."

"I'll get some blankets and try to warm some food," Lila said. She stepped around Reed and walked toward the wagon, drawn to look at the burden there.

"You don't want to see this," Sander said, looking even paler than before.

"Yancey and I are the closest to a doctor he's going to get," she said, steeling herself.

If Hector had been a fallen angel before, now he was simply blasted. The shell seemed to have hit him on the right side. There were holes of various sizes pocked through his clothing, with one bandage wrapped around his thigh. He was definitely missing fingers on that hand. The worst was his face. The right side sagged almost as if melted, the eye closed, the features blurred. His other eye was wide and panicky, and when Lila looked over the rim of the wagon side, the noises started again.

She looked at Yancey, who stood on the other side of the wagon. He shook his head slowly, without words, in a gesture she understood.

Lila went through the house, grabbing a shawl on the way, and stoked the fire in the cookstove. Automatically she put a pot of water on to boil. She wondered if Yancey was going to try to clean any of the wounds.

She could hear him behind her. For once they put away their animosity. "What do you need?" she asked.

"You put water on. Good. Is there anything we can warm up in the way of food? Reed's almost asleep on his feet, and he and the other two haven't eaten since Tuesday."

Lila thought. "Mush and sorghum is the quickest I can come up with."

"It'll do. We might even be able to thin some down and shove it in the patient."

Lila turned to look at him when the irony of his words got to her. "You're going to try and feed him? Isn't it useless?"

"As far as I'm concerned touching him would be useless. If he were on fire I wouldn't piss on him to put him out, but the captain thinks otherwise, so I'll feed him. And I'll clean his bandages before they start off again."

HALF THE BATTLE

Lila nearly reeled. "Start off again? Where, and how?"

Yancey's look of disgust was palpable. "Palmyra. We're giving them fresh horses. Ten to one he dies before they get him home."

"Home?" Lila echoed. The word and its meaning dawned on her slowly as she sifted meal through her fingers into the pot of water in front of her. She thrust it back on the stove and hurried past the startled Yancey.

Sander still stood next to the wagon, looking in but not seeing.

"You're taking him home?" she said.

His face was grim. "I don't have any choice. My father has never had a kind word for any human being except Heck. If I don't get him home, I can't ever go home again."

Given what she knew of his father, Lila was surprised he would ever want to. It was on the tip of her tongue to say so, but his anguish was so great she couldn't. She reached up and stroked his face, bringing the light of surprise to his eyes.

"Go and pull the throw off the chaise and wrap it around yourself. You'll catch your death out here otherwise. I'll stay here while you do."

He nodded and went into the house while Lila looked down into the wagon. She looked inside herself, trying to dredge up some pity for the man lying there. For Sander she could conjure pity. Hector just made her turn her head away.

Sander came back and stood beside her. Lila shook herself out of her thoughts. "I've got food on the stove," she said, trying not to sound curt. "I'll send Yancey back when it's done."

He nodded and looked down. "Fine." He took up

his place again at his brother's side, and Lila felt whatever they had gained in this night had been lost with the appearance of this wagon and its burden.

Sixteen

Before dawn Hector slept or was unconscious, and Sander went inside to dress and pack what he'd need for the journey. When he got to the bedroom, Lila was putting things in a bag.

"You don't have to do that for me," he said, feeling that he'd caused her enough pain in one night.

"I'm not doing it just for you. I'm coming with you," she said. The glitter in her eyes dared him to tell her otherwise.

"You can't," he said.

"This isn't any soldier's mission, and you need somebody to nurse him. Without that, you won't get anywhere near Palmyra with him alive," Lila argued.

"You're right," he told her. "And I need you anyway. I don't know if I can do this alone." It hurt to admit it, but Sander was tired of fighting his demons by himself. "I'm surprised you would try to keep him alive."

Lila shrugged. "He's your brother. If you can find it in your heart to forgive him, I should be able to. Besides, it wasn't him that did the worst of it, was it?"

"I don't think so. It was that pitiful excuse for a human being he rode with. I can't help thinking Price sent Hector along to be Virgil's keeper."

"He didn't do a very good job," Lila said quietly.

"He did it as well as he knew how," Sander said, unwilling to say more.

It was a cold morning to set off. Lila and Yancey packed things around Hector in the wagon to make him as comfortable as possible. They discussed the different things Lila would be likely to need on the trip, and Sander could see the urgency passing between them. Once there was a hint of daylight, he made sure the wagon was loaded, and they set off.

Lila could sleep sitting backward in the lurching wagon. She positioned herself in the wagon bed, near enough to Hector to care for him if needed, but far enough away so as not to jostle him. When he was silent, she slept. Sander marveled at it, wondering how exhausted she had to be to find sleep under these circumstances.

By afternoon they'd gone about half the distance, and the horses had to rest. At the next shallow creek bed Sander halted the wagon and unhitched them. The big beasts waded into the cold water to drink.

"Should I build a fire?" Lila asked.

He shook his head. "If there's one to be built, I'll do it," he told her. "You probably have other things to see to."

"I do. But I'll be back in a few moments." He helped her out of the wagon bed, marveling at her lightness. She staggered against him, and it was all Sander could do not to sweep her up and take her home, abandoning his brother.

He looked into Lila's eyes, and his feelings must have shown on his face. She reached cold hands up and caressed him. "We have to keep going," she said softly. He loved her more then than he ever had.

He made a small fire, and she heated up something

for them to drink. It was some awful herbal potion softened with honey, and she managed to get Hector to take a little of it as well. He was quieter now. Sander didn't know whether to be relieved by that or worried.

They stayed by the creek about an hour, and then Sander hitched the horses to the wagon again. They couldn't waste any more daylight.

Lila was silent in the wagon as they got closer to the country Sander remembered from childhood. They were maybe ten miles outside Palmyra, and the sun was setting, when she spoke for the first time in hours.

"We have to stop now, Sander. I know we're out in the middle of nowhere, but we have to stop." Sander halted the team, pulling off the road into a grove of trees.

Once the horses were quiet and the wagon still, he could hear Hector's breathing. It was ragged and ugly, and it told him what Lila had already tried to express. His brother was dying.

He stood by the wagon where Hector lay stretched out in agony. "I'm sorry we didn't get you home," he told him, unsure whether he could hear anymore.

"You did your best," Hector said in a voice that was hard to understand. "Better than I would have done for you."

"Any word for the old man? He'll know you were a hero," Sander promised him.

"Only words I need to say . . . are to you," Hector said. Lila was holding his brother's head steady now, unaware of her own tears. "You were the lucky one. You got away from him. Living with that hate . . . it just festers."

He turned his head, trying to find Lila. "I'm right

here," she told him, letting his head rest in her lap. "I'll take care of him, don't worry."

"Do that. He needs you. Maybe if I'd had someone . . ." His voice trailed off for a while. Then his eyes opened wider. "Instead I rode with the horsemen. Straight to hell." And then he was quiet.

None of them moved for a while. "I don't hate him anymore," Lila said finally. "I can't."

"Neither can I," Sander admitted. "But I can't go any farther today, and neither can those horses."

Lila looked at him. "If he dies, couldn't we just bury him here? Do we really need to go there, Sander? You heard what he said."

He nodded. "I heard. And I still have to do this, Lila. It's too dark to go farther tonight. But in the morning, we have to take him home one way or the other."

They slept in the grove, huddled together in two blankets. Sander didn't think he'd be able to sleep at all, but exhaustion took him and he didn't wake until near dawn. He was cold, stiff and sore, but his wife lay in his arms. For that reason alone this day would have to be faced. Unbelievably, Hector was still alive in the morning.

Lila worried that Sander would fail before they got to Palmyra. He looked pale and drawn, and his shoulder had pulled open again. He didn't look capable of continuing, but he pressed on.

Just past Palmyra, they pulled off the main road. In the next hour they found progressively smaller roads, until the last one was only two tracks in the dirt. The closer she got to the house, the more she wondered if there was anyone living there. Rank weeds, gray now with frost-kill, choked everything. There were piles of trash in the front yard, and the porch sagged. But a small plume of smoke came from one of the chimneys.

"This is it," Sander said, pointing to the house. Lila pulled herself off the wagon seat and went up the creaking front steps. She rapped on the door, as devoid of paint as the rest of the place, and just as gray with wear. Somewhere inside there was a shuffling and some muttered conversation. Just when she was ready to rap again, the door swung open.

Before her stood a man she would have recognized on any street as her father-in-law. He was tall and stern, his dark hair going iron gray from the temples back to match his beard. And his eyes held the same reptilian flatness as Hector's.

"Mr. MacCormack. I'm your son's wife. Sander and I, we've brought Hector home."

He looked out the door, past her to the wagon. "Wrong one's in the back of that wagon," he said succinctly and walked away from the door, leaving Lila speechless on the porch.

A small figure slunk into the light in the hallway. "I'm Dulcie. Heck's wife. That old man don't have no manners at the best of times. You get Sander in here; then we'll try to manage the other."

The starved-looking young girl came out on the porch. Lila looked at her, thinking that clean and with ten or fifteen more pounds on her scrawny body, she could be pretty. She didn't look above fourteen, and was obviously pregnant.

Somehow, between the two of them, they got Sander off the wagon seat. But he balked at the front stairs. "I won't go in that house unless he invites me," he said. Lila thought it was his fever raving now, but he was strong and meant what he said.

Dulcie sighed. "There's a room in the shed. It's got a cot in it. I get away from the old hellion when I can." She helped Lila walk Sander back to the shed.

Dulcie helped get Sander settled on the cot. "He's hot," she said, looking at Lila. "You got anything for fever with you?"

"In the wagon. There's a bag full of all the medicines I had for the trip. Hector's still alive, just barely. We tried."

"I know you did. He didn't deserve it either. Lord knows the old man is too mean to die." Her body might be that of a young girl, but her eyes were ancient.

Lila was torn between staying in the shed with Sander and helping Dulcie with the tasks ahead of her. Somehow she knew it was this slight girl who would get Hector into the house, not his father.

MacCormack himself forced the issue, coming into the shed. "Always thought I'd live forever. Never thought I'd outlive you two, especially your brother. He needs to be in the house. You going to help?" he barked at Sander.

Lila didn't think he was conscious, but he got up off the cot. Silently, he lurched up and got moving. Lila wasn't sure afterward how the four of them got Hector into the parlor. She didn't want to remember.

Once they had finished the hard process, Sander stumbled out. MacCormack stood impassive, watching him go. "Can't you say anything to him?" Lila asked, turning on the older man. "He brought his brother home when he shouldn't even have been on a wagon himself."

"Nothing to say." Andrew stroked the front of his faded vest. Lila noticed a watch chain in one pocket,

HALF THE BATTLE

and wondered that someone who could still afford that kind of small luxury lived in such a rattletrap old house.

Dulcie stayed as far from the old man as she could get, edging around the wall and keeping her back to it, but staring at him boldly. "You stop badgering her now," she said. Lila wondered what her life was like, living with him day in and day out. "Can't you see she's in no condition to stand in this old drafty hall and jaw with you. At least let her come in the kitchen and set, you old hellion."

He laughed, a particularly frightening sound. "Why you are right, Dulcie." His gaze settled on Lila, chilling her. "Now what do I call you? Mrs. MacCormack sounds too damned formal."

"Lila," she said, hating to tell him. There was the same acquisitive gleam to his eyes that Hector's had held, and it frightened her.

"Lila. How charming. As Dulcie says, we must offer you some hospitality. Dulcie, go put on the kettle."

Lila felt the hair on the back of her neck rise. "I can just go into the kitchen with Dulcie. Besides, I need to tend to my husband if nobody else is going to."

MacCormack's laugh was bitter. "You mean you're *Sander's* wife? Somehow when you said you were married to my son I naturally assumed you meant Hector. Having one wife back home wouldn't have stopped him. How on earth did the other one get you to marry him?"

"It was easy. I love him. He's a fine man, something you'd know if you'd ever given him half a chance."

"That's all he's taken," MacCormack said. "Half a chance. And look where it's gotten us all."

Lila forced medicine for fever and pain down her husband and made him as comfortable as she could.

After a while, Dulcie came in and stood by her. "Why are you here?" she asked the girl. "And how old are you, anyway?"

"Fifteen. Old enough to know being the oldest of five girls made me fair game for someone like him when he came calling. At home, we were starving."

The room spun in front of Lila. "You still could have said no. You can't have known what you were getting into."

"I knew. Our cabin at home only had one room and a loft. So I knew what getting married means." Her eyes saw something Lila didn't see, never wanted to. "And that old bastard made sure I couldn't say nothing happened. Ma and Pa wouldn't take me back anyway."

The finality to her shrug chilled Lila. Dulcie saw her shiver and put a thin hand on her shoulder. "You get out of here tomorrow when it gets light. No matter what happens, don't you stay."

"Don't worry," Lila said. She tightened her shawl around her, and they went back to the cheerless gray house. They ate in the kitchen. It was the only room warm enough to sit down in. Lila sat in the flickering lamplight and picked at a square of corn bread. That and cold bacon were the extent of the meal.

"Sander not joining us for dinner?" MacCormack said.

"He's too sick and tired to move," Lila snapped. "Besides, he said he wouldn't enter this house until you asked him to." She looked at MacCormack, running a finger around the rim of his coffee cup and smiling an odd smile.

"Oh, I already asked. And he's been in, to bring in Hector," the old man pointed out. "Still, we'd better have him in. I don't want his death on my conscience tonight."

Lila wanted to follow him into the darkness, but something in Dulcie's look kept her sitting at the table. In a few moments Andrew was back, Sander following him silently.

"You're cold," she said. "Let me get you a cup of coffee and some supper." It wasn't her place to do it, but no one else seemed to be offering so she turned to the shelf where the plates were.

Sander's hand on her shoulder stopped her. "I don't sit at table in this house, Lila."

Lila spluttered. "He brought Hector back here all the way, and got him here even after he was wounded himself, and this is how you thank him?"

His father quirked one eyebrow. "Wounded, are you? In all the excitement, it must have slipped your mind. Obviously not a serious wound. And probably not won in service like Heck's either. Fall off your horse, boy?"

Lila turned to face Sander, afraid of what he might say in response. But his face, though taut, was still. It was the very stillness that frightened Lila, made her reach up and touch him gently on the cheek. His skin was cool, and under her fingers was a tiny pulse of suppressed emotion.

"Oh, yes, gal," his father's voice crooned. "Go ahead and make up to him. That way maybe you can convince him that babe you're carrying is his."

The room swirled, and Lila dropped her hand to her side. The chuckle behind her was malignant. Sander's eyes held emotions in flickering succession. Questioning, doubt followed by a spark of anger once his glance had taken in her middle and then had moved back up to her face. "Won't do no good, gal." The voice behind her swirled in Lila's ears, and hearing it she knew that the coffee cup in front of MacCormack held more than coffee. "You and I both know you've been acquainted with both the boys. And we both know who's more likely to get a child on a gal, too."

"That's a lie." Her voice verged on a sob as she almost threw herself over the kitchen table before Sander dragged her back. He pulled her tight against him, and she could feel the roughness of wool rub her cheek. "Take that nasty talk back now," she said.

"Why? I'm sure it doesn't upset anybody here. Sander knows what I think of him." It was the softness of MacCormack's voice mixed with his malevolence that made Lila's gorge rise. "The Spartans always said good warriors came home on their shields or carrying them. Sander here managed to mess that all up. He came home dragging his shield with half of his brother on it."

"If that isn't enough for you, then nothing will ever be enough because that's the best I can do." Close to his side, Lila could feel him trembling.

"Without doubt," his father said. "And your best has never been good enough."

Sander held her tightly, refusing to release his heavy grip on her shoulder. "This is why I never wrote home, Lila. This is why I've prayed you'd never come here. All this poison."

Sander's hand slid from Lila. "Let's do it now, old man. Let's go out in the yard. I'll kill you with my bare hands and get it over with. Nobody wants an end to this more than I do."

"Ah, there's where you're wrong, Sander," his father taunted. "What do you think it's like for me?"

"I mean it," Sander said. "Let's do it now. Put on

HALF THE BATTLE

your shoes and we'll go outside. Not in here in front of the women. Outside."

Andrew's lip curled. "You couldn't do it. You've never been man enough to take me on, and you aren't now. Inside or out."

Lila looked at Sander, sweat breaking out on his forehead, then back to Andrew, gloating malignantly. Before she could say anything there was a flash of light at the front windows, and pounding at the door. "Andrew MacCormack?" a heavy voice called.

MacCormack gave them all one more look and headed toward the front door. "More company? Has word spread already we're having a wake, even before he's dead?"

He walked to the front door and opened it. "I'm MacCormack," they heard him say. Then the shots rang out.

Lila launched herself toward the front of the house, where the stamping of horses and jingling of harness seemed to be mingling with the pounding of feet, flashes of light and a strange high raspy breathing.

"Don't go out there, Lila," Sander grasped her arm, pulling her back. "They'll shoot anybody who does. Union men, and they don't know you're anything but one of us."

The footsteps seemed to be receding as Sander pulled her close to him and down toward the floor, motioning for Dulcie to follow. Neither of them made a move toward Andrew. Lila wondered idly if he was the one making the odd, bubbly noises that stopped abruptly.

A glow came through the front windows, making hellish lights around the kitchen, as the men outside shouted back and forth. Someone rode around the house, and there was a thud on the back porch before the hoofbeats pounded away. "Torched us in," Sander said. He got up quickly and ripped off his coat, pouring the basin of water on it. "We've got to get out."

Lila and Dulcie stood in the hall. Andrew's still body slumped in the open doorway, and down the road Lila could see riders disappearing. Sander stopped halfway down the hall. "Get her out of here, Dulcie. If the shed's still standing, go there."

Dulcie started pulling Lila away from the stairs, away from the growing cloud of noxious smoke that seeped in from the front of the house. "Come on. We've got to get out of here."

"No. Not until Sander comes with us," Lila said. She tried to shake off Dulcie's arm, but the girl was stronger than she looked. It took all of Lila's strength to pull out of her grasp.

There was a pop as one of the front windows exploded, and as crashing sounds came from the parlor, Dulcie mewed in panic. "We have to get out while we still can. Come on!"

The smoke was billowing in now, making it hard to see. Dulcie let go of Lila and went to Sander. "We can't move them. They're both dead. You come out of here while you're still alive."

"Heck's still alive. He may not be long, and moving him may do him in, but I can't leave him here." Sander pushed Lila and Dulcie in front of him down the smoke-filled hall.

Lila wouldn't go any farther. "I'm not moving until you're with me," she told him. It seemed an eternity until he came back, supporting his brother.

Hector seemed to have real comprehension in the eye that was open. "Is he really dead?" he asked, looking down the hall.

"Really dead, Heck," Sander told him.

"Leave him there. Promise me," he managed to say.

"If that's what you want," Sander told him.

"I do," Hector choked out. "If he burns maybe he'll go to the devil faster." He let the others carry him out of the house.

Seventeen

The fire was too intense for them to consider putting it out. Sander herded everyone into a shed away from the house, striking a match and lighting a candle that flared and sputtered in a lantern. There was a battered old stove, its door hanging perpetually open. Sander stoked it, motioning Heck and Dulcie to the tumbled cot in the corner.

Dulcie led Hector over there and pushed him down onto the cot. She crooned to him in a low voice, and unbelievably his rattled breathing stilled to that of a normal person.

Lila stood, watching Sander build a fire in the stove, looking out the open door at the blaze across the yard. "Will it reach over here?"

"Only if the wind shifts," Sander said, looking out, his eyes shaded with a hand. There was so much Lila wanted to say to him. She had so many things to tell him that she didn't know where to begin. She longed to pet him as Dulcie was petting Hector, but knew Sander wouldn't stand for it. In the candlelight she looked at him, his shoulders slumped, sagging with fatigue.

There was a battered chair in one corner, and she pulled it to a position near the stove. "Sit down before you fall down, Sander," she said softly. He sat, and the movement changed the shadows around him into dark patches on his shirt and coat. Lila hurried over, lifting one sleeve.

"You're burned." It was true. The material was charred away in spots, leaving angry red skin exposed. She took his hands, and he unresistingly let her examine each one in turn. Tears started in her eyes as she looked at the angry flesh on his palms.

"Why didn't you say anything?" she demanded.

"Didn't know it had happened. There's not much feeling yet," he admitted. Lila looked around for anything that might be of help. There was little in the shack that would have been useful to anyone. As she looked around, a new noise joined the crackling roar of the fire. Something was pinging on the tin roof.

"Not cold enough to snow," Dulcie said.

"Good." Sander looked out the half-open door. "Rain or sleet will only help us."

Lila went to the doorway. Outside was a bucket, half-filled with water. It was cold, and she heaved it inside. Sander sprang up at the sight of her pulling the heavy bucket. "Don't you dare," she admonished him, setting it down. There was a small tin basin, and she poured the chilly water in it, setting the bucket outside to gather more.

"Take off that shirt and coat," she ordered. "Then stick both hands in that water."

"I'll catch my death," Sander grumbled. He was faltering with the buttons on his shirt. Lila pushed him gently back onto the chair and started unbuttoning them herself.

"Mama always said cold drew the heat out of a burn. She said fire keeps on eating away at you even when you stop touching it," she said, easing his clothing off. She couldn't resist stroking the skin of his shoulders before finding a blanket to wrap around him. For now the touch was enough.

Deftly she pushed his hands into the basin and started moving one small section of the blanket away at a time while she looked at his arms. There were only two bad places on his right arm, where cinders must have burned through his clothes. The rest were mere singes.

She needed bandages, and thanked her stars that she'd left her bag in the shed with Sander. Rummaging in it, she found her one spare petticoat and started tearing the hem into strips.

"Better than I deserve, sweet," Sander said. She took his hands out of the water and dried them gently, wincing at the pain she was causing him. As she was tying the last bandage, the candle guttered. Heck whimpered at the darkness, and Dulcie tried to calm him before he started screaming.

The mixture of sounds—icy rain drumming on the roof, the fire burning out into a spitting pile outside and Dulcie trying to calm the incoherent man in the corner—melded in the dark to fuel Lila's panic. Sander, obviously sensing her distress, pulled her down onto his lap.

"This chair isn't going to hold both of us," he said softly. "We're going to have to move, Lila."

She slid off his lap and tried to find her way in the darkness over to the rickety table that held his clothes. By touch she found the wool of a tunic, the smoothness of a shirt, and brought them back.

Helping Sander dress in the dark brought a new variety of sensations, the sharp male scent of him and the aroma of horses and wood smoke still clinging to the tunic. There was the crispness of his hair as she slid the shirt around him, the warmth of his lips as he lifted her hand and pressed his mouth to the palm silently. The contact shot through her like a bolt of lightning, raising a whimper in her aching throat.

Once Sander was dressed they huddled on the floor, the blanket around them both. They passed the balance of the night fitfully, listening to the rain, the dying fire and Hector's nightmarish outbursts until a pale dawn roused them all.

Dulcie did the digging the next morning. Lila marveled at the wiry stubborn strength in her thin body. She had marshaled them all once it was light. Sander and Lila poked through the rubble. Two walls still stood, and there was some charred furniture still usable. They managed to wrestle a few things into the shed.

Lila, exhausted beyond what she thought was possible, didn't argue when Dulcie forced her to lie down on the floor, covered by both their blankets. Hector looked more like a living person with every passing hour. Lila watched Dulcie fry two squirrels for breakfast and make a pot of coffee. Then the girl made them all eat.

"Your daddy was the devil himself," she said, standing in front of the two men. "But we still have to give him something like a Christian burial." She marched out with a shovel and dug a shallow trench, then disappeared into the ruins of the house with a blanket.

When she came back she went beyond the barn, shuddering. Lila put on Sander's other tunic and followed her, held her thin form while Dulcie retched until she couldn't anymore. When she straightened, she took the tin cup of water Lila had brought.

"They couldn't do it," she said, her eyes a thousand

years old in the thin face. "Besides, this way I'll always be sure the old demon is really dead."

Without another word she walked away. She and Sander dragged the obscene thing in the blanket over to the trench and covered it with dirt. Hector insisted on a timber for a crutch and got off the cot. Sander made a rude cross and got his mother's Bible and read a passage from Ecclesiastes, while his brother stared wide-eyed.

When it was done he stood straighter, closing the book. Across the trench he looked at Dulcie. "We'll be leaving before it gets dark tonight. I'll sign anything you want before I leave to let you know that whatever is left here is his . . . and yours."

Dulcie swallowed hard. "Do you know what was in that box you rescued with him? The land deeds, the money?"

Sander nodded. "I know. I still have two hands and all my intellect, Dulcie. I don't want it ever said that Heck went without because of me."

"I never have before." The voice behind them croaked a little with the effort of speech. "You were the lucky one, Sander. Get out again . . . before the hate touches you."

Dulcie went over to him, putting one thin arm around his shoulders. "He'll never want. With the money and land behind us, even *my* family will take us in until I can get a roof over our heads again."

Heck shook his head. "Just buy food. The shed's good enough. Needs a window for light. There's one still whole in the kitchen."

Dulcie smiled at Sander and Lila. There were tears glittering in her eyes. "We'll get by just fine."

Lila still had things to say. Seeing Andrew MacCormack had told her all she needed to know about Evie and how she'd died. She stood in front of Heck and looked up into his face without flinching.

"You killed Evie, didn't you?"

He nodded. "Virgil did the shooting. And the killing. But I didn't stop him."

"I know that," Lila said softly. "And I can't blame you anymore. There're worse things than being hung for murder."

The expression in his good eye showed he understood everything she meant. She might never be able to think of this man as a brother, but from today she couldn't think of him as a monster.

Dulcie insisted they take the two horses that had been hitched to the wagon. She'd have foisted the wagon on them, but Sander had insisted that she and Heck would need it when spring came. "Go to the Perry farm and trade it for horses or mules. They'll be honest with you," he instructed Dulcie.

Lila couldn't imagine anyone successfully cheating the imp who nodded up at him, but she was suddenly being fussed over because Sander had refused the wagon. "Don't he know you can't ride long?" Dulcie said, standing on tiptoe to tighten a shawl around Lila's shoulders.

"He's not thinking much yet," Lila said, watching Sander see to the horses. "I'll make him stop if I feel tired."

"It may take a swift kick in the head to get him stopped. All these MacCormacks are damned stubborn, aren't they?" Dulcie looked across the yard to where Heck poked at ashes.

Lila turned back to Dulcie. "Can you write?"

"No, but my little sister can. Ma taught her when nobody was looking."

"Let me write down an address. Get word to us if you can."

"I will," Dulcie promised. "He really won't ever be back, will he?"

The harness was all tightened, and Sander walked back into the shack to get their few belongings. "I don't think so," Lila said. There was nothing he cared about here. She just wondered if there was anything going with him that he cared about.

"Let's go home, Sander," she told him.

He gave her a pointed look. "It's only home to you, Lila. I'll stay there long enough to make sure you're settled."

"You didn't believe that nonsense your father was saying . . . ?"

"Not for a moment," Sander said, looking away.

"Good." No more on that or any other subject was said for quite a while. They avoided Palmyra. Sander, in a Confederate uniform, didn't belong in the town where his father's killers were probably eating dinner.

After a few hours in the saddle everything blended together. Lila was numb with cold and weariness. Twice they came to a stream and rested the horses, letting them drink. Lila stumbled on unwilling legs, trying to ease the constant ache in her back.

The second time, Sander wordlessly removed the cavalry saddle from his horse and slung it and the baggage on her mount, leaving only the blanket on the broad back of his. He swung Lila up on it and mounted behind her, pulling her close into his body.

"You need rest," was all he said. "You're a funny color."

"I'm tired." And cold and hungry, Lila wanted to add. But Sander looked as drawn as she felt. Unless he had something she didn't know about, they didn't have any money between them except the coins in her pocket. That wasn't enough to buy feed for the horses, much less themselves.

When it got dark, Sander swore softly. The road they were traveling was sparsely inhabited. "We can't just sleep under a tree," he said, stroking her hair. "I never wanted this, Lila."

"I know," she said, past caring. "You never asked me to follow you. I just did it."

"Probably saved my life," Sander said softly. "I would have killed him, or he would have killed me."

In the darkness far back from the road a light flared on, showing the greased paper window of a cabin. They both saw it at the same time, and Sander kneed the horses toward the light.

The gaping woman who answered the door agreed to let them spend the night in the cabin. There wasn't a spare bed, but there was plenty of floor. Lila traded their night's lodging for some things in her pack.

Sander said little, but then he'd said little since they'd fled the house in the fire. She wondered when he was going to start coming back into the world.

Before they left the cabin in the morning, Lila insisted on unwrapping his hands. Holding the reins all day had rubbed more skin off some of the burned places. "How can you keep moving?" she asked him. "Doesn't that hurt?"

"It hurts," he admitted. "But the sooner we get you home the sooner I can stop worrying that I'm harming the baby you're carrying."

They rode most of the day, and still there was no

lifting of the mood that held Sander. He answered if spoken to, but to Lila he seemed miles away. The closer they got to home, the duller he seemed.

When afternoon began to turn to evening and they were still not home, Lila was ready to scream. They stopped to rest, and her legs wouldn't hold her. Sander's support was wooden. He couldn't look her in the face.

"It's nearly killing you, isn't it? Going back there. There's nothing there for you, is there?" Her voice trembled, and she had to force herself not to shriek. "Why are you going? Just because duty says I shouldn't be alone? Why don't you go back and find your troops? That's where you want to be, I know."

He still didn't look her in the face. "If you say so."

"Well, you don't want to be back at that house."

"Now there you're right."

Lila pushed his arm away. "Then don't go. Don't help me out of duty Sander. If you have duty, it's to the Confederate army. If you're going with me, go out of love."

His smile was a travesty. "Love? Now what part is that supposed to play in anything?"

She stepped away from him, feeling horrified. "If that's the way you feel, then go. I don't want you taking me back. Go wherever it is you'd rather be."

"Anywhere. Anywhere at all," Sander said softly.

"Then good luck in getting there." It was difficult for Lila to get back on the horse, but she did. And for a change she was the one not looking back.

After a while it got too dark to travel. Lila turned into a grove of trees off the road, guiding the horse into the space under the naked branches. When she listened she could hear water nearby, and she groped around until she found it. The horse actually found it first, but he didn't seem inclined to go anyplace once he'd had a drink.

Lila took the saddle blanket and wrapped it around her, praying that there was nothing else around more desperate than she was. And then she slept.

When it got light she found a way to get back on the horse and get going again. It was probably midmorning when things began to look very familiar. In another hour she was sliding off the tired beast and into Chloe's arms.

"You look like death. And you're alone."

"It's a longer story than I can tell," Lila said, looking up into her friend's concerned face. "Right now I need food and sleep. Maybe tomorrow."

Chloe led her into the house, where she was surprised to see Yancey. "Mrs. MacCormack. Good to see you. Captain putting away the horses?" He seemed cheerful.

"No, the captain isn't with me. We came part of the way back together, but then we split up."

"What for?" Yancey seemed puzzled.

"I made him go back to his company. He couldn't come back here."

Chloe and Yancey exchanged a look. "That just isn't possible, ma'am," Yancey said slowly. "Captain MacCormack, he didn't have a company to go to. Once he took his brother home, General Price gave him a discharge. I took care of it myself. He's no soldier anymore."

There was a loud buzzing in Lila's head, and Chloe and Yancey seemed to disappear down a tunnel before everything went dark.

Two days later Chloe let her sit up on the chaise in the parlor. She wouldn't let her go any farther or do anything more strenuous than sew for the baby.

"Shouldn't we be out looking for Sander?" Lila kept asking.

Neither Chloe nor Yancey had an answer for that one. She didn't know where to look herself. He would have had plenty of time to discover he was discharged by now, and would have come back to her if he were coming. She had to face the fact that he wasn't.

Sitting there, mourning and sewing, suddenly she knew. She knew where Sander was as sure as if he'd told her. That same kind of communication he'd talked about that led him to rescue her from Hector and Virgil was still working.

Lila wasn't sure she had the strength to do anything. Then someone else made the decision about what she would do next. An odd fluttery wriggle flashed across her belly. Then it flashed the other way and unconsciously she put a hand on her belly in communion. So he wanted his daddy, did he?

Lila smiled. She stood up and called for Chloe. "Hurry up," she shouted. "We've got a wagon to pack."

Eighteen

They covered the distance to Evie's ruined cabin before nightfall. Chloe had argued that they should wait until first light in the morning, but the minute the basics were packed, Lila had insisted that she go. She wasn't sure that Sander would stay where he was, nor would she lay odds on the shape he'd be in when she got to him.

Yancey, who would not be left behind, drove the team, looking over in worry each time a rut jostled the wagon. "You're sure you're going to be all right?" He must have asked it a dozen times.

"I'll be better once we get there and I see for sure if it's really Sander," she said, scanning the gray sky.

Dark was gathering when they got to the ruined cabin. No one came out to greet them. But the graves had been cleared, and there was an air about the place of someone living there. Not living well in the hardscrabble ruins, but living.

Lila came off the wagon seat gratefully when Yancey stood before her. They looked at both halves of the cabin coming off the central dogtrot. "He'll be in the left," Lila said, trying to stay calm. "Last time I was here, it had most of its roof."

Yancey walked to the dogtrot, close enough to raise

his voice and be heard inside, but not close enough to be in pistol range. "Captain MacCormack, are you in there?"

"Who wants to know?" The voice that answered was cracked and belligerent.

"Your wife," Yancey called back, still not moving.

"Not by the sound of it." At least he hadn't lost his wit. Lila gathered hope from that and pushed past Yancey. She stood in the doorway, waiting for her eyes to adjust to the dimness inside.

She had expected squalor, but this was beyond what she'd dreamed of. Sander lay in a corner of the dingy cabin. The close air was dank. There had been no fire in here for quite a while. There hadn't been any water or soap either.

He was huddled in a blanket, half-propped against the wall. "Really is you," he said. "Y'know, it's harder to drink yourself to death than I imagined."

Lila crossed the floor and knelt before him. "If we don't find you a doctor, this fever's going to do the job for you before the liquor does."

"That's good, because I've only got one jug left." He motioned to his side. "Never gave me nightmares like this when I was awake before."

"That's the infection—and not eating, Sander. Why are you doing this?"

His eyes were dark and clouded. "World will be a better place once I'm gone."

Lila resisted the urge to shake him. "You can't mean that."

"Can and do." He focused on her face, still not moving. "You could start a new life, Lila. Find a good man . . ."

"I've already found one," she said firmly. "The one

I want. Now get up and come with me, Sander. You may have been raised by relatives, but my son is going to have a father."

"You remain determined, don't you?" He wasn't moving.

Lila took one of his hands in hers. "I've got Yancey with me. I'm sure between the two of us we could haul you into that wagon."

"Just try it." His voice was low and dangerous. "I still have one bullet in the pistol."

"Which one of us would you aim for?"

"You?" His eyes glittered. "Who says I'd try for either of you?"

Lila gasped. "Sander, you couldn't. That's a sin."

"I've committed enough of them already. My father was right, Lila. I'm lost no matter what I do. Go away and let me die in peace."

She put both hands on his face. He was burning with fever. Lila turned him to where he couldn't look away from her. "I love you, Sander MacCormack, and I'm not going to let you do any such thing."

The doubt in his eyes wrenched inside of her. His saddlebags lay strewn within arm's reach of the rude bed he'd made out of the blanket and some straw. She let go of him and darted to them. On the second dive into them, she found the gun.

Dancing backward out of his grasp she got to the doorway. "Yancey," she called. "Take this and unload it, then throw it into the woods."

She tossed it to her surprised companion just as Sander lurched to his feet. "You can't do that, Lila," he said, weaving unsteadily. He put out a hand and crashed into the wall. With a groan he slid to the floor, the fever and the pain from hitting his burned hand creating more stress than his body could bear.

Lila went to him. He was unconscious, but breathing well. "All right," she called to Yancey. "We have plenty to do before he wakes up."

Yancey came to the door of the cabin. "Ye gods. Where do we even start?"

She took a deep breath. "We start with you getting me a cup and filling it with that liquor. If he comes to, keep him drunk." She grimaced. "I never thought I'd say that, but right now I want this man out of his mind until those infected places are cleaned out. The only way he's going to let me do that is if he doesn't know I'm doing it."

Yancey shook his head, looking down at Sander. "And you thought she was this sweet, placid creature."

"He never did," Lila said, smiling in spite of herself. "But now he'll know for sure."

There was too damned much light. And noise. Sander opened his eyes, trying to ignore the pounding in his head long enough to focus. The last few days were a painful blur.

Lila had been part of the blur, always before him, scowling sometimes, coaxing others. And Yancey, although he couldn't imagine the two of them working together. It was obvious he was alive, and judging from all the various aches and pains in his body, he was tenacious about staying that way. Killing himself didn't work.

His hands itched something fierce, which was better than the burning ache of before. Clean bandages swathed both of them. Sander let the room come into focus a little more, amazed at what he saw.

The windows had new oiled paper over them, and the door was open, letting in a bright stream of winter sunshine. He was lying on a rude bedstead, and it was far from the only piece of furniture about. A rocking chair sat in the corner, and two plank benches and a table sat in the middle of the room. There was a fire in the fireplace, which had been scoured and cleared of rubble.

He remembered Lila forcing some vile brew down him more than once and Yancey feeding him liquor. Right now there was no one in the room. They couldn't be far away, judging from the banging noises accentuating the pounding in his head. Sander sat up as best as he could, favoring his injured hands.

Sitting up made his head throb and brought a wicked bout of dizziness. Swinging his legs over the side of the bed was not to be contemplated yet. He leaned his head against the wall, trying to get his bearings.

Before he could, Lila came through the doorway, carrying a basket of something. "Oh, good, you're really awake this time."

"Is that good?" The effort of talking made his throat ache.

"It's marvelous," she said, putting down the basket and pulling the rocker over to the side of the bed. "Doctor Holcomb said we had to let your body fight the infection, then see how long it took you to wake up."

She was actually smiling. Sander found himself staring in dumb amazement at her face. It was unbelievably beautiful. "And how long did it take?" he asked.

She tipped her head back, thinking. "Two days, I expect you'd say. That was once we stopped giving you anything out of the jug. Do you know you can argue

Blackstone drunk, with a fever hot enough to fry eggs on your forehead?"

So those hadn't been hallucinations. "What day is it?"

Before Lila could answer, someone entered through the doorway. "Miz MacCormack," the tall, blond young man said, "Yancey says he needs more shingles."

"George should be done shaving them by now, in the clearing, Henry."

"So that's where he got to," Henry Davis was smiling. Sander wondered if all this was just more of his febrile wanderings. But Henry looked terribly real, a dark red shirt open over his long johns, and grubby with sweat.

Lila was smiling back at him, nodding. "I showed him how to use the tools, and he took right to it. You two ever have any carpentry training?"

Henry shook his head. "No, ma'am. Just trapping. George has always been good with his hands, though." He seemed to pause in thought. "Carpentry. You could do that mostly sitting down, if you did fine furniture and such, couldn't you?"

"That you could." Lila was positively beaming.

"You know what else Miz Wayne told me? There isn't a store or a church or a school left within ten miles of here." Henry shook his head.

"Why do I get the idea that the two of you might be scheming to take care of at least one of those problems?" Lila countered.

Henry laughed. "It'll have to be the store. I ain't getting dunked in the river this time of year for nobody, not even to start a new church. Better see about those shingles. Good seeing you awake, Captain."

"Good seeing you too, Henry," Sander said as the

young man headed for the door. Thinking this hard made Sander's head pound. "What was that all about?"

"Oh, George and Henry have been here about three days. They heard about your discharge, and wanted to stay since they were both at loose ends themselves."

"Oh." He didn't have a good explanation for the insanity that had gripped him when they'd parted, so he didn't say any more. Lila didn't press. She found her handwork and started in on a tiny garment. Before Sander could say anything else, there was another interruption. This time the visitor came thumping across the dogtrot and in. George, swinging along on crutches. And behind him a black woman jiggling a fretful baby. Chloe.

"Miz MacCormack, go ahead and tell her," George burst out as they came through the door. "I've got seven brothers and sisters, counting Henry. I can be trusted with that child while y'all get supper on."

"I expect he can, Chloe," Lila said softly. "And it would be a help."

Chloe snorted. "All right then. But don't you dare let me hear that child squall."

"You won't, ma'am," George said. He sat down on the bench and took the squirming boy. "Why don't you stir up those biscuits right here where we can watch. I still don't understand why yours come out so much higher."

" 'Cause I don't beat them to death," Chloe muttered. Sander looked at Lila again. The question in his eyes must have been evident, because she giggled.

"Chloe got here two days before the Davises, Sander. Yancey went back and fetched her and Freeman when he got the doctor. They've been setting the place to rights. By tonight I expect everyone can sleep under a roof without it being the same roof, the one over this room." She looked pink as she said that.

"I've woken up in a circus," Sander said, shaking his head as much as the pounding would allow.

"Well, you were the one who said you weren't moving, Sander," Lila reminded him. "I just brought our home to you."

It didn't get any better. A constant stream of people trooped in and out of the cabin. They joshed with each other, ate and pretended it was the most normal thing in the world to go about their business while Sander remained firmly enshrined in the bed in the corner.

Lila bullied him into dressing each morning, but even she couldn't get him to move off the bed. At night she eased in gently beside him, taking up as little space as possible.

Sander ached to reach out and touch her, to tell her how much all this meant to him. She had pulled him from the edge of an abyss so black he couldn't contemplate it, into a life he wasn't ready to rejoin yet.

She continued to try to force him to enter into life. One morning she and Chloe went so far as to plop Freeman on the bed while they hauled out the basin and did dishes. Sander examined the babe, who goggled at him and chewed noisily on a fist, wide-eyed and solemn.

He'd never held a baby before that he could remember. It was not an unpleasant sensation once he got over the fear that he was going to drop him. Freeman settled on his lap, seemingly happy.

He wasn't as happy as the two women who were at the table. To Sander's amazement they were actually singing. Chloe had a husky contralto, Lila the soprano he'd expected. Their voices blended with a sweetness that tore at his insides. Stroking the soft fuzz on Freeman's head, he listened to the words. As he listened Sander's amazement grew. Not only could they sing, they could sing this!

" 'Tis the song, the sigh of the weary,
Hard times, hard times, come again no more.
Many days have you lingered, around my cabin door,
Oh, hard times, come again no more."

And Lila went on, deftly scrubbing out bowls as she sang.

Come again no more? Sander thought to himself. "Lord in heaven, woman," he exploded, "the hard times have never left. If anything, they've just started. Can't you understand that?" Lila dropped her rag and stared at him, her eyes glittering, then ran from the cabin. His tone of voice made Freeman curl up his lip and cry.

Chloe came and snatched the child, but continued to stand over him. "She really thinks you're worth all this. Why, I can't understand. For her the hard times *are* over, you fool, because you're together and alive."

Sander couldn't find any answer to this monumentally angry young woman who stared at him. "There's nothing left," he muttered.

"Nothing? You've got all your limbs and a good head on your shoulders. Why you don't get out of that bed and join the men out there doing something is beyond me."

Sander looked at the wall. It was better than looking at Chloe. This way he could talk, try to find the words to explain to her. "They've all got something to work for. Henry says you all are going to start a store. If I get up, I've got nothing to look forward to except watching all this. What is she staying for? She got what she wanted."

Chloe spun him around, making Freeman wail again. "What in blazes are you talking about? No, don't answer yet. You really love her?"

"More than I could ever admit."

She put her face close to his. "Lila always said you didn't know anything about women. Lord, she was right." She eyed him sharply. "What is it you think she wanted?"

"To find out about Evie. And she found out."

"About Virgil? And your brother? I know, she told me."

Sander felt a growing sense of wonder pierce the dullness that had been enveloping him for days. "And she still wants to stay?"

Chloe snorted. "Of course. She loves you, fool. Why, I don't understand. But she loves you anyway."

"You know that for a fact?" he said, looking back at Chloe.

"Don't you?" She didn't say anything else before she turned on her heel and spun back to the dishwater.

Lila stood at the edge of the trees. The four grave plots had been weeded again, and stones put around the perimeter. She wished it were spring, and there would be something growing there to make them look less naked.

But there wasn't. It was the beginning of winter, and the gray air was as dead as the ache inside her. She was a fool to think Sander would come around. She couldn't even stop anymore to wipe the tears off her face. She looked down at Evie's headstone.

"You can have him, I guess," she said, feeling more like she was talking to her cousin than at any time since Evie had died. "I can't keep him. I can't get him interested in anything, and he won't come around."

"Oh, yes he will. He has." The voice behind her was a shock. The hands that pulled her around firmly to face Sander were an even greater shock.

He stood, tall and upright. Digging a handkerchief out of his pocket, he wiped her face gently and thoroughly. "You can stop that now. I'm up. And I'm staying that way. Lila, I've been a fool."

She tried to say something, but he hushed her with kisses, taking her mouth with a fervor that nearly lifted her off the ground. The ache she felt was replaced by hope, fragile as butterfly wings. "I love you, Lila." Sander's voice overwhelmed her. "I couldn't tell you how I feel even if I took the rest of my life."

His dark eyes were alight. Lila's tears threatened to start again, and it was hard to ignore the odd feeling in her belly. Sander made a pained noise deep in his throat. "Oh, don't cry again, sweetheart. Let's have done with the crying." He slipped an arm around her tightly. "How bad do you want to stay here?"

She looked up at him, puzzled. "As badly as you do, I guess."

He smiled, a smile that lifted Lila's heart. This was the man who had ogled her in the middle of a creek in another lifetime for both of them. "And if I want to go back to the farm and read law with my brother-in-law?"

The wind pulled tendrils of her hair. Lila hardly dared to speak. "Then I expect we could go. Can you live under the same roof as a Union man, once he comes home?"

"I can. And to show you how determined I am, I'm going in and throw away that last jug."

Her face split into a grin. "You're too late. I did it yesterday."

"Well, thank you. Both of you." Sander picked her up this time and swung her around in a tight circle. The sudden movement made it impossible to ignore the pain she'd been wishing away. Lila could feel her skin get clammy with the sweat that broke out on it. Sander's eyes darkened in concern when he lowered her to the ground, and she could feel her own face tighten into a grimace. "What's the matter, sweetheart?" he asked.

"I hurt," was all she could choke out. "Get me inside."

Lila didn't know what hurt worse, the pain grabbing her midsection from the backbone forward, or watching Sander pace beside the bed. "It's not your fault," she told him, trying not to grimace. "These things just happen."

"You've worked yourself nearly to death on my account," he said. "I should have been taking care of you instead of feeling so sorry for myself."

"What's done is done," Lila said, trying not to gasp when the pain built again. "Let's go on from here."

He was at the bedside in an instant, clutching her hand. "I want to. I want us to have years together, Lila, to go on from here. To take this love and make it as strong as you're making this cabin again. You can't go now."

"I'm not going anywhere," she said, trying to sound firm. "But we may lose this baby."

He swore, putting his head down on the quilt beside her where she could tangle her fingers in his dark hair.

"This place is cursed for me. First Evie, now you." He sat up, resolve firming his already hard features. "No, I won't let it happen. If that doctor's anywhere within twenty miles, I'm going to find him and bring him back. If we lose this baby, we'll just have to deal with that. No child you could give me is as important as you are. I love you so much. Give me a chance to show it."

The tightness was gripping her muscles again, and Lila tried not to cry out. Chloe burst through the door, brandishing something. "I found it, finally. Yancey packs with no sense at all. At first he tried to tell me it wasn't in the trunk. Do you know where it was? In with the horse liniment."

Sander looked up at the bottle she was waving. "What is it?"

Lila and Chloe answered him at once. "Arlie's tonic." Lila made a face. "Give it here and let's see if it will help."

Chloe stood over her, handing down the bottle. "What will help most is your not getting out of that bed for a week if we can get your labor to stop."

"I'll see that her feet never touch the floor," Sander promised. He held the bottle and tipped it up for her. She swallowed once, fighting the desire to retch, then pushed it away. Sander looked up at Chloe. "Should she have more?"

Chloe frowned. "Better see if she keeps this down first. If she does, we'll worry about more. That is the worst-tasting stuff on the face of the earth."

To Lila's amazement he sniffed the bottle, then tested it by wetting a finger and bringing it to his mouth. "Oh, God. You're right. And you just drank a whole swallow of that?"

"I'll do it again if I have to, if it means we'll all three

come out of this alive." She watched the tears spring up in his eyes as he set the bottle down gently and sat on the edge of the bed to cradle her.

"You would, too. You'd do anything there was to do for me, wouldn't you, Lila? You've fought raiders, faced down my father, and built us a new life. It's going to take the rest of my days for me to pay all this back."

The pain seemed to be receding, and in its place blossomed warmth fueled by Sander's arms around her. "Both our days, Sander. We'll do it together."

He leaned down to burrow his face in her hair, and Lila was surrounded by his love. "The hard times really are over, no matter what happens next, aren't they?"

She lifted her face up to his for the kiss he offered. "I truly believe they are."

"Say that after another swig of Arlie's tonic," Chloe dared.

"She can do it," Sander murmured into her hair. "She can do anything."

She laced her fingers into his. "We can do anything. And we will." She reached out for the bottle, and this time the bitterness was gone, lost in the sweetness of what life had to offer—a life together, one they had fought for. It was more than half the battle, and they had won.